The Scarlet Forest:
A Tale of Robin Hood

THE SCARLET FOREST:

A TALE OF ROBIN HOOD

A. E. CHANDLER

To Dawn:
Enjoy the journey.
Amy Ch

thistledown press

Thistledown Press Ltd.
410 2nd Avenue North
Saskatoon, Saskatchewan, S7K 2C3
www.thistledownpress.com

Library and Archives Canada Cataloguing in Publication

Chandler, A. E., author
The scarlet forest : a tale of Robin Hood / A.E. Chandler.
Issued in print and electronic formats.
ISBN 978-1-77187-138-9 (softcover).—ISBN 978-1-77187-139-6 (HTML).—
ISBN 978-1-77187-140-2 (PDF)
I. Title.
PS8605.H3558S33 2017   C813'.6   C2017-905311-6
C2017-905312-4

Cover: *Festival of the Archers,* 1493 (detail), Master of Frankfurt
Cover and book design by Jackie Forrie

Canada Council   Conseil des Arts
for the Arts   du Canada

SASKATCHEWAN
ARTS BOARD

Canadä

Thistledown Press gratefully acknowledges the financial assistance of the Canada Council for the Arts, the Saskatchewan Arts Board, and the Government of Canada for its publishing program.

Find book club questions, bonus
material, and more titles at:
aechandler.wixsite.com/author

CONTENTS

Part One

Chapter One
Oak

A LONG THE FOREST PATHS A fair youth strode for Nottingham Town. Sherwood kept special watch over this newcomer into its kingdom. The merry month of March had come in the night, and all was uncommonly blithe as the birds clamoured amidst the branches.

The youth stood tall and wore fine yet simple clothes. A red feather extended back from his cap, and a broad sword was girded at his side. He carried a stout longbow of English yew, and a linen bag slung from the back of his belt held a sheaf of arrows. The arrows' crests showed they belonged to the Earl of Huntington's second son.

The law banned the carrying of bows in the greenwood, lest someone should poach the king's deer. Yet Robert found he could think better when alone amidst the trees. No one could be seen upon the paths today, so he walked silently on to Nottingham. His thoughts cycled far away from the forest upon this most important day of his life.

Robert was journeying to a shooting match in Nottingham. He expected to win, for none could match his skill at archery, the closest competition being his friend Marian, the eldest of Baron Fitzwalter's five daughters.

At age seven, Robert had been sent away to serve the ladies of Baron Fitzwalter's household as a page, before his mother and her ladies could spoil him. Upon turning fourteen, he had become the baron's squire, receiving instruction in courtesy and combat, in the hope that at twenty-one he would show himself worthy of a knighthood. His elder brother, David, would inherit the title of Earl of Huntington, thus he was free of that charge.

Robert and Marian were the best of friends. Whenever the two had a moment free they would hunt or shoot or he would teach her what he knew of combat. They had dreamt that once Robert became a knight she would be his squire, and thus they would continue to have adventures together all their lives. Yet such a life could only be a fancy.

Six months before the day of this shooting match, Robert's long-ill father had passed into heaven. David was being schooled in France, and their elder sister Margaret was married to Squire Gamewell. Thus the youth, two months from being eighteen, had temporarily given up training as a knight to aid his grieving mother in governing the family's lands. Though she entreated him to continue his knightly training, Robert insisted upon caring for her until his elder brother could return.

One month ago his life had undergone yet another change, when Marian turned eighteen. Neither of them told a soul what had happened, yet today at the shooting match Robert was to meet with his mother as well as the Fitzwalters and Marian. Then they would reveal their secret.

Around the next bend a group of green-clad foresters lazed at food and drink, with kegs of fine October ale. When they saw the youth coming toward them, they called him back to the plane he walked with every manner of taunt they could muster in their drunken states. The slur of alcohol sounded stronger in some voices than in others.

"Ho, lads! See how the fledgling dresses!"

"Learn to crawl before thou dost walk, boy!"

"Art thou too ignorant not to bring thy bow to the greenwood, young hood?"

Being of an age when he considered himself a man, and his pride giving him a sour temper, Robert's anger beat hard against his chest. He had not expected to be ambushed yet kept his tongue, remembering the foresters were drunk and did not mean their insults.

A shout went up: "Let us take him to the sheriff! To be punished for his crime!"

"Nay," quoth a forester with red hair. He seemed to lead the party. "Let us have sport with him first. Three marks thou canst not e'en pull that bow, little robin."

"There done!" cried Robert, finally losing his temper. He would gladly have all his limbs broken before he let a man breach his pride. "Name the mark."

Not thinking the arrow would fly so far, or perhaps not thinking at all, the lead forester stretched out his arm. "Seest thou that herd of the king's deer ten-score and more yards down the path, young hood? If thou canst fell one, all our coins to thee."

Robert pulled back his bowstring. The weight of it felt akin to lifting a man above his head. His anger was rampant and the foresters insisted upon insulting him even now, but his skill was such that this rated as no distraction. The string sang, sending forth the shaft. Struck even as he tried to leap away, the life of the herd's lead stag fled whilst his body could not.

The foresters stood so amazed they scarcely moved. They had truly not thought this lad would make the shot. The deer were for the king's pleasure alone, to be hunted and eaten at his will. No one else must kill or even touch one of them.

"Your coins now, fellows. I have won them all."

At last the lead forester spake. "Dost thou know what thou hast done, boy? Thine eyes are forfeit, and it is our sworn duty to arrest thee."

Robert felt himself go cold, so he might start to shiver. "Do not speak of mine eyes. The new law says I must pay a fine to the king, and I shall pay it."

"Nay, but we like the old law." Another of the foresters crept toward Robert, his limbs rolling like those of a wolf stalking its prey. "And we shall take thine eyes before bringing thee to the sheriff. It is good sport, and one we like to see."

Panic welled in Robert's breast. Almost without thought he nocked another arrow. "The next to move shall die!"

Fear pushed all else from the lad's head. In his anger, it had not occurred to him that he might be signing away his life in the stag's blood. A man with no eyes could never be a knight, nor could he be anything else. There was no place for a man without eyes. The bow felt rude in Robert's hands. It had always been a friend to him, and a link to his father. Now it felt alien to him and he doubted his accuracy if forced shoot.

The frozen foresters stood spread around him, as numerous as the shafts in the linen bag upon his belt. They watched, waiting for a good chance to spring forward and bind him. Without a sound, an arrow rose from the rear of the group. It flew high, arcing down toward Robert. This same moment the foresters parted, revealing the lead man as he who had shot.

The shaft missed Robert's throat so narrowly that the feathers scratched his neck. On instinct, as he had practised so often at Baron Fitzwalter's, Robert loosed his arrow upon the attacker.

The shaft flew true. The man fell writhing upon the greensward with the arrow through his heart. He sprawled in pain a moment; then only the shakings of death stirred him.

None moved. The foresters stood shocked to see their leader fall. Robert felt a dark claw at his throat. He panted hard, so that his breath would not stop, willing what he had done not to be true.

At last one forester stepped forward, his face etched in contradictory lines, his eyes slit. He looked at Robert, whose arms hung limp at his sides, with such anger and hurt that not one day would pass in the lad's life when this face did not echo back to him, the words ever circling his head. "Blinding is too good for thee. Hanging is too good for thee. Thou art not worth the rope. The forest is thine home now. Here starve and freeze and die alone. Thou hast killed thyself. Now run! Run to save thy murderous hide!"

Robert turned, running deep into the forest, not knowing what else to do. His mind whirled with frustration, terror, shame, and hope that he might find relief within the trees.

Branches and leaves whirled about him. He fled aimlessly, mile after mile.

By sunset he felt exhausted, his yellow hair in disarray and his beard coated with sweat. Pits of shadow deepened all around him. His playful blue eyes were carved hollow with grief and fatigue. He walked a little farther, finding himself in an especially large clearing with an ancient giant of an oak at its head. Spotting a path leading out of the clearing, Robert followed it to a small opening in the forest. Overhead, the branches converged, almost closing out the sky.

He lay down beside a fallen log. His last thoughts before he slept were of his friends and family, and how they would feel to know that he was a murdering outlaw. He prayed God that they not despair. Surely the foresters had deciphered the cresting upon his arrow by now and discovered his identity. They would tell his mother, and she would be alone now.

Mostly, however, he thought of Marian, and then of the wife of the man he had killed. What would she think when she learned of her husband? Most likely what Marian would think, only she might take satisfaction in it. For, as far as the law was concerned, both he and the forester were dead.

Robert lay sleeping in the clearing until noon the next day. The sun was shining directly overhead where the kindly leaves could not shelter him. He awoke aching in both limb and mind.

Lying still a moment, he relived the scenes of the day before. These would have made him vomit, had there been aught in his stomach. All the same, convulsions ran through his body. After a moment they passed, and for the first time he heard running water. Following the sound, Robert came upon a stream not a hundred yards from the two clearings. He drank his fill, splashing his face that he might be rid of yesterday's stains.

His mother must now fare without him. Perhaps his brother David would return from his schooling in France upon hearing that Lady Huntington was left alone. Still, Robert could not shake the guilt of abandoning his mother.

What of Marian? From the first day they had met, they had been the firmest friends. The last month with her had been the best of his life. This was over now.

In childhood, Robert and Marian had often played with two other boys. One, Will Stutely, had become a forester. Robert had been the tactless Stutely's hero, the latter gladly willing to carry out any task required of him. Robert decided to find Will, that he might hear what the sheriff, who kept the peace in Nottinghamshire, planned to do about him.

Strapping his sword to his side and stringing his bow, Robert left his mantle behind in the clearing, the green surcoat underneath providing better camouflage. Thus he started off rather unsteadily, with his right foot foremost.

The Blue Boar Inn was the centre of all that went on in this part of the forest, and it was here he thought to find Stutely. The inn was nestled in a clearing off the main road through Sherwood. Men were laughing and drinking outside the Blue Boar, enjoying the warmth of the sun. Robert cringed as he walked past them. The air breathing through the inn door carried with it the smells of sweet ale and fresh bread. Even this was not enough to persuade his stomach to embrace hunger.

Fortune, who had so cruelly abandoned him the day before, repented and so he found Will Stutely inside, sitting alone. Robert approached him, never thinking his friend might turn him in.

"Will."

Stutely jumped upon seeing who spake to him. "Heaven save us! — Quickly, out the back — art thou *mad*?"

When Robert's sense caught up with him, he and Stutely were having a hastily whispered conversation behind the inn, amidst a grove of saplings. Answering the questions asked him, Robert managed a few of his own.

"My mother, Marian — how are they?"

"The news is all over the county, Robert — all know. No one expects such crimes from the son of a nobleman. Thy mother was horribly shocked, yet she is a strong woman and will soon recover."

"Will David return?"

"He cannot have heard yet, but worry not: thy father's advisers are able enough to govern until thy brother arrives. 'Tis Marian I worry over."

Robert's hand shot out, grabbing Stutely's shoulder. "What dost thou mean?"

Will hesitated. "She took it into her head to become an outlaw herself. Knowing her she would have, yet this morn she and her family had to rush to attend a sick aunt." He paused. "I have only just come from there. I had to tell them. Marian fell to crying, for she knew thou wouldst not be well with what thou hadst done. I never saw her shed a tear in all my life;

'twas terrible." Will hurried on before Robert could digest this information. "Listen, Robert, thou wilt not survive alone, I know. Let me gather those foresters I know can be trusted, and wish to seek a new life. We shall join thee."

The last thing Robert wished to see was more men in his position, yet Will presented his case well, saying he had often wished for an outlaw's life. He spake of roaming free, and never worrying for wages. Robert led the forester back to the clearings where he had slept. Before suppertide the next night, Will returned with thirty men.

Lone outlaws, wronged peasants, and poor men of every profession joined the ranks until they numbered four-score-and-ten. Thus the outlaws possessed many disguises from their past lives. They could go forth in these, gaining supplies such as leather and iron. Former bowyers, fletchers, and tailors now plied their trades in the greenwood.

A code of honour was sworn. The band vowed never to menace woman nor child, to always give aid to the poor, to be plain in their dealings, and to value all men at their true worth, regardless of rank. They vowed to fight fairly and lay down their lives for woman, king, or honest man.

Foresters in the main let the band alone, for they feared facing such a congregation of criminals. Thus the outlaws, dressed in Lincoln green, roamed Sherwood Forest largely as they would.

Now, the High Sheriff of Nottingham knew of this growing threat, and he intended to end it by eliminating its leader. Robert had been chosen for this station due to his deft hand at archery, and because he had united the outlaws. The sheriff saw them as no different than any other bandit hoard he had ensnared. A warrant was issued for one Robin Hood. The sheriff thought this name clever, for not only was Robin a nickname for Robert, but as the young man had been described to him, the outlaw was "no more than a hoodlum" and "a robin that sought to fly too soon." If one said the name quickly, it sounded like "robbing hood." For his part, Robert took a liking to the name and adopted it.

Word spread that any man wishing to earn fifty pounds (a generous sum worthy of the outlaw's former rank) could come to the sheriff for a warrant. Despite gossip that this was no more than a nobleman's cocky young son grabbing for fame, none accepted the sheriff's invitation that month, or the month after, or its successor. Not only did the outlaw help those in need, but the Sherwood band contained doughty fighters who had pledged loyalty to their leader, even to death.

A shepherd came up from the south, so tall he towered head and shoulders over every man he met. He had naught save the clothes upon him, a few farthings, and the quarterstaff in his hand. Having spent his days travelling, this giant was bearded and bronzed. His hair and beard were so tangled, one could barely discern his features. He knew he must find work soon or starve for, though he always had been rather thin, his ribs now began to wrinkle his tunic.

When this giant heard of the sheriff's warrant, he said to himself, "Never would I have thought such a large sum real. I must busk me to Nottingham Castle before another man accepts the commission." Thus the stranger came before the sheriff, concealing his shaggy hair and dirt-stained face beneath a hood.

The sheriff, upon seeing the shepherd's height and hearing that he had never been beaten at the quarterstaff, gladly gave him the warrant.

Robin Hood was oblivious to this and had set out that day in search of adventure. E'en as a boy this had been his addiction. He had grown weary of the routine of establishing camp. The band warned him of the sheriff, but Robin contended that he could meet any challenge put his way. At the urging of his men, however, he took a silver horn to call upon if he fell into danger.

The past three months had seen the outlaw grow in mind as well as muscle, his temper no longer so sharp over trivial things. Killing a man had shown him much. He had sworn his men not to take a life even in battle for, not only was the consequence bitter, but also the reprisals of conscience.

Happening down a path by the forest edge, Robin doffed his cap to all, rich or poor, for it mattered not to him. After walking a ways he began to daydream of Marian, thinking of how she could be there now to walk with him, and what she would say. Hopping upon a log serving as bridge over a stream swelled by heavy rains, he failed to notice another daydreamer, who had stepped onto the log from the opposite side.

Both walked to the middle, not seeing one another until no more than a hand's breadth perched between them. Each leapt back in surprise in the same moment.

Angered, the stranger grumbled in a voice not much deeper than Robin's, "There is but room enough for one. Give over, say I, and let the better man pass."

Robin looked this stranger down and up, wondering if the man might be good for a jest. He stood tall in height, yet the stranger stood taller. He spanned broad of shoulder, yet the stranger's spanned broader by two palms' breadths. Robin was able in muscle and yet, if he were any judge, the stranger was not unused to defending himself.

Robin decided to have fun with this behemoth and responded, "I agree the better man should pass first, yet who is to say which of us is he?"

"This," quoth the stranger, brandishing his oaken quarterstaff.

"A fair judge indeed. Allow me to cut a staff for myself, and I shall attend thee in a moment, sweet chuck."

So saying, Robin retreated to his side of the bank, where a sapling thicket grew. Choosing one amongst them, he felled it with his sword, and trimmed away the branches. Returning to the log, he said, "Here I am, friend, to show thee how we north men fight."

"My staff is longer," quoth the stranger. "I shall abide here whilst thou cuttest thyself a better one."

"Nay." The outlaw's eyes twinkled with boyish pleasure. "If my staff be shorter I shall only further prove myself the better man."

"As thou wishest, fellow. Now begin, say I!"

The stranger swept his staff forward in a fury. Robin ducked beneath the blow, glad to have found fair game.

Ever and anon they would stop their battle to sit down and rest, their staffs idling upon their laps whilst their feet dangled just up from the water's reach.

At first they sized up one another from the corners of their eyes, each thinking the other the stoutest knave ever to hold a quarterstaff. Soon they fell to talking.

Robin asked, "What dost thou do in Sherwood, friend? Surely thou art ill-suited to nomadic life."

"Aye, that am I," returned the other. "I was a shepherd, but my sheep became unwell from eating brown grasses, and those that did not die I sold for the slaughter. I have spent nearly all my money travelling the country to find work."

"Thou art a ragged vagabond, forsooth," quoth Robin.

"Make not light of it, friend. 'Tis a sorry strait. Thank heaven I have found employment with the Sheriff of Nottingham."

"Oh?"

The giant hardly noticed his companion's sudden lack of talkativeness. "The task is easy enough: I am to capture an outlaw leader by the name of Robin Hood."

"Many outlaws have roamed the forest, friend."

"Aye, but never united in such great numbers. If their chief is caught, they will be simple enough to dispose of. We are brothers in a quest in that sense."

"How?"

Robin's blank stare confused the giant a moment. "Why," quoth he, "from thy clothes, thou art a forester, art thou not? Is thy first charge not to keep safe the king's deer? These outlaws prey upon the herds."

"Come," motioned Robin, "let us continue our sparring."

Both men battled more fiercely than before, eager to follow their separate ways after being reminded of the world beyond their quarterstaffs.

The outlaw's still youthful nerves jangled him. He put all his energy into the fray, becoming overanxious and not taking proper care in his defence.

The giant struck Robin's ribs, nearly toppling him into the gurgling waters below. The outlaw was light of foot and recovered quickly.

Before Robin could block it, the giant swung again, striking the outlaw's head with such force that Robin was knocked senseless. He fell into the water as though he were a boulder and was pummelled by the current.

The stranger crossed to the bank the outlaw had been defending. When Robin pulled himself to the water's surface he saw his conqueror laughing mightily. The giant fished Robin from the stream, setting him sopping wet upon the shore.

"Truly, friend," quoth the stranger, "thou art wetter than a foxhound shut out in a storm by its master."

"More like a sparrow in a bare birch tree," returned the outlaw with a wry smile, cradling his side. "I tell thee, friend, thou art the best with a quarterstaff that e'er I hope to meet. If thou dost will it, I would make thee my right-hand man. Thou wilt receive fifteen marks a year in pay,[1] as well as three suits of Lincoln green. Thy life will be full of adventure, and thou wilt feast upon venison as sweet as any the king hath set to his lips. What be thy name, friend?"

"John Little," quoth the giant, amazed the forester offered that which so many had died for taking. "May I inquire as to *thy* name?"

"Why, thou dost know me already, friend. I am Robin Hood."

---

1   One pound is twenty shillings. One shilling is twelve pence. A groat is four pence. One mark is one hundred sixty pence, or thirteen shillings and four pence. An archer could earn six pence a day, or more than thirteen marks a year; Robin's offer is generous.

"Thou didst deceive me!" John thundered, starting forward.

Robin held up his hands. "Nay, friend. The dunking into yon stream hath cleansed me of all deception. Truly did I speak of thy skill, and truly am I offering what I have said. Wilt thou not join our band? O'er time, 'twill pay thee better than the sheriff's warrant."

The giant considered. "I shall join thee," he answered, "if thou canst beat me at archery. I have heard of thy prowess. Hm, I see thou hast no bow about thee, nor arrows either. What say we hie to Nottingham Town? Someone there will have what we need."

Robin replied with a laugh. "There is no need to trouble ourselves, thou crafty fellow, for mine attendants will bring what we seek."

Clapping his horn to his lips, Robin blew both loud and shrill. Soon sixty men — dressed in green hose, tunics, surcoats, and hooded capes that reached their elbows — came crashing through the underbrush.

Will Stutely led this party that roamed the forest. "What be your bidding, master?"

"Yon fellow hath challenged me to a bout at archery. Lend him any bow he doth wish."

The giant mingled uneasily with the outlaws, choosing the largest and thickest bow.

"Give me thy word," quoth he, returning to Robin, "that if I win thou wilt let no harm come to me."

"Be not fearful, friend; that thou wilt win is not as likely as thou thinkest." Robin handed the giant an arrow, which the latter carefully examined before setting it to the bowstring.

"Choose the target."

Looking 'round askance, Robin nodded. "Seest thou that dead tree across the stream? 'Tis a good fifteen-score yards distant. The knot upon its left side will be the mark."

Without a word the giant pulled back the string, aiming overlong. The shaft twanged forth.

"Hah!" cried John, nearly flinging the bow to the ground. He had not fully expected the arrow to pierce the tree, let alone the knot, yet it had landed dead centre. "Match that, my saucy friend!"

"As thou wishest."

Taking the same bow John had used, Robin selected the choicest arrow from the band's quivers. He gave himself little time to aim.

When the pointed bird had flown the band cheered, and John thought he might never move again. The young Hood's arrow had split his own in two, from one end to another.

"Thou didst shoot fair, as thou didst handle thy staff," quoth Robin.

"Aye, yet never could I shoot as well as thou hast. I shall join thy company, friend." The giant felt not altogether sorry he had lost, for the life sounded fair, and the clean forest air was heartier than any he had yet breathed.

"Then welcome, John Little."

Will Stutely spake up. "Methinks a better name for yon scant lad would be *Little John*."

As the outlaws laughed, the giant might have been swayed to anger had not Robin said, "Ah, the name doth suit thee well. Come lads, such a day deserves to be feasted upon."

They journeyed back to camp. The clearing where the outlaws made their home spanned a hundred yards in length, and forty in width. In the right rear corner dwelt the head of the outlaws' table. Beside this were fire pits and pots. Wood for the fires was never cut from a living tree. The stream behind the camp provided water for cooking and washing. Longhouses built of branches lay hidden amongst the leaves. Many paths spread from the clearing's front, closest to the king's highway. Through the thicket at the right of the camp sat a hollow rock, large enough to encompass five men. This became the band's treasury, guarded by a locked oaken door hidden under a pile of branches.

The crowning gem of the outlaws' camp was the great greenwood tree: a truly massive oak, the trunk so wide three men with their arms outstretched could not fully surround it. Its branches spread far, and never did its leaves bear any colour save a shady green. The men regarded this tree as almost sacred. They sat beneath its shade telling jests as the sun burned down, and upon clear nights slept under the stars shining through its boughs.

At this feast, carved cups the outlaws had made of silver birch held the finest ale the Blue Boar could offer. Edgar, the Blue Boar's innkeeper, was glad to have them as patrons. They never drank overmuch, ran into debt, or cheated him. Berries and seeds from the forest — as well as bread, cheese, and spices purchased with coins taken from dishonest travellers (who were always left just enough to help them home) — were spread along the board. Roasted venison from the spit dripped with sweetness. Food was plentiful, for deer were ever close at hand, the band never hunting for sport.

After the feast dissolved into crumbs, Will Stutely proposed they christen their new companion.

Henry o' Lincoln Town stepped up with a sober face, deeming himself priest of the ceremony. Little John was brought before him. Some of the band gathered 'round, whilst others preferred to recline where they were.

Henry pursed his lips, rolling his eyes about as he talked. "We gather here this day to welcome into our honourable company this tiny babe. Who amongst you brings this young one to be christened?" The mock priest peered into the crowd as though short-sighted.

"That do I," quoth Will Stutely, a smirk upon his face in a rare show of humour.

Henry continued, his face still sober, though the mouths of others were beginning to curl. "What is this child to be named?"

"Little John," called Stutely, smiling broadly now.

"Then, by the power invested in me by the outlaws of Sherwood and Barnesdale, I pronounce thee Little John, henceforth to live with us until gracious pardon from our good and noble king."

Henry motioned for the giant to kneel, and the latter did as bidden. A group of outlaws crept up behind John. The next instant he was dowsed from head to toe in nut-brown ale. He stood up amidst the outlaws' hoots, soaked to the skin.

Robin came forward, tears of laughter in his eyes. "Thou didst need a bathing. Now thou art fresh and new for thy life in the greenwood."

"And repaid for thy tumble into the stream, I suppose." The giant wrung out his beard. "I must trim mine hairs if I would keep them from turning into a nest for the birds."

The rest of the evening passed with singing and jests. This is how Little John the shepherd became the right-hand man of Robin Hood, King of Outlaws.

⊖⊷⊖

The sheriff paced his great stone hall. Its trestle tables and benches lay stacked against its walls, for the evening meal was over. His black hair matched his mood. He was puffing, unused to exercise, as his growing stomach evinced. "I was a lad of fifteen whilst Robin Hood still cried for the breast. Why cannot I capture the brat?"

"This outlaw is more cunning than the average peasant caught trying to shoot the king's deer." The sheriff's wife sat upon the dais at the high end of the otherwise empty hall.

"The longest a peasant hath evaded me hath been a month or two."

"Yet it is . . . nearly six months now, of Robin Hood plaguing you?" His wife smiled sweetly.

"He is robbing rich clergymen, taking them to his camp to feast, and demanding scores of pounds as payment. Yet none can tell me where exactly the camp doth lie, for the victims are blindfolded and led in circling paths until they no longer know which way is up, let alone north."

His wife shrugged. "Though the clergymen make a fuss, none worth worrying about hath yet been stolen from — none able to persuade the king of your unfitness for this office, at least."

"The king may still remove me if I fai'
Hood. Nottingham's fair approaches.
will be held, and men throughout th'
Nottingham Town to shoot. I shall order a go.
the prize."

"Can ye risk Robin Hood stealing it from the winner?"

"What if Robin Hood were to win? All proclaim the outlaw
the best archer in northern England. I recall having seen him
shoot at Baron Fitzwalter's castle when he was younger, and
indeed he had talent. I shall send out criers with this message:
'If the coward outlaw Robin Hood would have fame, glory,
and a golden arrow to boot, then let him come to the archery
contest at Nottingham, to be awarded the prize he deserves.'
All that need be done afterward will be to wait for the outlaw
to tumble headfirst into my trap."

CHAPTER TWO

Fir

WE HAVE HEARD FROM WILL Stutely how Marian Fitzwalter was taken by her family to attend a sick aunt. Happily, the aunt recovered. Now Baron Fitzwalter, his wife, and their five daughters have come home.

Whilst away, Marian had contented herself by practising at archery, broadsword, and quarterstaff with any who were willing in her aunt's household. Her sisters, meanwhile, spent their days at gossip and embroidery. Marian had long given up such activities in favour of learning combat. She had also sustained a lengthy campaign against being married. Her parents felt a twinge of shame that their eldest child preferred running over the countryside with a horde of boys to learning the ways of a lady, for there lurked a chance she would be chosen to wife some lord or earl who would take her to live at court. The Fitzwalters had hosted a grand feast for suitors upon Marian's turning eighteen. Yet she behaved as much like a boy as like a girl and was stubborn to boot. No marriage could be forced without her consent, only pressured, and the pressure had indeed grown great.

Now a visitor came to the baron's castle: Harold, the youngest son of another baron and a childhood friend of Robin and Marian. He was shown into the great hall, where the Fitzwalters sat at meat beside the fire.

"Harold, lad," cried the baron joyously, "come, join us."

"Many thanks, sir, but I am come with news. It seems at Nottingham Fair tomorrow the sheriff plans to capture Robin Hood by luring him with an archery contest."

Marian scoffed. "He is daft if he believes himself capable of so much as picking out Robert from the crowd."

"Thou thinkest Robert will attend?" Lady Fitzwalter looked up from her meat in surprise. "Surely he would not risk such a foolish thing."

"Robert is the best archer in all the world, Mother. Why should he not go?"

"Indeed," quoth the baron, "I hold great faith in the lad. Odds are he will carry off the prize from under the sheriff's very nose."

"Will ye be attending the match, sir?" Harold asked.

The baron thought a moment. "I fear we have business to catch up, yet I know Marian would fain go. Wouldst thou escort her?"

"'Twould be my pleasure." Harold glanced at Marian, who smiled her approval.

The next day, Harold and Marian set off for Nottingham Fair, in plain clothes and on foot, for they preferred fresh air and a brisk pace to sitting inside a cart as it bumped along.

"Wither do ye go, children?" quoth one of the men guarding the castle's entrance, in a teasing voice.

"To Nottingham, to see the notorious Robin Hood," Marian answered with mock apprehension.

"Be careful, children," warned the man-at-arms. "He is the deadliest archer in all the land."

"Fear not." Harold drew himself up. "I shall protect her." To his dismay the others laughed at this.

The two youths continued upon their way, buying bread and cheese for their lunch upon arriving at the fair. They saw clowns, minstrels, bouts at quarterstaff, plays concerning battles between angels and demons, juggling, and bear-baitings.

Marian brimmed full of impatience. At last it came time for the shooting match. Opposite the stands built for the nobility, a fence was set up to keep back the poor and the yeomen. Here she and Harold found a place to watch from near the shooting line.

The sheriff came riding to his box upon a white mare, his wife trotting along behind. He wore black silk, with the crest of his office embroidered in golden thread upon the sleeve. Upon his head sat a black cap with a scarlet ribbon, and a white plume so long it drooped over his shoulder. Around the sheriff's neck hung a thick, golden chain, and about his fingers perched many rings. The sheriff's wife rode a palfrey with a fawn mane. Her grey dress showed blue and gold embroidery, and a white cloth held her hair. She appeared bejewelled with light.

Once the two riders were settled upon cushioned thrones, a gaily dressed herald recited the rules of the contest: "Each man is to shoot a single shaft. Those hitting the centre ring may stay. The target will be removed twenty paces, and all those again piercing the centre will remain. This will be repeated until the final two archers are left, whereat each will send three shafts, and the better will claim the prize of our gracious Sheriff of Nottingham: a silver arrow with head and feathers of red gold."

The spectators cheered, for the rules were fair to their minds and the prize even fairer. The archers lined up upon the field, making ready to shoot. Many had come: farmers and coopers, tinkers and beggars, the sheriff's own archers, and those men whose deeds are preserved in ballads. The most famous was Clim o' th' Clough, whom many considered the best archer alive. Before being pardoned by the king, he had been companions with the northern outlaws William o' Cloudsley, and Adam Bell.

Marian sought to search each face, yet there were too many, and she could not find the one she wished.

What breezes arose were few and slight, thus it was a good day for shooting. After the first round, only a dozen archers remained upon the field. They rested whilst the target was moved back and the shafts removed from it.

The sheriff scrutinized these twelve. Leaning toward his wife, he asked, "Madame, do ye see Robin Hood upon yon field?"

The lady responded, "To my mind, Robin Hood hath not shown himself, for look: there are seven famous lads, two of your own guard, and the chief forester. Of the other two fellows the farmer is not only too short but too old. The beggar is blind of one eye and hath a brown beard, whilst the outlaw's is gold. My liege, he stands not here and thy plan hath failed."

"The coward-heart durst not show his face — blast him! It is shameful for a nobleman's son to be so timid. How have I not before captured this arrogant, false outlaw?"

Marian knew Robin was there, for he could not resist the challenge and, of all the archers, only the beggar's face was hidden. He wore a torn cloak of faded red, and breeks encrusted with mud. His shoon showed bits of his feet, and over his left eye he wore a patch. The hood of his ragged cloak cast a shadow over his face, though one could still see the smudges upon it.

As the archers shot a second time, Marian noted something familiar in the beggar's manner. He loosed his shafts quickly, letting them fly where they listed.

Six arrows struck the clout, five from the famous shooters. The sixth was the beggar's. Whilst the other archers went to rest (for pulling a longbow greatly strains the shoulder) the beggar stayed upon the field.

First he scanned the stands of the richer folk. Then he turned his attention toward the poor, who were enjoying themselves as much as the nobility. Almost immediately his eye alighted upon Marian.

When the beggar saw her, his face seemed not to know whether to flush red or drain white. He stepped to her, speaking with a south country accent. "'Ello, milady. Right fine day for a shooting match. Truly, ye are the fairest lass 'ere. I make it a custom to kiss the fairest lass at each contest — gives me good luck."

"Back, scoundrel," quoth Harold. "Thou knowest not to whom thou speakest."

"It is thou who knowest not to whom thou dost speak," snapped the beggar. He turned back to Marian. "Please, love?" This was whispered and the accent had vanished.

"To help a rascal," she whispered back.

The two leaned together and, though not for long, they kissed.

A horn summoned the archers back to the mark.

The beggar held her hand a moment longer. "I love thee."

Marian smiled. "And I love thee." Longingly was the tattered form looked after as he returned to the field.

Harold leaned closer to her. "Was that Robert?"

"Thou art in luck he doth not wish to draw attention to himself, else thou wouldst find thyself engaged in combat for what thou didst say to him."

"But when . . . "

"Hush! They are to shoot."

Had Harold finished his question, he would have asked when the two friends had fallen in love. Yet he could only stand there in puzzlement, for Marian's attention now focused fully upon the match.

The first four archers failed to strike the clout, partly due to jangling nerves. When Clim o' th' Clough shot, a breeze sprang up, causing the arrow to fly to the mark's very centre. A great cheer rose up.

The beggar took his stance, undaunted.

Quickly was his arrow loosed. The crowd laughed even before the shaft reached its mark. The beggar had aimed wide, and would miss the target altogether.

At the last moment the arrow swooped down and lodged itself in the dimpled clout, forcing out Clim's shaft and taking its place.

Not a sound was heard until the herald regained himself and announced, "The final pair containeth Clim o' th' Clough and the beggar. Each will send three shafts. The winner carries off the sheriff's prize."

The target was removed twenty paces. Both archers examined their bowstrings and arrows. The very best shooting was yet to be seen, for now each archer knew the other had a keen eye and steady hand.

A coin was tossed, and the lot fell to Clim o' th' Clough. He took his place.

His first arrow landed a hand's breadth from the clout's centre. Luck flew with the second shaft, and it lodged in the exact middle. A cheer went up, and Clim let go a deep breath. His third shaft alighted but an inch and a half from the second. The beggar stepped up to shoot.

Some in the crowd jeered him, calling his last shot a fluke. Hoots lapped upon bellows.

Everything was silenced as Robin drew back the string. His shaft sped, landing immediately beside Clim's second arrow, slicing the fletching off the right side.

The crowd thought to taunt the beggar again, for his arrow had failed the centre, yet before any-a-one could get a word out, the beggar launched his second missile, landing it upon the opposite side of Clim's shaft, severing the left fletching.

None moved as the beggar nocked his final arrow. To cut off the third fletching would cause him to lose, for the shot would not better his opponent's.

Pulling back the string, the beggar paused a moment longer before bringing it fully taut.

A sonorous roar arose. Clim's arrow, which had pierced the very heart of the clout, had been shattered, the blind man's shot vibrating in its place. The feathers of his three shafts clustered together, looking like the fletching of a single arrow.

The crowd of archers, who had remained upon the field's edge to watch, rushed forward, engulfing their champion and carrying him upon their shoulders to the dais.

The sheriff and his wife rose to their feet. Handing the beggar the golden arrow, Nottingham's protector spake. "Good beggar, thou hast shot fair this day. Truly, thou art better than that cowardly scourge Robin Hood. What be thy name?"

"My name be Ralph o' Worcestershire, sir, and I think Robin Hood the better archer."

"We never shall know, for the faint-hearted knave stays within the forest walls."

The beggar remained silent.

"But let us not speak of outlaws," the sheriff continued glibly. "Wilt thou join mine archers? Thou wilt receive two-score-and-two pence every sennight, clothes better than thou art wearing, a roof, a bed, and more food than thou canst eat. What sayest thou?"

"I say there be no man i' th' world worthy to be my master save good King Henry. G'day m'lord." The beggar turned upon his heel and quit the field.

Marian forced her way through the crowd, leaving Harold behind. Reaching the edge of the ocean of people, she whipped her head in every direction, catching sight of a bit of red disappearing into the bushes some hundred yards away. Running softly, Marian took a deep breath. For months she had planned this, and now she must not fail.

Through the forest she followed Robin for miles, never letting him know she was there. She knew he would not countenance her living in the greenwood with him, where she could be killed by anyone who passed by. The first part of her plan was to track him to his camp and memorize its location. The next day, she would return to carry out the second part.

Twilight came upon the forest, and the trees' shadows deepened. Marian lost sight and sound of Robin. She spun in confusion, trying to pick up his trail, yet this proved useless. Marking the way in her mind, she proceeded back toward the king's highway.

Well doth the greenwood hide those who dwell within it.

⊹⊹⊹

Arriving at camp, Robin was greeted by his men, now some five-score. Stripping away the eye patch and the beggar's garb to reveal the suit of Lincoln green beneath, Robin Hood held aloft the golden arrow to a grand cheer.

"We shall hang this arrow upon the greenwood tree, to remember how the Sheriff of Nottingham was put to shame. Prepare a feast, my men, though the hour be late, for this deserves celebration. Come, Little John, let us see if we can remove the walnut stain from my beard."

The men chuckled as they went about their master's bidding, whilst Robin and Little John retired to the stream.

"How good to be home in Sherwood, hey master?"

"Sherwood, both home and prison together," Robin murmured.

"Yet we stand free in the forest air."

"John," quoth the outlaw, once they were well away from earshot, "there are two matters troubling me."

"Speak thy mind, master. Mayhap I can aid thee."

"John," quoth the outlaw, as soon as they were away from earshot, "there are two matters troubling me."

"Speak thy mind, master. Mayhap I can aid thee."

"The first matter," quoth Robin, "is that, when the sheriff did give me the prize, he cursed us as cowards for not falling into his trap. I would have him know 'twas Robin Hood won the prize from his very hand."

"Leave that to me, master. I shall send the sheriff word. What else perplexes thee?"

Sitting upon the greensward, Robin's eyes slowly rose to meet his companion's, and he whispered, "Not another soul in all the world knows. Promise me, upon thine honour, Little John, that thou shalt tell no one."

"I promise, master."

Taking a deep breath, Robin began, "Today at the fair I saw one I have not seen these six months past. Thou hast surely heard that, whilst I dwelt at Baron Fitzwalter's, his daughter Marian and I befriended one another."

"Aye, true," quoth the giant.

"Five days before I turned outlaw . . . we were married."

Little John stayed silent.

"We were to tell our parents at the shooting match, yet upon the way ill befell me, and I became outlawed."

The Hood's right-hand man regained himself and asked, "Did she recognize thee?"

Robin smiled softly. "We have been best friends since the age of six; no disguise have I ever donned that she could not see through."

"What wouldst thou have me do, master?"

"Nay, Little John. This I must unravel myself, yet I thank thee for listening."

⊗ ⊗ ⊗

That night, whilst the sheriff dined with his guests, he again spake ill of Robin Hood.

"I cannot believe the fiend stayed away." A piece of bread hung from his mouth. "The haughty wolf's-head durst not show himself for fear of me."

Even as the sheriff spake, a blunted arrow sailed through the window, clattering onto a plate before his wife.

She gave a small start, yet reached out and took the shaft. Tied near to the head was a small scroll, which Lady Nottingham unrolled. It was a warrant for the capture of Robin Hood. An outlaw who had been once a clerk had aided Little John, who could neither read nor write, in adding a message behind the warrant. The sheriff's wife read aloud, her lips curving into a smile at the jest:

Thou hast given freely
Gold arrow from thine hand,
And it has gone to feast
With Robin Hood's stout band.

CHAPTER THREE
Birch

ROBIN SPENT THE NEXT MORNING ranging about the forest, trying his best not to seem lovelorn. When he arrived back at camp late in the afternoon, Will Stutely had news.

"Master, there is a stranger who hath found our camp, and boasts great skill at the bow. A garland is set up, and the stranger awaits your presence underneath the greenwood tree."

Too troubled in heart and mind to attribute anything to Stutely's odd manner, Robin approached the great greenwood tree, now adorned with the golden arrow. Many of the band sat or stood nearby, having gathered to see this new archer.

"Greetings, friend," quoth Robin.

The stranger bowed, not uttering a word. A hooded mantle of coarse brown wool obscured the face from view. One could tell the stranger carried a broad sword beneath the mantle, along with broad shoulders and six feet of height.

"Shoot at thy will."

Easily pulling back the bowstring, the stranger loosed three shafts, one fast upon the other, that sailed through the garland at eleven-score yards, the last arrow splitting the wand that held the garland.

"Well done," exclaimed Robin, surprised at this show of skill. "Thou hast shown thyself worthy of joining our company. What be thy name?"

Removing the hood so that all might see the face beneath, the stranger quoth, "Anne o' th' Hood."

Marian Fitzwalter stood before them, her dark brown hair clipped above her shoulders, face bright.

None dared move, Robin and Marian staring at one another, the merry men in turn staring at them. Then the two lovers came together and either laughed or wept, burying their faces in each other's shoulders.

Little John, who had been sore at ease for his master's happiness, thought this the fairest scene he had e'er laid eyes upon. Smug Stutely stood next to him. Having known Robin and Marian in childhood, he appreciated the bond they shared, yet he knew nothing of their loving one another.

At length, the outlaw and his wife leaned apart a slight bit, to stand kissing each other eagerly. The merry men looked away, for they felt this a private scene.

Will Stutely's face nearly fell from his skull. Marian had always been one of the boys, who could fight and whoop and climb as well as any of them. The love she and Robin shared had ever been companionable. What could have happened to make them fall in love?

At last the outlaw and his wife drew apart enough to talk without being overheard.

Robin brushed hair past her face. "Marian love, how didst thou find our camp?"

"Yesterday, dearest, I followed thee into the woods and yet lost sight of thee. Today when I returned, Will Stutely was there and showed me the route. We devised a plan to fool thee, and show myself worthy of joining thy band. Art thou angry, lover?" Marian looked up at him, exercising her power to seem innocent.

Robin smiled back at her, for he could not summon strength enough to be severe. "Nay, love. I am not vexed, for how could I be so with thee?" A slight crease, though, came into his brow as he slid her hair between two fingers. Turning toward his men, who were all stock still and leering in the most awkward way, the outlaw leader spake. "My men, may I present here . . . "

"Anne o' th' Hood," Marian interjected. To Robin she whispered, "I' 'twill take me awhile to accustom myself to saying always Robin instead of Robert, and by this I even the score."

He smiled and continued, "She is my wife. I trust ye will treat her with the great loyalty and respect all women deserve. Now, lads, prepare a feast. This is somewhat to celebrate!"

As his men hurried about his bidding, Robin took Anne aside. They followed the path to the small clearing where he had passed his first night as an outlaw. "Thou hast no need to invent an alias, Marian."

"An outlaw would not continue under their true name."

"Thou shouldst not have cut thine hair. 'Twas verily down to thy waist before, my fair one."

"I know how thou didst admire it. Yet 'twas best gotten rid of since I am to live in the forest. 'Tis a great weight gone."

"Some might see such short hair as immodest."

Anne smiled. "I wished to shock thee." She drew a cloth of light green from one of the two purses hanging from her girdle. This she wrapped over her forehead, and tied at the base of her skull. "I shall modestly cover mine hair, now that we are no longer covering the fact of our marriage. Besides, i' 'twill help keep out the twigs. I also intend to wear the same Lincoln-green suits the men do. Yet, if thou dost wish, lover, I can wear the tunic and surcoat longer, except they interfere with walking through the hedges."

"Marian, enough. Dearest, thou canst not stay here, for it is by far too dangerous."

"I cannot leave. I robbed a monk upon the king's highway." Anne untied the second purse from her girdle, passing it to Robin. "I told him my name, and afterward followed him to the edge of Nottingham. By now he hath reported my felony to the sheriff. I am an outlaw, love."

He saw that one of the purse strings was cut and six shillings lay inside. "Dost thou know what thou hast done? Outlawry is no life, but death on earth."

"Nay, love. Death on earth hath been spending the better portion of this past year always parted from thee."

Robin stared at Anne and did not know whether to cry for joy or sorrow. The one person he cared for most in the world would have a death sentence upon her head, and yet this meant they were reunited. There was silence before he at last asked, "Hast thou told anyone thou art here, love?"

"I left two letters, one for my father, and one for my sisters. They detail our falling in love and marriage, as well as my coming to the greenwood."

Robin grinned. "Thou soundest belike to thy mother."

Anne smiled back. "I missed thee, love."

"As have I thee." He took her in his arms.

"I knew thou wouldst not be well with killing a man, though thou wouldst think the price upon thine head the most fashionable thing it had ever worn. Didst thou know thy life is now valued at two hundred pounds, lover mine? With the warrant thou hast thwarted and the archery contest, 'tis no wonder."

"Only *two* hundred?" Robin considered. "We shall have to remedy that. Though I am sorry, love, if my being outlawed hath worried thee."

"As long as thine head is upon thy body I shall worry for thee. Heaven knows thou didst have more sense when thou wert six, for since then it has either leaked out thine ears or been beaten out by another man's quarterstaff. Thou goest into all manner of adventures without first knowing what they are about."

"True, love," quoth Robin, "but thou dost follow."

"Only to keep thee from being sliced into a thousand pieces, burnt to ashes, and flung over the breadth and width of England."

He laughed, kissing Anne's forehead, and then the rest of her face. Soon one of the men came to tell them the feast lay ready.

Robin led the table prayer, thanking God that Anne would now live in the greenwood as queen over his men, and imploring above all protection for the band. During the meal Anne was introduced to each outlaw in turn, and told somewhat of his reputation. Some were spies from local towns, coming in to relay news. Others were men returning from delivering spoils to the poor, and some worked as long-range patrol, bringing guests whenever they might. Most stayed at camp, occasionally patrolling, and alternating such chores as hunting (which was more a joy than a chore), preparing meals, skinning, carving bows, and fletching arrows. Each outlaw received her with kindness and thought their master fortunate.

Afterward, all were eager to hear how Robin and Anne had fallen in love, most of all Will Stutely, who felt quite irritated at being left out of the secret.

As a storyteller Anne was exemplary, so the two Hoods, Robin lying on his side upon the ground and Anne sitting close at his head, talked of the night Marian Fitzwalter had turned eighteen, and how Robert of Huntington had loved her.

"The curtain rises as the afternoon air tints a redder gold," Anne began. "Two mates sit by a silver stream. The forest around them hath grown much over their eleven years of friendship.

"The one is a lad of eighteen with hair of sun, eyes of sky, and a spirit floating with the clouds. The other is a lass with hair of tree bark, eyes of sunset, and a spirit sinking through the earth. All her life she hath been one with the lads, romping about. Tonight her father hosts a feast to encourage these lads as suitors, so that they will seek her hand, friendship forgotten. The sweet lad who accompanies her is the dearest of all her companions. She knows he at least will keep their friendship well.

"They discuss all as they sit, and when the lass leaves to get ready, he calls after her, 'If thou wilt be in need of anything this night, Marian, be not hesitant to ask.' And so she treads home."

Robin continued, "That night the lad comes to Baron Fitzwalter's castle dressed in his finest. The walls of the great hall are decorated with colourful tapestries, and minstrels play in the gallery above. Inside he finds his chums, neighbours, and even strangers. He sees many a man who could easily be father to her. They have all come to court his friend. He vows he will not let any one of them lay hand upon her.

"Of a sudden the music is silenced and Marian's father ascends the dais. He speaks so that all might hear: 'Attention please, good lords. I am not a man of many words, yet it doth please mine heart to see so many noble men taking an interest in my daughter . . . ' Here the lad sticks out his tongue, making a face as if he had drunk sour ale. ' . . . May I present Maid Marian Fitzwalter.'

"Here a graceful, well-plumed bird enters from the head of the hall. She hath dark, oaken hair that is swept back, leaving in view the tops of her milk-white shoulders. Her lips are scarlet, as is her dress, this with white silk and golden embroidery. Her hands are clasped, and her eyes shine as emerald as the greenwood. An air of remorse floats about her. She looks unsure and uncomfortable.

"All this our lad takes in with great interest and, in the very moment he doth set his eyes upon this fairest of fair creatures, he falls in love." Robin kissed Anne's hand, and it was as if they relived the moment.

Once more the she-Hood took up the tale. "After the meal, her father bids her rise, and the maid Marian stands with feelings mixed. Her father orders the minstrels to play a lively tune, and each man present offers his hand for the first dance. In all their eyes is the same thing. They only see her; none care how she feels.

"'My lady,' a tall, handsome youth bows before her. It is her dearest friend. There is such a look in his pure eyes that makes her wonder and draws her in. Whilst looking into the sweet lad's eyes, she herself falls in love without realizing it.

"They dance the whole evening without ceasing, and though the suitors are nettled, they dare not interrupt. The lad and lass dance without knowing the night passes. At last the minstrels refuse to play another note, as they are tired and their hands cramped.

"The two sit by talking. Once all the others have gone to bed, at last the lad Robert makes ready to part."

"Says he," quoth Robin, gazing at Anne as if speaking only to her, "'Tomorrow at sunrise I shall come to seek thee, and caress thy face as the sun doth caress the east sky.'"

The merry men had no need to guess at what happened next, for Robin and Anne touched lips so lovingly, there could be no mistaking.

⊖⊖⊖

For the three weeks after the feast at Baron Fitzwalter's castle, Robert and Marian had kept their love a secret. The lovers in romances always did so, to protect their bond. It made for more fun, and prevented anyone's mentioning that, as a second son, Robert ranked appreciably below Marian, who was heir to her father's title.

One day, Robert and Marian were reclining by their stream, beneath the white saplings that had grown up with them, when the subject of marriage peeped out. Marian's father had been receiving noblemen's requests for her hand.

"And what has he said them?" Robert asked.

"None have been accepted, yet he hassles me increasingly."

Robert stretched. "Why dost thou not marry, then?"

Marian's eyes widened. "How dost thou mean?"

"Choose a suitor and settle down. Clean house. Cook meals." Robert hit upon each idea with new enthusiasm. "Have children! Change the babes, and feed them at all hours of the night."

Marian cocked her head to one side. "Art thou quite finished?"

"Nothing of the sort." Taking her hands, Robert raised her to her feet and knelt. "Marian . . . I love thee, sweetheart. Thou art the only one I could ever love, could ever dream of loving. Fair one, wilt thou marry me?"

For lack of another response, tears stung her eyes. After a moment she spake. "Of course I shall . . . but thou must e'en cease to be wild. Clean the house, cook the meals — have the children! Change the babes, and feed them at all hours of the night."

"Keep this up, dearest, and thou wilt see no ring."

Marian dropped to her knees and kissed him, both grinning.

The next day they made their plans, enlisting the aid of a local churchman, for a price. Each young lover cut a lock of their hair, braiding these into rings. Gold and a silver coin were melted, and the braids dipped, Marian's in gold, Robert's in silver.

At first light the morning after, Marian met Robert upon the highway, she wearing a simple, green robe. Robert handed a bouquet of white roses to Marian, who smiled in return, and off they set. Laughing along, they did not meet many upon the road. They reached the church and came home by supper, wearing their rings upon leather thongs about their necks.

The two determined to announce their clandestine marriage the next week, returning from the archery contest at Nottingham. As we have seen, Robert's disappearance went unexplained until the next day. By then the Fitzwalters were preparing for their journey. No amount of pleading would persuade Marian's father to leave her behind, and for the six months away she planned. The solution she found to regain her life was to give it up. She left family, comfort, and safety to live in a cave in the freezing wintertime, and be hunted like an animal in the summer. Let it be known that she never regretted it.

CHAPTER FOUR
Aspen

THE LOCAL PEOPLE HELD NO qualms with Sherwood's outlaws. In sooth, they rejoiced in the outlaws, praying for their safety and the further humiliation of greedy lords.

The sheriff was consumed with capturing Robin Hood, to the detriment of his other duties, his reputation suffering each time he failed. After two months of planning, he vied one last time to capture the outlaw. He sent out parties of armed men. They entered the greenwood with orders to lie in wait for Robin Hood and his band and bring them before the sheriff, if possible, alive.

When Robin Hood received word through Edgar o' th' Blue Boar Inn of the sheriff's plan, he withdrew his men to Barnesdale, in Yorkshire.

Earlier that month Little John had gone to Nottingham Fair. No word had come from him in all this time. Robin sent Will Stutely to find the giant and bring him to Barnesdale.

Over his suit of Lincoln green Stutely donned the cloak of a travelling friar, kept with other disguises in the band's treasure store. Strapping a broad sword beneath, he left for the Blue Boar to gain news.

The morning clouded over, the sky telling of dark times to come.

Arriving at the inn, Stutely saw a band of two-score men bearing Nottingham's crest. They brooded about, half drunk. Stutely sat upon a bench outside the door, wondering how he could speak with Edgar without them becoming suspicious.

The innkeeper did not recognize Will. He thought him a weary traveller, and let him be.

One of the sheriff's men called to Stutely, "Ho there, friar! Come drink with us!"

"Nay," quoth the outlaw, lowering his voice to disguise it as well as his body. "My vows permit it not."

An ill gust of wind sprang from the maw of the incoming storm, flying up Stutely's robe and revealing his Lincoln green hose. The sheriff's men saw this, and knew what it meant. Rushing upon Will with a battle cry, they drew their swords.

Stutely unsheathed his own blade, resolving to die before he was taken.

He warded them off as best he could, yet twelve were they, quickly joined by more. Though not all the sheriff's men came away without injury, the outlaw caught the worst of it, collapsing from lack of blood.

Imprisoned under Nottingham Castle, Will Stutely barely survived the night. Edgar's wife had been asked to bind his wounds as best she could, but no other aid was given. In two days Stutely would be hanged, thus teaching all outlaws to beware the sheriff's justice.

⊖·⊖·⊖

Late that afternoon, when Will had not reappeared, Robin Hood grew restless. The storm that brewed, contriving to hit upon the morrow, put the outlaw further on edge.

"Let me seek him, love," Anne volunteered.

"Nay," quoth Robin, "I sent Stutely to seek Little John, and now he, too, hath disappeared. I shall venture no one but myself this time. Thou art chief until I return."

Anne would have liked to argue, yet the remorse in Robin's voice made stay her tongue. As leader of the band, he felt responsible for both the actions and fates of his men.

Donning a traveller's clothes, and catching up his quarterstaff, he set out toward Nottingham. If there were a piece of news in England, it would not take long for the country to come alive with it.

When Robin came to the border between Nottinghamshire and Yorkshire, he observed an aged pilgrim, back from the Holy Land, resting by the roadside.

"Ho there, good fellow. Have ye any news for me?" Robin called, with a wave of his hand.

"The whole of Nottinghamshire is abuzz with tidings of a hanging two days hence," replied the old man. "They have caught one of Robin Hood's own band — Will Stutely!"

For a moment Robin could neither speak nor take breath. "Where doth this execution take place?"

"At the gates of Nottingham Town, as warning to all outlaws of the sheriff's great power."

"My thanks to you, old man. Ye may have saved a life." Robin turned his toes, hurrying back whence he had come.

The pilgrim thought this strange yet dismissed it from his mind, striking up a ballad and continuing his journey.

⊹⊹⊹

Back at their temporary camp, the outlaws awaited their master's return. Some noticed a rustling in the bush, and hurried to the spot, eager to see if 'twas one of the strayed.

A stooped, wrinkled figure clothed in tatters appeared to their sight. Long silver hair beneath the faded kerchief told of a woman. She seemed to have no flesh, but only bones upon which to hang her rags.

Anne approached. "Greetings, stranger, what dost thou do in these woods and with no escort besides?"

"I seek Robin of the Hood to help me in my troubles," replied the woman, with an age-cracked voice. "I heard he hath moved to the north. Could you direct a poor widow?"

Anne nodded. "Thou art in luck, for though thou hast not found Robin Hood, we are his band and shall help if we can. What be thy troubles?"

"'Tis urgent I find aid for my sons William, John, and Lester. Mine husband died two years ago, and since my sons have poached the king's deer, for they could not get honest work. This very morn were they taken by the sheriff's men. They are to be hanged with a fourth . . . by the name of William Stutely, if I remember me right . . . two days hence at the vile gates of Nottingham Town."

At the mention of Will Stutely the outlaws tensed. When the widow finished, a great whisper like wind amongst leaves swept through the band.

A tightness choked Anne's voice. "Prytell, what be the story of this other man?"

Raising an eyebrow as if to ask what difference it made, the woman answered, "He is a local outlaw, I have heard, caught by the sheriff's men. He fought them and lost much blood. There is doubt whether he will survive to be hanged."

"Thankee, good woman." Anne started off between the trees, for she could bear it no more. "Henry, thou art in command; give our guest somewhat to eat." She was gone to find Robin Hood.

As it happened, Robin was none too far away, having hurried back after learning what was to become of Will Stutely.

Anne glimpsed a traveller coming toward her. Scanning him from head to foot, she recognized her husband beneath his disguise and pulled back the hood shadowing her face. "We have a tangle, my love," quoth she.

"Aye and that I know right well. Stutely is to be hanged."

"And with him the three sons of a widow who hath found us."

"Where is this widow now?"

"Feasting with the band."

Robin craned his neck. "Thank heaven for this storm, else Stutely might have been hanged upon the morrow."

The band, as well as the old woman, were glad to see them. Robin listened to every word she spake, and one could see he thought of a plan.

"We have much to do," quoth the outlaw, "and much waiting. For now, as the fair widow hath begun to feast, let us also."

There was wisdom in this, for premonition weights the mind, whilst feasting lightens the mood if not the stomach. A grand feast was spread and all ate, despite misgivings bubbling in their guts.

Afterward, the widow was called upon to select entertainment. Every night the band enjoyed some form of amusement, be it ballad, story, contest, or otherwise. The widow declared she would take pleasure in a ballad. Henry o' Lincoln Town was chosen to favour them, for he had a fair voice.

Hark to the tale of a maid
Whose spirit never was swayed.
She boasted she'd marry never —
For she was skilled and clever,
And did not need a man.

'Twas a young lad known as Ned
Who vowed that he would her wed.
She refused him many-a-time,
Claiming he was born of swine;
She was content alone.

Ned gave her father treasure.
This gave the old man pleasure,
So he promised Ned his daughter.
For years now Ned had sought her;
At last she would be his.

She loathed his proposition,
And golden exhibition,
So she fled to the forest well,
Where she met good Adam Bell,
The outlaw good and true.

"Harken to my woes," said she,
"Ned's own wife I was to be,
But I have no wish to tether
Myself with strap of leather
To that repulsive man."

"'Tis bravely spoke," quoth Adam,
"Yet Ned will be quite saddened.
Are ye sure of your decision?
Your eyes have been his prison,
And he doth love you so."

At this speech the maiden saw
Ned's own strong and handsome jaw,
And knew she would be his lover,
Upon his needs to hover,
'Til parted by cold death.

A cheer of appreciation rose up at this fair singing, the loudest being the widow's, for she thought the song a charming one.

When this praise subsided, Anne spake. "What be the reasoning for that last verse? Surely no woman could give herself over after such a fight to be free. What happened to make the independent maiden turn slave?"

One of the band piped up. "Pardon, but is that not the idea of marriage, milady?"

"Nay, heaven forbid," quoth she. "A man, also, must be reverent to his wife. 'Tis to be a partnership, not a submission."

Seeing an argument upon the horizon, Robin dove in. "Aye, 'tis true. If a man wishes for fawning submission he should find a dog. Ho! fair widow — wilt thou stay the night with us?"

"I bethink me I should return home," she answered.

"Then thou wilt be escorted by Anne and I," quoth Robin, catching up his staff and receiving a knowing glance from his wife.

The black trees in the northern forest enjoyed contorting into beasts. Sherwood had been home to the outlaws for nearly a year, and they missed the warmer greenery. No forest in the world was as alive.

The party came upon a small hut, none too far from the end of the leaves. Outside were scattered bones, likely those of the deer the widow's sons had killed, the house acting as a tombstone. The widow strode to her door, motioning for the two Hoods to enter.

By now the stars had nearly taken the sky, yet a slit of sun remained to see by. Hardly a thing sat within the walls of woven wood but a table, and four stools. There was no floor to catch crumbs, only dirt, and no crumbs anyway. Rushes and grass stacked upon the ground formed a bed. The rushes held dust and insects; belike some mice as well. The widow would not survive if her sons did not return to attend her. She had no one else in the world and would starve to death. At the outlaws' feast she had eaten more than three men together, for she had not eaten in days. Robin and Anne had seen many such as her. Some of the band had been in her position, joining to avoid starvation.

Robin offered the woman a bag of coins. "For thy pantry," quoth he.

"Thankee, kind sir. Ye are generous indeed."

"Not I, mistress, but God whispering good deeds into men."

"Good morrow to you."

The outlaw and his wife walked in silence after they left the widow's hut. Thoughts of starving, and helplessness moved Anne to speech. "Tha' 'twas kind of thee, love."

Robin smiled. "Outlaws know little of kindness, my fair one; 'twas merely some taxes needing to be returned."

"We cannot let that woman lose her sons."

"Aye, and we shan't."

⊹⊙⊹⊙⊹⊙⊹

The next day was a busy one. One outlaw was so anxious, Robin called to him laughingly, "Do not sharpen thy sword further, friend, else only the hilt remain."

The band laboured over weapons, mail, and helmets. They had vowed the sheriff would never hang one of their own, and all were prepared to die fighting for this promise. Hanging was an agonizing death. Outlaws pray for a sword in their flesh before a rope 'round their necks.

Evensong brought a late meal. The men gathered in a circle. Though all felt tired and hungry, their jaws and stomachs were made tight by thoughts of Will Stutely and the morrow. Robin deemed a story the best way to calm nerves. He asked Anne to do what she could.

"This is the tale of two young friends who, whilst travelling, came upon highwaymen so lacking in honour they robbed children."

Shouts arose in condemnation of this practice.

Anne continued, "The two children are aged fourteen years. One is a lad with hair of golden wheat and eyes as clear blue as a crystal stream. He goes to visit Squire Gamewell's manor. With the lad is his dearest friend, come to keep him company.

"The ground is speckled about with the sunlight peeping through greenwood leaves. A slight breeze plays in the canopy. The pair come upon two men standing in the middle of the road.

"'Hold there, young ones,' calls the lead man.

"'Wherefore, sir, and what may it be?' the lad Robert asks.

"'All who travel this road must give o'er every penny else they are beaten.' The man twirls his staff above his head, making it whistle.

"'We have not a groat between us,' returns the lad. 'Furthermore, it doth ill-beseem grown men to set upon those weaker than they. It shows them as cowards.'

"'Ye will pay, else a right stout beating is in order,' the second man chimes in.

"Robert returns with anger in his voice, 'Verily, we have no money, and if we did, we should not give thee a lead penny.'

"'Thy beating is well earned by thy saucy tongue, boy!' The leader charges forth in a rage.

"Robert has leapt to the ground, staff in hand, whilst his companion has nocked an arrow. The shaft flies true, piercing the second man's arm. He had been drawing a knife on Robert.

"The lad and the lead man battle fiercely. Each strikes the other once, the highwayman with a mighty buffet in the ribs and Robert with a stout box o' the ear. Despite what

Robert lacks in height, he makes more than a match for the highwayman, who soon finds himself equal to the dust.

"'Now, sweet sir,' says Robert, out of breath, 'I hope thou wouldst think twice ere again robbing those who have nothing to give. He who takes from the poor will soon find himself in a like position.'"

Chuckles were heard amongst the band, for this saying was one their master all but governed his life by.

Anne went on. "The pair rides for Gamewell Hall. Upon seeing them the men-at-arms sound a horn. A stately man, a gentrified woman, and a bright-eyed lad appear from out of the castle.

"The squire is decked out in a fine black surcoat, a silk cap upon his head, his wife in a richly embroidered robe. They both stand erect and, though he is solemn, she hath a twinkle in her eyes belike her brother Robert.

"The lad is four years younger than the riders, yet hath a dignified air about him. Although he holds a manly stance, he appears dainty, with thin blonde hair and a slender jaw. The measure across his shoulders is wide, and he hath good height, yet his arms are ill-hung. Whether he grows to be a wight man remains unseen.

"As the riders near, the squire hails them with a crafty smile. 'Ho there, Cousin Robert, who hast thou brought with thee? A lady friend?'

"Robert laughs. 'Good brother and sister, this is Marian Fitzwalter. She and I have played together since the age of six. Surely ye have heard of her?'

"'Ahh, yes — the troublemaker.' The old squire chuckles.

"Robert glances meaningfully at Marian, and she repeats the speech rehearsed during their journey. 'I hope 'twill be no inconvenience, yet I would much appreciate thine allowance to stay as long as Robert is in thy charge.'

"'Of course,' the squire answers jovially.

"Young William leads the visitors to the stables, where the animals are unsaddled and taken into the ostler's care.

"Jumping down from their mounts, the two travellers take their bags and weapons, starting back for the house with the boy.

"'Will, how hast thou fared since last I saw thee?' asks Robert.

"'Very well, sir. Mother said thou mightest teach me to fence and the like.' Will's young eyes shine.

"'Aye, that will I,' says Robert, 'and Marian will assist, she being my former student.'

"Will looks at Marian with curiosity, which she returns with a nod.

"The next days, Will Gamewell shows great promise with longbow and quarterstaff. After paired weeks of targets, the trio betake themselves to the forest, that Will might practise with rabbits.

"They walk until nigh noon, yet no game is seen. Not even the king's own deer."

A few of the outlaws smiled at this.

"Upon entering a thicket, the three hear voices. They crouch behind the thick plants, careful to snap no twigs beneath their toes.

"'The fact is, mates, we can be no use as highwaymen as long as we are wounded.'

"'Didst thou hear that *boy* scorn me? If ever I meet him again, I shall beat in his head!'

"Robert's eye gleams. Before Will can ask him explanation or Marian can lay hold of his heel, Robert shoves through the thicket and into the company of three highwaymen, two of whom tried to rob him not two weeks agone.

"'Ho there, sweet fellows. How have ye faired? Healing well, I trust?'

"'Here is the part where Robert gets beaten,' Marian whispers to Will. 'Nay, stir not. We must be patient ere he needs our help.' Indeed, at the Fitzwalters', watching Robert wedge himself into plights had become as common a diversion as hearing a ballad sung.

"Will stays and, although he is nervous for his uncle, no other seems to be — including Robert himself.

"The lead highwayman rises to face the lad. 'So, thou hast returned to gloat.'

"'Nay, heaven forbid! I sought you out to see how ye mend. Gloating I leave to the pompous.'

"'Leave, else ill befall thee.'

"'Shall I have another beating? Truly, I enjoyed the last one right well. Come, we shall see who gets his crown cracked.'

"Each draws his sword, and they begin a right stout bout. Clashing metal rings for miles through the trees.

"It is fortunate for Robert his friends lie in the brush. Approaching from behind, the other two thieves think to behead the lad with a wicked sword.

"'Will,' whispers Marian, 'here is good game for thee. Nock an arrow. I shall aim for that man's sword arm. Do thou take his left.'

"When the traitorous man gives his back to them, preparing to strike, both shoot fair and the man, crying in pain, drops his sword. Seeing his companion fall, the third knave runs in fright, soon followed by the second.

"Swords clash on. Robert possesses great skill for his age, yet the strength of anger is with his opponent, and the lad's guard is beaten down. Robert surely would have died then had not young Gamewell broken cover to block, with the second bandit's sword, the deadly blow with might and main.

"Will buckles under the force and falls to the ground.

"Raising his weapon again, the highwayman prepares to strike death to both boys.

"'Hold!' Marian shouts, stepping forth and loosing an arrow that skims the man's neck. Blood trickles to his shoulders. She fits another shaft. 'I would fain not slay thee, yet if thou dost not put up thy weapon, I will.' She half draws.

"The highwayman flees after his comrades.

"Standing, Robert and Will raise their swords, yet all danger is passed.

"Approaching Robert, Marian glares. 'This time I *mean* it. Thou doest that again, Locksley, and I shall lash thee to a tree.'

"Robert smiles wearily. Will is too wide-eyed to do much of anything. When he can finally speak, he gasps, 'Thou hast done this before?'

"'*Constantly*,' Marian rolls her eyes good naturedly, smiling in spite of herself. 'He ever finds fights, and someone must come to his aid. Usually Struts[2] or I.'

---

2   Struts is the name Anne called Will Stutely in childhood.

"'Thou didst do well, lad,' quoth Robert, attempting to shake the focus from himself. 'Thy future is sealed — thou wilt be a great fighter.'

"So if e'er ye are near to Gamewell Hall, keep out an eye for a dainty lad with a fine maiden air, but beware, for *no* man trifles with his uncle."

❦❦❦

The band woke as morning broke. Each struggled into a coat of mail, placed a cap of steel under his hood, and clapped a good sword by his side. They then disguised themselves, some as friars, others as beggars, more as tradesmen.

Like many great leaders before and after him, Robin gave a speech before his followers marched forth. He stood upon a stone and addressed them all. "My men, ye must crowd around the gallows to which Stutely will be carted. Armed men guard it, but ye must get as close as ye can. At my signal, draw your swords and fight with might and main. I have killed a man, and would fain not do so again. Yet if we must strike, let us strike hard, so there be no need to strike again. May God have mercy upon us."

The outlaws jogged the miles from Barnesdale into and through Sherwood, hardly resting. They came to Nottingham and lay in the brush beside the city wall, awaiting news of what time the hangings should take place. They saw the gallows from where they hid. Four places were set, the wooden platform standing beneath a tree thick with branches, just outside the city gates. All sneered to see the hateful thing. The gallows was the resort of the coward, who killed men dishonourably by leaving them to dangle 'til their breath ran dry and the birds pecked away their flesh. Every man of Sherwood burned to set fire to the gallows, that false tree.

An old man stepped out of the city and started down the road. Robin called upon Henry o' Lincoln Town to ask news of the ancient, for Henry was a personable sort, and unlikely to be recognized.

"Helloa, thou silly old man. Helloa, say I," cried Henry merrily as he climbed out of the leaves. "Tell unto me, hast thou any news this day?"

"That have I," declared the old man. "The sheriff hath need of a hangman ere the executions can take place. It seemeth no man doth wish the ill will of Sherwood's outlaws. Now I must be off, for even *silly* men have their business."

Henry smiled, doffing his cap and disappearing back into the foliage.

"Well, well," murmured the old man as he hobbled along his way. "Perhaps there will not be hangings this day, for I wot that lad was an outlaw of Robin Hood's."

Upon hearing Henry's report, Robin proclaimed, "We must help our good friend the sheriff. I shall be hangman, and the rest of ye will bide amongst the crowd until my signal. Be sure to stay close to the sheriff's men, and keep them back long enough for Stutely and the others to be loosed. Do not enter the city all together, but in smaller numbers."

Robin Hood departed from his men and, entering the city, wandered it as though he had ne'er been inside before. When he circled back to the gate, he made conversation with one of the sheriff's men stationed there.

"Truly, sir, 'tis a wondrous city that thou hast," quoth he in a dust-cracked voice. "Tell me, where is the hangman for this entertainment?"

"Verily I tell thee, the sheriff hath no man for the job, yet mayhap thou shouldst be he, for thou dost seem a merry sort withal, and I trust the sheriff will take a liking to thee. See! he comes." The man straightened. As he did so, the rings in his armour clinked.

Robin bowed his head, smiling beneath his shadowy hood. "Give you good den, my liege."

The sheriff seemed like to pass them by without even a nod, yet the man-at-arms spake up. "My lord, here is a fine fellow. As like he would serve your purpose."

The sheriff looked over the figure, as if noticing him for the first time. "What is thy name, man?" he asked. "From whence dost thou come?"

Robin replied in the same cracked voice. "Most call me Blaine Crocker, and I come from Shrewsbury Town."

"Then, Blaine Crocker of Shrewsbury, thou wilt be mine hangman. Take this fellow to ready the prisoners."

The sheriff's man stepped forward, leading Robin up the hill toward Nottingham Castle, and 'round to a cave entrance that delved deep beneath the fortress. The air ran cold and the way was steep and slippery, darkness lying in wait to swallow the light from the man's torch. The carved steps proved more stumbling blocks than stairs.

The stone passageway echoed with raucous laughter from below. Though usually jovial when in disguise, Robin felt distantly but mortally fearful descending this hole. He could think of few things worse than suffering alone in a place without sunlight or trees, knowing death might come before another sight of the sky.

They reached the last step and saw a small enclave in the rock, where members of the sheriff's guard sat and took their time obeying orders. The urge to reach up and feel whether his hood still shadowed his face prodded him, but he resisted, lest the gesture seem suspicious.

The man-at-arms turned his back to his comrades, following the passage to the right. At first, Robin thought it odd that he breathed the luscious smell of warm bread. Then he recalled tell that prisoners were kept chained below the castle's bakery, so the scents from above could sharpen their unrequited hunger.

The gaol was a putrid place. The hay strewn for bedding had not been changed in years. Everywhere raced a rat or a gaggle of fleas. Men like scarecrows decorated the walls as so many tapestries, and many a rat feasted upon human flesh, both living and dead.

Here was Will Stutely. At first Robin feared they had crippled him; he lay in a helplessly confused heap upon the cold stone. Chains hung from the rock wall, but none shackled Will. The guards knew him too weak to escape. His skin looked paler than snow. A great gash seared his head, hair matted across it. The yeoman's face was gaunt, his eyes closed, his breath shallow. He appeared for all the world to have been dead the past two days.

"Surely this shadow of a man be not worth the rope to hang him," gasped Robin to the man-at-arms. Kneeling beside Stutely, he whispered, "Come, Will. Is there pain in thine head? Canst thou speak, friend?"

Opening his eyes at the familiar tone, Stutely strove to sit up, and Robin assisted him. "I can fight. Give me a sword and I shall take on a dozen men — or give me no weapon, I care not. I shall not die a common thief's death."

"Quiet now," quoth his master. "Come, lad. 'Tis time."

The man-at-arms bound Stutely's hands behind his back, repeating the task with three sour-looking young men chained against a wall. These were the widow's three sons: William, John, and Lester. They were in better condition than Stutely, looking as though if given the opportunity they would rip to shreds anyone who provoked them.

More of the sheriff's guard entered. The three brothers were led out before their hangman, who was supporting Will.

It was next to impossible, lugging Stutely up the passageway with so little light. Robin summoned all his strength to the task, never loosing his grip upon his friend. Determination and God's grace carried them upward faster than effort alone. As they went, Robin vowed within himself that whilst he breathed none of his men would ever languish in such a place again. Will flinched against the sunlight when it struck him, leaning the heavier upon his master.

The four men and their hangman rode to Nottingham's gate in a wagon surrounded by men-at-arms, to keep back the people. The greenwood made such a fair sight for Stutely's eyes that they filled with tears, and he bowed his head lest anyone should see. Though Stutely had recognized his master's voice before, he thought it only a dream now, and gave himself up for dead.

Four nooses slithered down like vines from a gibbet. The four men were taken from the wagon, and shoved into carts beneath each noose. The sheriff's men helped the hangman close the braided mouths around the four necks, then hurried to push back the crowd. Much of Nottingham had come to the hangings, and the people jostled nearer to see.

At the sheriff's signal, the executioner would lead the carthorses toward the crowd, leaving the condemned men to drop off behind with their legs thrashing for the ground below. Such a short fall rarely broke necks, for death was forbidden quick arrival. The law demanded that men suffer for their crimes.

Two of the brothers kept stony faces, confident they could get through without undignified flailing, though the youngest began showing fear. Will, too, defied death, though he cringed involuntarily as the executioner approached him at the sheriff's signal.

The hangman gripped the carthorse's reins, preparing to heave.

Then he seemed to think better of it. "Sir sheriff," he mused, "since I must hang four instead of one, mayhap my pay should be raised."

"Out upon it!" cried the sheriff. He well knew Robin and Will had grown up nigh as brothers, and felt eager to see Stutely die, as revenge upon the outlaw king of Sherwood. "Thou shalt find not a single farthing if thou dost address me so! Be quick, the crowd awaits."

"Aye, yet killing with rope is the coward's way. Blood must flow for the death to be noble."

So saying, the hangman drew a sword from beneath his mantle. All assembled gasped with horror as the executioner leapt up behind Will Stutely. Some had come to be entertained, others out of pity, but now all felt fear climb inside them at the sight of the mad executioner.

"Wouldst thou kill a man from behind?" quoth Will, striving to clear his mind of illness. He wished to look his last upon the earth with clear eyes.

Without reply, the hangman struck. The ropes fell from Stutely's hands, the noose released from his neck.

Pulling back his hood, Robin of Sherwood sailed down the line to the widow's sons. The same instant, five-score men in the crowd drew swords, and set upon the sheriff's guard. A mighty clamour of shouts and steel arose, the noise causing the forest trees to sway. Screams and pounding feet fled in every direction. The sheriff shouted orders no one could hear. Chaos fell complete.

In the midst of all this, a man standing head, neck, and shoulders above the scrimmage shoved to the fore, striding to Will Stutely.

"Come, friend, here is no place for thee." The giant plucked Stutely from the cart and carried him away from the gates of Nottingham into the greenwood.

The false executioner then sprang down, leading the widow's sons, and blowing three times upon his silver horn. The sheriff's guards pursued Robin Hood's men, but lost sight of them amidst the fleeing spectators. The outlaws disappeared into the trees, leaving none of their fellows behind, living or dead.

༺✥✥✥༻

After much experience, Anne's fingers were as deft with blood-matted hair as they were with the bowstring. For this

69

reason, she had become the band's surgeon. With her skill and woodland air, Stutely emerged from his sickness.

Back in Barnesdale, a relieved Robin spake to the giant who had rescued Stutely. "Truly, friend Little John, we feared some great ill had befallen thee."

Little John, standing once more in the midst of his brethren, looked sheepish. He stared at the grass, which shone silver in the late sunlight. "I am sorry I troubled thee, master. I have been abiding with the Sheriff of Nottingham."

"We must e'en hear of this," quoth Robin, and all gathered 'round to hear the tale. "Pray, tell us thine adventures, for the greenwood is always athirst for a stout tale."

CHAPTER FIVE
Alder

IT HAD BEEN THE TIME for the Nottingham Fair again. The sheriff hesitated to give notice, fearing Robin Hood and his band might attend. If an outlaw again won the prize at archery, it would rack his reputation. Yet if he did not announce the fair, he would be marked as a coward.

After much deliberation, the sheriff concluded to hold the fair, offering such a prize as only peasants would want.

"Now out upon it!" cried Robin when he heard the news. "What is three beef cattle when we have all the deer in the forest?"

"Master," quoth Little John, "an' it please thee, I would still go to the fair."

"Nay, Little John. I would have naught of ill befall thee, especially for such a trifle."

"Yet I have not tried my bow against those without Sherwood for sometime, and I crave adventure."

Robin inclined his head. "I know how loudly adventure may call. Look to thyself, Little John."

The giant donned a peddler's cloak and set off for Nottingham Town. The day was calm, good for shooting. Leaves rustled now and again in conversation. They filled the air with a scent softer than freshly cut hay.

The fair lay within Nottingham's walls this year, and one could smell rubbish rotting in the streets. A multicoloured brown-clad crowd clamoured around a platform. A man stood upon the stage, pacing, a quarterstaff clenched in his fist. Little John paused to see what was afoot.

"Where are the men of Nottingham?" cried the man. "Here stand I, Eric o' Lincoln, and one such as we of Lincolnshire call a man hath yet to step up. Hath no one a fair lass to fight for? Are they all ugly crones?"

A splash of heat dashed along Little John's spine. "Thou saucy braggart! Let us see if the men of Nottingham are here yet, and the women fair. I shall fight thee! Hath anyone a good staff?"

A dozen staffs were offered. Little John chose the stoutest. He clambered up upon the stage, tripping over and becoming tangled in the ropes around the ring.

Many in the crowd felt their hearts sink, for they wished to see Eric o' Lincoln drubbed.

The man in charge of the sport ordered both combatants to their corners. Then the two came together, Eric stealthily and Little John with faltering steps.

Eric's face shone. "Come, take the first swing."

Little John swiped his cudgel in a slow arc. Eric barely ducked to avoid the blow. His laugh caught between his teeth, however, for Little John swung back with such might to knock Eric down upon his face.

The crowd shouted laughter to see him brought to the ground, as if bowing an apology.

Regaining his feet, Eric gasped with rage. When he joined with Little John again, he found a fleet, sturdy match.

Each struck hard and fast. Though Little John tried his best, Eric o' Lincoln now took extra care on the defensive. This caused him to lack on the offensive, so Little John fared none the worse for it.

The Lincoln man grew frustrated. He began raining down a mighty shower of blows. Little John parried left and right.

At last, finding an opening, Nottingham cracked Lincoln a blow to the jaw.

Eric fell to the platform unconscious.

Now where'er Little John went the people stared and pointed. When he stopped at a stall for ale it was given free of charge.

In the afternoon, 'twas the shooting match. Little John made his way to the butts. With the other archers he entered the field and strung his bow, examining each arrow in turn.

Chattering onlookers filled the area surrounding the targets. After a nod from the sheriff, who sat in a covered box nearby, a herald proclaimed the rules. "Each man will send a flight of three arrows. The ten who shoot fairest will shoot another three shafts, and the best man will win the three head of cattle."

The archers took their places, and cheers arose at the shooting that followed. Even the sheriff joyed to see such men in his shire.

Once the ten best archers were deciphered from the cresting of the arrows scattered over the clout, their names (or rather descriptions, for they were all poorer folk) were announced. These lined up to shoot again. Of the ten, all were grubby sorts: two peddlers, three beggars, four yeomen, and a traveller.

First shot the traveller, who did well, yet not so well as the four yeomen following him. The beggars shot shrewdly, and 'twas one of these who seemed like to take away the prize. As the first peddler loosed his shafts, the beggar who had shot best grew cocky.

The beggar's shafts were two in the clout and one in the ring just outside. When Little John stepped up, all hushed for his concentration. He took careful aim.

The crowd cheered, for the arrow landed in the clout, beside one of the beggar's. The second shot bettered the first.

All was silence for the third shot. If Little John were to once again strike the clout, he would be winner. Many in the crowd wished him victory, hoping their hero at the quarterstaff to be also their hero at the longbow.

Pulling the bowstring, the tall archer loosed his third and final shaft. This alighted closer to the bull's eye than any other yet that day.

To cheering and waving of banners, the giant was brought before the sheriff, whilst those who crowded 'round told of admiration.

The sheriff was overjoyed. He had not expected such fine archery with Robin Hood and his band in the woods. He did not know Little John, for the giant's appearance had changed much since the day he had asked for a warrant to capture Robin Hood. Now his face was clean, his hair cut and well kempt. His beard no longer reached to his chest, but was shaved close to his jaw.

"By my troth," quoth the sheriff, "thou art the fairest archer I have laid eyes upon for many a day. Is it true thou didst crack the crown of Eric o' Lincoln?"

"Aye, your worship," Little John replied, the corners of his lips creeping toward his ears.

"By my whiskers!" the sheriff shouted. "Thou art a stout blade. Wilt thou join my service? The pay is six pence each day, and three suits in a year of better cloth than thou hast about thee now. (No mention made of food and shelter.) What sayest thou to that?"

Little John bethought himself, 'A merry jest shall I have with the sheriff, for he is to gain the worst servant he ever had.' Aloud he said, "Ye ask too many an archer to join you, methinks. I accept, good sheriff, for it pleases mine 'eart to serve so noble a man."

"Well spoke, sir," quoth the sheriff. "Now that this matter is by us, what might be thy name?"

"Men call me Reynold Greenleaf."

"Then, Reynold Greenleaf, I wot I have gained a stout soul this day! Come, let us to the castle."

Thus did Little John away with the sheriff to Nottingham Castle. He left his prize for the people, to be roasted and devoured as their pleasure dictated. All rejoiced at the gift, and many pledged their everlasting friendship to the giant, though 'twas the sheriff who would come to need it more.

⊕⊕⊕

Over the next month, Little John was servant to the sheriff. His only duty (that he performed) was to run beside the sheriff's horse when his new master went a-hunting. Thus, when the sheriff required Little John as a hangman, the giant lay in bed snoring.

At last, deeming the notion of awakening worthy of attention, the giant dressed and went down to the pantry. He arrived as the head steward was locking up.

"Hold there, friend," quoth Little John. "I have eaten naught this day."

"The meal is over," the steward replied, "and thou hast missed it."

"What means this? Bring me meat and drink in quick season, for I am hungry enough to eat a deer, with room beside for a hogshead of malmsey."

"Am I thy slave to fetch thy meal? Get it thine own self!"

Little John tried the pantry door.

When it failed to open, the steward burst out laughing. "Not so fast, mighty Greenleaf. Thou must e'en wait for suppertide."

"Thou knave, wouldst thou deprive a man of food and drink? Unlock this door, or 'tis like to go ill with thee."

The steward only roared the merrier. Upon catching the look in the yeoman's eye, he ceased all noise.

Drawing back his fist, the giant crashed it through the planks of the door.

A buffet to his ear made Little John shrink whilst the steward chimed down blows with his heavy keys.

"How now, Reynold Greenleaf? Hast thou nothing to say? Thine head be emptier than thy stomach!"

As the steward raised his arm to strike again, Little John grabbed him by the wrist, giving him such a buffet as would fell any man alive. The steward dropped to the floor with a clatter of keys. Little John walked into the pantry saying, "Mayhap the next time an hungered man approach thee, thou wilt show compassion."

Inside, Little John laid out a feast: veal pasty, pigeon pie, fresh bread, a wheel of cheese, a leg of mutton, and many a cup of sack and malmsey.

In the room beside, the sheriff's cook prepared the coming meal. When he heard shouting, he came by the doorway and saw the battle between Little John and the steward. He had gone to retrieve his sword from the kitchen and now knelt by the steward. "Friend, I have a good mind to beat yon knave. Get thee gone, lest thou be in the way."

Still dazed, the steward hurried from the room.

Striding to the pantry door, the cook entered through the hole and spake. "How is it thou hast invaded our master's pantry? Rise up and let us decide thy fate as men."

Little John set aside his bread. "If thou dost wish it, then look to thyself."

Grasping their swords, the two exited the pantry. Back and forth they fought, neither landing a blow. Each looked with admiration upon the other for his skill in battle.

At last they came apart and Little John spake. "Friend cook, thou art a stout hand at the broadsword, and we have been working up fair appetites. Wouldst thou join me in feasting? It is a poor thing for hungry men to let good food grow stale."

The cook leaned upon the hilt of his sword, considering Little John's proposal. He himself had eaten naught since early that morning.

Entering the pantry, each fell to without one word to the other. Hands shoved into flaky pigeon pie. Sacks of sweet malmsey were opened. At last the cook could eat no more and tipped his stool back to lean against the wall. He loosed a breath akin to a sigh.

Little John lay back also. "I have been thinking, friend, there is no need to continue our battle. I know not why we fight in the first place."

"Truly, good fellow, neither do I," quoth the cook good naturedly. "What say we let the matter rest?"

"Exactly to my mind. I bethink me thou hast as fair a voice as I have heard in a full moon's time. Wouldst thou sing us a song?"

"Aye, that will I," quoth the cook. He hemmed and hawed, then set to.

In the good old summer time,
When deer trip o'er the lea,
And birds sing in the trees,
My love doth come to me.
She says, "Hum dillim dillim,
By the fish that swim,
I pledge my love to thee."

In the rusty autumn time,
When flows October wine,
And all birds south do fly,
My love doth venture nigh.

She says, "Hum dillim dillay,
By the leaves that play,
I pledge my love is thine."

In the crystal winter time,
When fat priests gorge and dine,
The snow shows hunters sign,
My love doth come beside.
She says, "Hum dillim dilluver,
By the snow that hovers . . . "
She says her love is mine.

In the blooming of spring time,
When roses raise their heads,
The poppies grow in beds,
My love doth come to me.
She says, "Hum dillim dillee,
By the deepest, bluest sea,
I pledge my love to thee."

"Now 'tis thy turn. Strike up thy ditty."

Little John tapped a fist to his mouth and cleared his throat. "I have but a poor voice, friend, yet shall endeavour to troll worth hearing."

I sit by the old oak tree,
And watch the sun in its ark.
My sheep feed on meadows green,
As I lean against the bark.
Though I am away from thee,
A shepherd I'm proud to be.

I guide my flock by the day,
Fight off the wolves and the bears,
Go after all those who stray,
For I am the one who cares.
Though thou art across the sea,
A shepherd I'm proud to be.

To streams clear, cold and so sweet,
Far from the thorny thistles,
Wool whiter than other sheep,
They recognize my whistles.
Though thou art now not with me,
A shepherd I'm proud to be.

At night when my sheep do sleep,
And when the pale moon doth shine,
The wind floats whispers to me,
That do cause mine heart to pine.
Though I am away from thee,
A shepherd I'm proud to be.

"A right sweet tune," quoth the cook.
"Tell me," quoth Little John, "what be thy name?"
"Men call me Roger Wilkinson."
"Then, Roger Wilkinson, harken to me. If thou wouldst leave thy kitchens and come to the greenwood, Robin Hood will give thee three suits of Lincoln green a year, with fifteen marks beside. Moreover, thou wilt have five-score-and-three of the merriest companions England hath to offer, of which I shall be one, for I am Robin Hood's own right-hand man."

"The sheriff is no generous master, and I wonder often about a free life amongst the trees. Yet if I am to join thee, friend Greenleaf — or Little John — I think it poor manners to approach the great Robin Hood with naught but mine own self. Let us collect the sheriff's silver kitchenware."

Gathering all they could, the pair filled a sack. Upon their way out of the city, they found the melee about the gates, and so met the outlaws sooner than they had thought to.

⊸⊷⊸⊷⊸⊷

"A jolly tale," called one of the band, "yet how do we know thou hast not switched sides, and the sheriff does not close in at this very moment?"

The other men showed grins. Little John's sour expression soon sprouted them into laughter.

Robin Hood spake to Roger. "Welcome, friend cook. We are glad to have thee. Ready a feast, men. We must e'en show our new comrade a merry time."

Whilst all busied themselves starting fires and skinning deer, Robin took Little John aside.

"What dost thou need of me, master?"

"Little John, thou art a true and loyal friend and a right brave lad. I am glad thou art well and that thou hast brought so worthy a man as the cook. I am not so glad at thy stealing the sheriff's plate. He trusted thee, and thou didst repay his hospitality by cheating him."

"I am sorry, master. I thought thou wouldst be pleased."

Robin gave a small smile. "Come man, let us put this gift to good use for the nonce."

So the outlaws feasted upon their victory, the recovery of Little John and Will Stutely, and the addition of Roger and the widow's three sons to their band.

The sheriff was near madness when, after the humiliation of the failed hangings, he discovered his huntsman, cook, and silver missing. He knew the culprit must somehow be Robin Hood, and descended into such a rage that he issued a manhunt as was never seen before.

CHAPTER SIX
Holm

Whilst the sheriff gathers his forces for the onslaught, it is well to hear how, before becoming outlawed, Robin Hood had thought he would spend his life.

Robert walked beside Marian through Baron Fitzwalter's castle toward the courtyard. Each was armed with a sword and a buckler shield. "Thy father, Marian, would hardly approve of our practising with real swords."

"Thou art six and ten years of age, Locksley — too old to impress anyone by continuing to practise with wooden wasters, least of all thy lady love."

Robert smiled. "Pypa is most beautiful, is she not, when her brown eyes peer up through her yellow lashes, and her small mouth smiles ever so slightly, as though to show and hide her admiration in the same moment."

"I would hardly know, seeing that in the ten weeks she and her father the earl have been our guests, Pypa hath never once favoured me with such a look."

"She will of a certainty be watching?"

"Aye again and again. She told my sister that she would spy upon thee from a small window in an upper room, Mirabelle told me, and here I am assuring thee that mine own spy be reliable. Pypa wishes to see how bravely thou dost comport thyself, and we shall give her a show, never fear."

"Her hair is so beautifully golden one could bathe in it."

"Love certainly softens one's brains, does it not?" Marian looped her free arm about Robert's waist.

He caught her neck in the crook of his elbow, tugging a moment as though he would wrestle her, then relaxing as if embracing her instead.

The sun poured into the courtyard as into a bowl. The ground was too well trodden to boast much grass. Robert and Marian drew their swords, setting aside their scabbards, and faced one another using the longpoint guard. Their blades pointed to the ground far out in front of them, their sword hands overlapped by their small, round shields.

Robert's gaze was up, sweeping over the windows above for some shadow that might tell him where Pypa watched.

"Keep thy mind where it belongs," Marian whispered. "'Twill not impress thy lady love to see me pander to thy distraction. Nor will it impress her to see me fell thee in the dust."

Robert's eyes lowered and he smiled. "The dust is thine, my sweet friend. Allow me to show it thee."

Marian grinned. "Show me, then."

The clatter of blades filled the courtyard. The dust sprang up as though roused from sleep.

Both bucklers rang. Robert and Marian's feet moved as quickly as if they half ran, taking them all about the courtyard.

The pair practised together often, and so were fairly matched. More eyes than Pypa's gathered at the windows to witness the combat.

Robert swung at Marian's legs, his blade pointed to the earth, his hands yet overlapping. Marian stepped back, swinging her own blade likewise to block the strike.

She stepped forward again, pushing up her blade's tip whilst keeping its forte, nigh its hilt, against Robert's. He stepped back even more hurriedly than she had done, her sword tip nearly grazing his chest and chin. Rolling his sword out to the side so it now pointed up, he was barely in time to swat away Marian's blade, so she had to tuck it back under her shield arm, in the first guard position.

He rotated his buckler over his sword hand so it now faced out to his left, in the half-shield opposition. She whipped out her sword, pointing it into his face. Robert dropped his hands, meeting the middle of her blade with the forte of his, avoiding being skewered through the head.

They shoved their blades against one another, the steel screeching as the swords rose up, pinned together at a point coming nearer and nearer their tips.

Suddenly ceasing to press, Robert brought down his blade. Marian pushed it aside. Not quite as quickly as he anticipated, for he brought his sword down faster than hers could turn it away, and the end of his blade sliced into her hand.

The buckler dropped out of it in the instant. In the next, Robert's own sword and buckler followed it to the ground.

He started forward, grasping her bleeding hand. "Marian?"

"'Tis fine." She still held her sword, though her face had gone deathly white.

"Help!"

Servants came sprinting into the courtyard at his shout.

"'Tis fine." Sweat slicked Marian's skin.

Robert glanced under his own hand at hers. "'Tis less than three fingers' width, yet it is deep. We must get thee to bed, call for the surgeon."

Marian winced, curling as though she fought the urge to vomit.

Robert moved to catch an arm around her, but she was picked up off the ground, the sword finally slipping from her grasp and her from his. He stood a moment, as though not understanding what happened about him, then hurried after the retreating, clamouring crowd of men with Marian in their midst.

⊹⊹⊹

That evening, Robert crouched in a corner of the courtyard, covered by the growing shadows. His elbows rested upon his knees, his brow upon his forearms.

"Sweetheart?"

He looked up at the small voice. "Thou hast found me."

Pypa stood looking down at him. "Marian thought it strange thou didst pay her sickbed only a short visit, yet she confided in me that thou wouldst be here."

Robert's eyes strayed to the blood-strewn dirt. "She knows me very well."

"I heard her tell her father that it was her own idea to use sharp blades."

"It matters not. I struck her. The fault lies with me."

"Thou didst offer her the sincerest apologies."

"It doth not matter."

Pypa fanned her fingers softly through Robert's hair. "I see thou dost require a penance."

Robert reached up, taking her hand and kissing it.

"I shall offer one. Thou and thy friends play that Marian is one of thee. She is a lady, and thou wilt treat her as one. It will be for her own good as well, saving her from injury and a wild reputation. It will see her married the sooner."

Robert kissed the hand again. "Thy counsel is always sensible, my love."

Pypa petted him with her free hand. "Then it will please thee to follow it?"

"Always." Robert rose, folding her in his arms.

⊹⊹⊹

The new day hung clear if not bright. A fortnight had passed since the unfortunate sparring match. Robert walked with Pypa through the sparse, young trees. Upon their gloved left hands, each carried a sparrow hawk: brown and white birds with bright yellow eyes. Many paces behind walked Marian and Harold, he with a sparrow hawk also, she with a slender stick to flush out smaller birds for prey, such as larks and quails, partridges and young pheasants.

Marian stared ahead at Robert's back, beating her stick about the tall grass. "Dost thou recall two years ago, when we passed out of childhood, how Robert decided he ought to treat me as a *lady* rather than his friend?"

"Thou didst convince him otherwise."

"Yet he hath become unconvinced."

Harold threw his sparrow hawk into the air.

"It hath been a fortnight of chess games and reciting poetry. Robert will hear nothing of shooting or sparing."

"Thine arm is still too injured, surely? Thou canst not even carry a hawk."

"That is not the point."

Harold shrugged, watching his bird as it settled in a tree to survey for movement below.

"It is Robert's manner, as though a wall stood between us. Such a wall is far worse than my father's empty threats to thrash Robert, or my mother's constant admonitions to take Pypa's feminine behaviour as mine example."

"Perhaps the wall is in fact the Earl of Chester's daughter." Harold motioned toward Pypa.

"Why should it be?"

"Robert hath always been thy favourite."

"He hath always been the one who understands that my favour is no more than friendship, despite my being a *lady*."

Harold slowed, staring up at his sparrow hawk. Robert and Pypa sent theirs into the air.

"As a woman, am I so delicate that my friends must always be reserved in my presence?"

"When unreserved, they nearly take off thine hand."

"One cut will not dictate mine actions."

"Were it to thy neck, it might."

Marian quickened her pace, moving farther from Harold, and closer toward Robert and Pypa.

Robert was speaking in a low voice, matching the quiet tone that Pypa habitually used. His breath caught in his throat at a sharp stroke across the backs of his legs.

Marian whipped him again with her stick.

He glanced over his shoulder. "Stop, Marian."

"I see no reason why I should."

Robert turned away.

She caught him across the shoulder blades.

Pypa's eyes pounced wide.

"Such sport is much more amusing than chess, is it not?" Marian snapped him in the small of the back, then across the kidney.

Robert lost his temper, whirling, catching her wrists and pinning her against a tree. Then the temper blanched from his cheeks, and he looked unsure of himself.

Marian laughed. "Come now, are there truly no larks in thy tunic? We seem to have beaten throughout the rest of this field."

Robert smiled. "Mayhap some reside in thine hair. It is long enough." He pinched a lock, twining it 'round his finger and giving a tweak.

"Promise me, once mine hand is all healed, that we shall duel again and determine a champion, for our last bout was never finished."

"Marian — "

"Please. It is by far more painful for me to endure thy guilt than it was to endure the blow."

Robert stared into her eyes. "Aye. I am sorry, Marian."

"Promise me."

"Very well. A rematch, but with wasters." Robert let her go. "Wouldst thou walk with us, then? It seemeth poor Harold hath grown tiresome company."

"It is his way." She smiled at Pypa, who did not smile back. "Surely some tale of Robert's childhood antics would amuse thee? It is only right that two lovers should know all about one another."

"I know he prefers to walk through the trees," Pypa replied, "when riding would have proved more comfortable."

"Look!" Robert pointed as the sparrow hawks dove down from their branches, speeding with a single-mindedness that was awing to see. "Come."

He and Marian raced through the trees.

⊹⊹⊹

Late that afternoon, Marian alone walked into a field, its grass brushing halfway up to her knees. Nearing a tall oak near its middle, yet farther than its middle, she stopped, lying upon her back in the grass, where no one could see.

"How is it thou knowest always where I am?"

"I do not always. I thought thou shouldst be under the tree."

Robert lay upon his back, staring up at the sky. His feet pointed the opposite direction to hers, though their heads lay side by side.

"Thou hast quarrelled with Pypa? If she is not a fool, and loveth thee as she ought, then i' 'twill be mended."

"She wished me no longer to be thy friend."

"And so thou didst treat me as a mere lady?"

"She wished it carried further than that."

Marian watched the wisps of cloud pass by, as though joined to some larger, invisible mass. "Confide in me as thy friend; do not shield me as though I were a child."

"Pypa averred that thine insistence upon behaving other than is proper reflected upon me as thy friend and so upon

90

her as my love, wearing upon our modesty and reputations. She said that she could no longer associate her good name with mine should I neglect to set a proper boundary between thyself and myself."

"Thou art made happy by Pypa. I could perhaps endure some boundary, were it for thine happiness."

Robert sighed. "I could bear no such complete boundary as Pypa desires. I love her, yet I do not love every turn of her mind . . . I feel I cannot breathe without thee — I should rather be killed than harm thee, Ivy."

"If I did feel the need to forgive thee, Robin, I did so in the same instant the blade found me. Pypa seemed the embodiment of the lady I imagined thou wouldst wed, yet thou wilt find another love and be happy."

Robert loosed a long breath. "I am not so certain now. What wife could I find who would never be irked by the closeness of our friendship? Once each of us is wed, how can we ever find the means to see one another as oft as we would wish?"

"Being tethered to a man would not grant me the freedom I require to remain in any way happy. I do not intend to wed."

"Thou wouldst go mad in a convent."

"I do not intend to enter one."

"That is the only way for thee to escape marriage. Thou wilt inherit the barony. If thou art yet unwed when thy father dies, the king can direct thee to marry whomever he chooses."

"A marriage requires consent."

"Thou shouldst not dare, Marian, to defy the king."

"Because God made me a woman is no reason to be such a woman as men wish to make me."

Robert exhaled sharply. "I shall marry thee."

"Nay, my sweet friend. Thou wilt marry a fair lady with long, golden tresses, soft-spoke, and rightly admiring of thee, who can raise happy children. And thou wilt love her in turn so much that even her footsteps will be precious to thee. Thou wilt think of her as perfect, she likewise of thee. Thy love will grow as thou dost see hers, and her happiness will grow as she sees thine. I know thee. I have foreseen it."

"Where art thou in this future world?"

"I am here, administering my lands. Not for my life would I deny thee the happiness I know thou wilt have in love."

Robert rolled his face toward hers. "How shall I feel happiness, knowing thou art parted from me? Knowing thou hast roused the king's anger? No matter how much I loved my wife, I should never be contented."

"So thou thinkest to marry me and never know love? My father would not approve of thy lack of title and wealth to make thee his successor."

"He would approve of our marriage more than he would approve of thy remaining unwed. I am in his favour, and he indulges thee. I would not order thee about; we should be equals, and always together."

"So could we be once thou art a knight, and I thy squire."

Robert again faced the sky. "That is a children's dream, Marian. We are old enough that we must think of realities."

"The reality is that I have no place, excepting I carve out one alone."

"I shall be a knight and take my wife upon my journeys, excepting they be to war. Then she would administer my lands in my stead. We should administer together when at home, sharing all."

92

"Thou dost dream still. Thou wilt have lands only if thou dost wed them or win them."

"This is best for us both. An' thou art alone when thy father would die, I shall marry thee."

"Unless thou art already in love. Do not lock away thine heart for my sake. Pypa may have injured it, yet it will heal."

"Though it aches with all that has just happened, thou art in mine heart already."

"That ache doth cloud thy sense at the moment."

"I shall do what I have said, Marian."

She blew a deep breath up into the breeze, watching the clouds disappear beyond the trees at the field's end.

Chapter Seven
Poplar

Robin and Anne had walked to Watling Street, where it ran through Barnesdale, to watch and see who might happen by. They were keeping but a poor watch, however, for their eyes were all closed as they held one another, kissing and leaning upon an ash tree. Thus they remained a long while, until hearing the approach of a great number of horses.

Robin looked over his shoulder.

"'Tis truly a great mass of monks, my love."

"Aye, and mounted well."

"They do not look to be upon pilgrimage."

"Much the better. They must then form an escort for some treasure they would keep from outlawed hands."

Anne watched carefully. "They must number an hundred."

"Yet unarmed. Will Stutely's patrol cannot be too far." Robin slipped the horn from about his body. "Wouldst thou, dearest, seek them out or call them once farther into the forest, so as not to startle our guests?"

Anne took the horn. "And thou wilt engage them in conversation so they do not hurry their heels overmuch?"

He kissed her throat.

She smiled, stroking her fingertips through the hair by his ear, and ducking to kiss his lips. "Monks have been known to carry heavy clubs, my love. Keep that well in thy mind."

Robin watched her vanish into the leaves. He turned then to the road. Wading through the ferns lining Watling Street, he emerged in plain view of the monks, walking toward them to see what they would do.

The monks neither slowed nor sped, but kept their horses' pace, not caring a wit for his presence.

Robin smiled, hailing the party. "Greetings, brothers, and God's favour, an' He wills it. Are all of ye vowed to silence, or is there one amongst you that might tell unto me where ye go?"

"We go north," murmured one of the monks, from beneath his hood.

"Plain enough, brother, yet for so many of you to travel in company, it must mark some occasion, mustn't it?"

"We have business."

The monks came abreast of him, and still did not slow their pace, so that Robin had to turn about and walk with them. "This business must be worth a great sum."

The monks seemed to hasten, so that he was engulfed by their number.

"Will ye not abide a moment, friends? I know of an inn nearby where your brethren can refresh themselves."

The monk astride Robin leapt from his mount, pinning the outlaw against the next monk's horse with a dagger to his throat.

"Be easy, friend." The horse halted, and Robin stood with his hands raised, to pacify or to snatch for the dagger. "I mean no harm and only wished to succour the church's chosen."

"Thou art no friend, however little harm thou meanest."

Robin squinted at the voice, staring up at the tall monk.

The man took his empty hand from the outlaw's shoulder a moment to push back his hood.

Robin stared wider. "Baron Fitzwalter!" He smiled. "Sir, welcome with all mine heart to the greenwood."

The dagger stayed at his throat. All the monks halted.

"Sir, what means this?"

The baron, his dark brown beard unable to hide the tightness of his jaw, glared at Robin. "Where is my daughter?"

"She left me but a moment ago, sir. She is gone to fetch Will Stutely." Robin still watched his mentor with concerned puzzlement, rather than any fear.

"Call her back, with thy famous horn."

"She carries mine horn, sir." Robin raised his arms farther from his body, to show that the horn was not about him. "We shall take thee to our camp and give thee a great feast, sir, and our men will show thee all the entertainment thou couldst wish. We have missed thy company, and Anne will joy to hear all thou canst tell of her sisters."

"Marian. Her name is Lady Marian Fitzwalter, not whatever play name thou hast invented for her. This is far more serious than any of thy children's games."

"What is, sir?"

"Thou hast stolen my daughter."

"I have never stolen aught from thee, sir. I would first see mine hand severed."

"Marian left me a letter, saying that she fancied herself in love with thee, that thou hadst whisked her off to marry — as thou hast whisked her into all of thine ill-thought-out ventures — and that she intended to join thee in the forest. Thou hast deceived her with romantic fancies and lured her away from her home and family."

"Sir, even were I ever minded to deceive her, Marian would never be taken in by aught that I could dream up."

"Thou didst think it a great jest to dance with her all night and prevent any other suitor from venturing near her, and yet Marian believes that thy motivation was love. Ye kept the affair a secret, and now thou hast persuaded her into thine outlawry, just as stubborn girls with ill-suited lovers re-enact the romance stories when they have their lovers pretend to abduct them."

"The last thing we are is ill-suited, sir. We grew up side by side; we have been together in everything; we know one another's thoughts at a glance."

"Marian is my chief heir. She will be a baroness in her own right, and thou art not even a nobleman. Only an earl's second son, with no title and no lands. Thou didst spy thine opportunity and take full advantage."

Robin's muscles eased, though his face darkened a shade. "I have loved her since the first day I saw her, thinking never to love her more, and yet I do now, for I am in love with Marian, sir. Mayhap 'twas somewhat fanciful to re-enact the romances by keeping our love secret, yet as the lovers in romances always fear that others will seek to destroy their love if it be known, and as I hear thee now, I do not regret it. Moreover, be assured that I had no knowledge of Marian's plan to trap herself in the forest until after she had carried it out. She doth know me. She knows that never would I consent to what might lead to her harm. She ensured 'twould be more harmful for her to return than to stay."

"I shook out of Harold all that happened at Nottingham's archery contest. Dost thou deny meeting Marian privately afterward and conspiring to have her condemn herself? How else could she have found thee in all these woods? I had to lure thee out with an hundred men-at-arms disguised as wealthy monks."

"She tracked me after the contest without my knowing, sir. Harold only saw us kiss; he cannot know what happened afterward."

"Thou art a deceiver."

"I omit the truth at times, yet hast thou ever known me to lie, sir?"

The baron turned his head, for another figure had appeared ahead upon the road, in Lincoln green from top to toe. "Marian." The dagger finally dropped from Robin's throat.

Baron Fitzwalter hurried out ahead of his men.

Anne caught sight of him and missed a step. She grinned and ran toward him. "Father!"

They collided in an embrace.

Robin ventured out from the false monks, though two in the front rank caught him before he could step quite clear.

Anne drew back. "Father, what is this? — Leave him be!"

The false monks ignored her.

"Marian, my child, I am come to bring thee home."

"I could not go home if I wished to; I am outlawed."

"No, my child, it is not so." Baron Fitzwalter held her by the shoulders. "Come with me to the county court when next it meets in two days' time. Don again thy woman's weave, as the church commands. We can answer the accusations against thee before thou art officially and finally waived."[3]

"I committed a robbery upon the king's highway. Such an answer will only see me hanged."

"I know the sheriff and have spoke with him. Thou art a baron's chief heir and a woman. Thou wilt not be hanged."

"I have committed a good many crimes since entering the greenwood. I bear no intention of leaving unless pardoned by the king, along with mine husband."

"A moral man would not allow his wife to gad about in men's clothing, as though she smiled upon the devil. He is not thine husband, Marian."

"He is. We made our vows before God and a friar."

"It can be annulled."

Anne stepped back entirely from her father.

He ducked forward, his voice lowered. "Thou art not with child. It can be annulled, for it has not been consummated. Tha' 'twas wise of thee."

"Robin would not have me large with child and having to run from the sheriff's men. He would not have our men endangered by our infant's cries. We would not have our children born into danger."

"I would not have mine own child in danger. I have already had to disinherit thee so that thou canst not be distrained. A writ of exigent hath been sued out. If thou dost not now obey the sheriff's order to appear, thou wilt be surely waived."

---

3   A woman is not "outlawed," but "waived."

"Then at last I shall be a proper outlaw. Thou hast disinherited me for the benefit of thine own lands, yet I would rather be an outlaw of the forest than a baroness all my life. Truly, I should rather be hanged than have my marriage annulled."

"Marian, thou hast entered into a clandestine marriage, against the pope's own council and without calling the banns three weeks before."

"Whatever the pope's council says, when hath a clandestine marriage, or one without banns, ever been dissolved against the will of those wed? The friar would suffer more for performing the ceremony. Moreover, though it is permitted to annul an unconsummated marriage — should there be one — it is nonetheless yet as valid as thine own union boasting five daughters."

Baron Fitzwalter reddened. His voice rose. "Thy mother often said that I raised thee as a firstborn son, with every indulgence. I could never see the harm. I wished mine heir to fight, hunt, and shoot. Thou didst have thine head in everything, and I was proud, at the time, for my daughter would rather learn the sword than the needle. Yet it was dangerous, to treat thee and Robert as the sons I did not have. It hath led to this pigheaded impulsiveness. I have waited long enough for thee to see reason, Marian. If I must lead thee by the nose in this, then I shall. Due to the disgrace and theft the sheriff had to endure at Robert's hands the day he would have hanged young Stutely, he is now searching every foot of Sherwood Forest, and every other park and wood throughout Nottinghamshire and Derbyshire. It is a mere matter of time."

"I shall not deny mine husband, and I shall not leave him. Until he is pardoned, I am an outlaw."

"Could she truly be safe?" Robin called.

The baron turned. "I would not have come if it might place her in further danger."

"Anne, 'twould not prove necessary to undo our marriage in order to undo thine exile. Would it, sir?"

The baron hesitated a moment, then shook his head.

"Surely then, my love, this is worth more thought than thou hast yet spent."

"I shall not contemplate it."

Baron Fitzwalter motioned for his men to release their hold upon Robin.

Anne walked past her father, meeting Robin halfway, and speaking in a low but sharp tone. "From thy manner one would believe it hardly pains thee at all to think of sending me away."

"Please, love, do not worsen my pain with thy venom."

"Is my venom any cause for exile?"

"My fairest love, surely thou must know that 'twould break mine heart to part from thee. Yet I break mine heart gladly, an' it doth mean thy safety."

"Yet it means not my safety, for it doth break mine heart also, and causeth me no end of pain. For thou shouldst not show thy face to me, thinking it should endanger me, and I would not see thee even once more until thou wert pardoned."

Robin's gaze dropped, and he clasped her hands. "Aye."

"I shall be a prisoner in my father's house, or I shall be free with thee."

"This is not freedom, but exile. I would have thee out of harm."

"I pray thee, my dearest love, to use reason rather than impulse. Parting should break not only thine heart, but mine. Staying risks my safety, but not mine heart. Were I to die, I should await thee in paradise. Parting places us both in an agony, yet by staying together thou dost risk thine heart alone. Mine shall be safe, whatever may happen to my body. Robin, thou art mine husband. I love thee. I shall stay with thee always."

He nodded, pressing Anne to his chest.

"Marian," called the baron, "if I must take thee away by force, then I shall. If thou wouldst not have Robert brought to face his own crimes, then come with me freely."

Anne turned back, one arm still about Robin. "Harm but one hair of his head, Father, and I shall have mine outlaws destroy everything under thy care: castle, crops, lands — all."

"Thou shalt be in my castle, Marian. Under lock and key if necessary."

"Then I shall shout day and night to be allowed to enter a nunnery. I shall appeal to the church and to God, and I shall have my way. Once in a nunnery, Father, thou shalt never see me the more — no word in speech nor in writing — thou shalt lose me more thoroughly than thou hast e'en now, and that forever."

"Yet thou shalt be safe."

"I am safe now. Either side of the road is lined with outlaws, arrows nocked upon their bowstrings, awaiting a word."

"Thou dost lie."

Anne eyed her father. "Men, shout."

Such a great bawling sprang up upon either side of Watling Street that made the false monks jump, draw swords from their robes, and strain to peer through the leaves to the outlaws beyond.

"This is mine home, Father. Return to thine."

Baron Fitzwalter looked about. His gaze then rested upon Anne a long while. "This is a great mistake, Marian. I only can hope that when thou dost realize the depth of it, thou art not half as disappointed in thyself as am I at this moment."

Anne's eyes glistened, yet she held Robin tighter. "Farewell, Father."

"Sir." Robin nodded, his own arm about Anne's shoulders.

The baron watched them a moment longer, then lowered his head and his hood, not looking up as he passed them to remount his horse. The party of false monks turned about, as Baron Fitzwalter rode through their midst to lead all back by the way they had come.

As the party began to disappear 'round a bend in the path, Will Stutely and the outlaws emerged from the leaves. "I never could imagine thee as a proper baroness, my lady. Not like thy mother."

"And thou art fortunate, Stutely," quoth Robin, pressing his shoulder, "that thou art no forester, for then thou mightest be expected to speak tactfully to any ladies thou wouldst escort hunting."

"We have all of us found our calling," quoth Anne. "We stand in our own kingdom."

"Aye, yet we can miss England."

"Were I pardoned, I should miss Sherwood and Barnesdale infinitely more."

Stutely nodded. "Long live the greenwood."

Anne pulled Robin nearer. "And all those within it."

"Thy father hath warned us well," quoth Robin. "The sheriff is hunting us more diligently than he hath before. We must remain in Yorkshire, practising at the sword, the cudgel, and the bow, until we might break cover and announce ourselves in Sherwood once more."

Part Two

Chapter Eight
Willow

MANY FORESTS GROW IN THE world, yet all are shadows of Sherwood. A person may be content to walk amongst the trees of their own country, yet these become drab after one has strolled through Sherwood's verdant leaves. This beauty may explain why, despite danger, Robin Hood and his band returned from Barnesdale.

Two years keeping themselves to themselves in Yorkshire seemed to have spent every coin in their treasury. The outlaws now robbed more and more passersby. In a short time, not one but two wealthy merchants were deprived of all they carried, the one receiving an arrow through his shoulder, the other nearly having his head beaten in by a quarterstaff. Some said the merchants must have drawn their swords and attempted to kill Robin Hood or one of his closest companions — perhaps even Anne herself — in order to merit such treatment. Others said the seed had been planted when the sheriff had attempted to hang Robin Hood's childhood friend, prompting Stutely's blood-soaked rescue. Still, from then on, any who could afford to do so travelled through Sherwood Forest with retinues of men-at-arms. Two outlaws were killed and more wounded, when they attempted to attack one of these parties. Their bodies were brought to Nottingham, and suspended in cages for all to see as the birds picked them apart, as proof that the outlaws of Sherwood were no longer untouchable.

Afterward, the band turned to stealing only from those travelling unarmed. This meant that journeymen could not travel where their skills were needed and would be remunerated. Farmers could not bring their surplus crops to market in Nottingham, and so lost their slender incomes.

Not only were the poor deprived of the outlaws' former charity, but of the forest's plants and animals for their tables, for even poachers were set upon and robbed of their bows. Some resisted when told to hand over their goods. The outlaws began beating their victims, cooperative or uncooperative. Foresters were wounded in surprise attacks, some lying in bed close to death afterward. The outlaws had discovered that disabling an enemy before he could hunt them down was more effective and better peace of mind than hiding for years at a time. Sherwood Forest, for all the splendour God gave it, was thrown into chaos and bloodshed.

The band had been lying in wait at the roadside since midmorning, yet no traveller happened by. It was now midafternoon and their stomachs hung so empty one could have dropped a stone amongst them, and they would have fought to devour it.

Along the road came three horses. Two were ridden by nuns, the third by a serving man. The nuns' habits and cowls, inside their travelling robes, were black, showing them to be Benedictines.

The outlaws broke their cover, blocking the path.

One stepped forward, staff in hand. "What business have ye, sisters, outside the nunnery walls?"

The nuns slowed their horses, looking about at the men surrounding them. They stopped before the one who addressed them. The older nun spake. "We have ventured forth upon the business of Wallingwells Priory, and now we return."

The eyes of the lead outlaw lit. "Priory business. Perhaps the collecting of tithes, from those farmers who sought to keep their small wealth to themselves?"

The younger nun looked stricken, whilst the older one pressed her lips together so they whitened.

"Ye must have thought to collect a fair amount, considering ye have spent much to hire three horses and a serving man to do so. I doubt, however, whether ye have paid this man so handsomely that he would spend his body in your defence. Give us the tithe money."

The younger nun turned to the older one, her eyes pleading for direction. The older nun would not meet her gaze.

Now along the road came a fletcher, carrying a staff and whistling a merry tune. He was clothed all in brown, but for a dusty red feather sprouting from his cap. The colour of his dress did nothing to stifle his spirits, for his step held a merry jaunt.

He confronted them all with a grin. "Greetings. Is it not a glorious day to travel through the forest leaves?"

"It is no glorious day, fellow, for my men and I need coins to fill our stomachs. Give us all the wealth in thy purse, or we shall give thee a beating such as the Romans gave Our Lord.

Then these nuns will know not to hesitate in granting our request."

"Wherefore shouldst thou demand such a thing?" asked the fletcher. "Knowest thou not this is Robin Hood's territory, and that women and the honest poor have his protection?"

The lead outlaw's mouth dipped almost into a smile. "Hoard no fear, fletcher, for I am he of whom thou dost speak. I am Robin Hood."

"Art thou indeed?" quoth the fletcher, his eyes growing wide.

"His very self."

"Yet, if thou art Robin Hood, how is it thou dost seek to rob a poor tradesman? Is thy prey not the nobility and the corrupt of the church?"

"That is only rumour. One cannot count upon the rich to keep one in bread and ale."

"How about this beating? I heard thou dost feast thy victims."

"A fairy story from romantic minds and dreamy minstrels."

"I heard also that thy men numbered seven-score-and-ten."

"Exaggerated, all of it. Back to the matter at hand: thy purse."

The fletcher looked thoughtful. "For all the myths thou hast laid bare, surely thou canst not begrudge me a trial by combat. They say thou art the greatest archer in the land. I practise with the bow myself. Let us compete. If thou dost win, I shall give thee all my wealth, and gladly. Yet if I win, thou and thy band shall surrender to me."

"I accept no such fool's wager. Thy purse, or I crack thy skull."

"I heard thou wert a nobleman's son. Surely one of such rank would not refuse to fight for his prize."

"Thou hearest many lies, fletcher."

"Then what of *this*: we two battle with our quarterstaffs. If thou shouldst win, thou gettest my purse. If I win, thou gettest half my coin only."

"Why? When I can take all thy coins with a word to my men?"

Anger flooded the fletcher's face. "Art thou truly such a coward? Thou needest thirty men to confront a single foe? Woe that England ever birthed such an ignoble braggart!"

"Those be thy last words, fletcher."

The nuns and their serving man urged their horses to the roadside as the outlaw leader advanced, his staff raised. Behind him, his followers cried out encouragement.

The leader's staff crashed toward the fletcher's head — deflected. The two fought with leonine ferocity. They leapt at one another, lips pulled back. If they snarled, 'twas not heard, for their pounding staffs drowned all other noise.

The leader gouged with the butt of his staff. The fletcher dodged, turning his own staff and thumping the leader across the shoulders with such force the latter dove to the dirt.

The outlaw leader lay upon the ground a few moments. The fletcher stepped back. The band stayed as they were, awaiting orders.

"It would seem I may keep half my coin," quoth the fletcher. "Or dost thou wish me to give thee a second drubbing, that I might keep all?"

The leader grunted as he picked himself from the dust. "Thou shalt die."

The fletcher turned his attention to the band. "Is this all of thy number?"

"Aye," spake one.

"But where is the giant?" asked the fletcher. "Where is Little John?"

A man stepped forward, barely taller than the fletcher himself. "I am Little John."

"Surely not. For I have heard the giant stands head, neck, and shoulders above all other men. Next wilt thou say that fellow beside thee is Anne Hood? Come now, where is Little John?"

"Here I am." The giant emerged from the leaves to stand amongst the outlaws.

The fletcher smiled. "Ah. I suspected these fellows did jest with me. And where is Will Stutely, that loyal soul?"

"I am here." Will Stutely came from the ferns.

"And where is Anne Hood?"

"Only here." Anne slipped from behind a tree, as though from the trunk itself.

"I bethought me these were not all the outlaws Sherwood could boast."

"Indeed," quoth Anne, passing between the fletcher and the lead outlaw, "for here are all the rest."

The forest came alive with men. They surrounded the smaller band of outlaws. A cloud passed and the sun came clearer.

The fletcher turned to the lead outlaw. "Dost thou know who I am?"

The man trembled; perhaps he nodded. "Ye are Robin Hood."

"Aye, and who art thou?"

"Sir, I was Randolf Fitzooth. I did not pay my taxes nor appear in county court. I only wanted to live free."

"Thou didst want power to which thou hast no right. Thou didst wish to steal and drink and frighten women. Knowest thou that Wallingwells Priory, whose tithes thou didst covet, is dedicated to St. Mary? Thou hast sought to rob the holy Virgin herself."

The false outlaw fell to his knees. "Please, master. I know we must be beaten, but I pray you to spare our lives."

"I should give thee to the sheriff! Yet, for the sake of the Virgin's Son, I shall show mercy, hoping thou wilt show mercy to others. Those despoiled and beaten must needs be compensated. To that end, thou wilt surrender all the money stolen."

"We have none left, sir. We spent all upon meat and drink. That is why we sought to deprive the nuns. Please, merciful sir, allow us to go in peace and we shall never return."

"Search them," Robin commanded.

This was done. Robin's men found many a coin concealed about the imposters.

"Ye have proved yourselves dishonest in every way, even in the midst of mercy. Ye shall face the law."

⊖⊖⊖

The Fox and Glove Inn was far from the Blue Boar, yet still within the realm of Sherwood. It sat above a sloping glen coddled by tall trees and feathered ferns. The sheriff's men often gathered at the Fox and Glove for ale and merry company, and a good many reclined at drink today, together with the king's foresters. All lazed about within the inn and without, reciting tales and jests, allowing their eyes to loll closed and absorbing the sun's warmth as so many lizards upon a rock.

None noticed when the ground first began to shake, nor the trees to tremble. Soon men were rushing out of the Fox and Glove to join their fellows, one half asking the air for explanation, the other silent and trembling.

Two hordes of men broke from the ferns, charging up the glen. The first horde had not one stitch of clothing to split amongst them. They ran forward, screaming and sweating. The second horde, clothed in Lincoln green, drove the naked men before it, shouting encouragement, prodding laggers with quarterstaffs.

The sheriff's men and the foresters stood mesmerized, watching the hordes bear down upon them.

Halfway up the glen, the green-clad men broke off, and the forest absorbed them.

The naked men kept on, fear flowing from their eyes. They ran into the midst of the lawmen, who recovered themselves and clothed the indecent with bruises.

Only later did the sheriff's men learn who it was they had beaten. By then the men had fled, and could not be hanged for their crimes upon the highway.

The people, too, learned the truth, and were duly compensated from the band's own treasury for their ill usage. Thus the merry men came back to live in Sherwood Forest, and no false outlaw ever resided in the greenwood after that day for fear of that noble robber, Robin Hood.

Chapter Nine
Elm

Robin was ever the venturesome sort. The call for adventure overpowered him and he set off with Anne. 'Twas not long before they spied a butcher driving his meat cart, pulled by a greying palfrey.

"Hold there, friend," called Robin, Anne laying hold of the bridle rein. "I would have speech with thee."

"Let me be on my way, good sir, lest I be late to market."

"Be easy, friend, I have a proposition for thee. At how much dost thou value thy meat and cart and horse?"

"At three marks."

Robin held out his purse to the butcher. "Here are four. Wouldst thou sell to me?"

"That will I!" cried the butcher, jumping down and seizing the purse. The coins' jingle was hushed between his palms.

Knowing Robin's mind, Anne spake up. "If thou wouldst be a butcher, love, thou must needs look the part. A crown for thine apron and hat, sir?"

The butcher agreed and was on his way richer than before.

Coming into Nottingham, the outlaw and his wife turned toward the marketplace, the liveliest part of town, where all manner of goods were sold, and all manner of cutpurses lurked.

Once they had set up a stall, Anne went to look about. Robin, dressed in his butcher's garb, began calling his wares.

To the peasant women he sold as much for a penny as those around him sold for three, to friars and usurers six pennies, to townsmen three, and to the poor and the old women he gave the meat for naught.

One maid, too poor to keep coins and noting this butcher's looks, asked if she might pay with a kiss upon the cheek. Robin agreed, and before long came many a giggling maid, for his blue eyes were playful and his yellow hair neatly combed.

The other butchers whispered. Some guessed Robin was a thief and had stolen the cart and horse, others called him a fool for a pretty lass. Most contended he was a rich prodigal wasting his wealth. It was not long ere Robin heard this, too.

He sold all his stock before suppertide. Once the last buyer left, some other butchers approached.

"Greetings, brother," called one. "There is a feast in Nottingham Castle this night for all of our trade, hosted by the sheriff himself. Wilt thou join us?"

"Aye, that will I," returned Robin, his heart quivering for joy at the invitation.

The other butchers returned to pack up their carts.

Anne came through the vanishing crowds to Robin's side. Said she, "The whole market doth buzz of a mad butcher who sells his meat for a kiss. Hast thou met this fellow, love?" A glint leapt in her eye.

"Methinks I have heard somewhat of him. But listen, dearest. If 'tis well with thee, bid the band prepare a feast, for I bring the sheriff at noontide. I am off to Nottingham Castle to break bread with these brothers in butchery. Await me upon the morrow."

One corner of Anne's mouth twisted into a grin. "I shall be sure the good silver is used. Mind thy manners, dearest."

"Do I not always?"

To prevent her answering, Robin pressed his lips to his wife's, then was off for the castle.

⊹⊖⊹⊖⊹

Robin played the prodigal fool, telling how he and his brothers had inherited land and cattle. When the party reached the castle hall, word of the mad butcher tickled everyone's lips. The news was whispered to the sheriff. Finding Robin a merry sort, he sat the false butcher at his right hand. Fortunately for the outlaw, the hall was dimly lit; he pulled his cap over his face and, side by side, made an awkward angle for the sheriff to look him in the eye.

"I hear thou sellest a herd of cattle, my good fellow," the sheriff cooed.

"True, m'lord," Robin replied, with an accent and a smile. "They're bonny hoovers, numbering over five 'undred 'ead. As for my land, never asked 'ow much I own. Truth be told, sheriff, I 'aven't a notion what price to pose. To your mind, is five 'undred pound too much?"

"That is exactly to my mind, and I shall give it thee, though I should like to see the cattle first."

"Save you! Save you, sheriff! 'Eaven save your soul! Your coins will be well spent."

The sheriff grinned at his own false generosity. This butcher had no mind for money. Why, he was practically stealing from the butcher's pocket!

The sky grew dark, and the butchers grew drunk. The sheriff took his leave. The outlaw lay down upon a straw pile with the other butchers. Thus the King of Sherwood slept the night in Nottingham Castle, right under the sheriff's nose.

⋅✧⋅✧⋅✧⋅

The sky blued and light flowed over the land. The forest was still or seemed to be from the city. Already bees flocked to flowers, trees opened leaves, and the king's deer grazed amidst the towers of the woods. Not least of those busying themselves were Robin Hood's men.

The sheriff met Robin outside Nottingham Castle. The outlaw had sold his horse and cart, and gave the proceeds to those he passed.

"Thou shouldst show more care with thy money," quoth the sheriff.

"Yet before the day be spent, me lord, ye will pay me a fair fortune. What need have I, then, of these little coins?"

He walked upon the king's highway beside the sheriff, who rode a white horse. The two journeyed for hours, the butcher nattering the while about that and this and some other, enjoying the sunlight, which seemed purer in the greenwood than anywhere else.

The farther they stepped into the forest, the more the sheriff wished for silence. He felt every moment the leaves giving birth to shapes of men. At last he could stand it no longer, and hissed, "Cease thy chattering, fool. Knowest thou not Robin Hood may be about?"

"But, sir, have ye not driven 'im out yet?"

The sheriff quaked. "Is thy land in Cathay that we *journey so long*?"

"Calm yourself, me lord. We have not much farther to go."

Around the next corner a herd of deer blocked their path. These lazed in the roadway, snatching at the greenest shoots, sunlight glistening off stray hairs along their backs.

Quoth Robin, "Here are mine animals. Speak low, so as not to frighten them."

The sheriff burst out, "Look here, cur — I have no wish for games. I return to Nottingham this instant!"

With hands faster than the dun deer leaps, Robin grasped the sheriff's bridle rein. "If ye would not buy my beasts, good sir, have at least the courtesy to meet my brothers."

Three notes sounded, and in the time it takes to wink to a friend, the pair were surrounded by three-score men clothed in Lincoln green. These were headed by a tall woman wearing a brown mantle. She smiled menacingly, yet her tone was sweet as morning dew. "Greetings, sir sheriff, from Robin Hood's band of outlaws. 'Tis an honour to see thee face to face."

"Doff your caps, men," cried Robin. "The sheriff is worthy of our respect. My lord, these are my brothers, and this my good wife Anne, whom ye may recall seeing at Baron Fitzwalter's castle. Since ye have given me meat, I would fain return your favour."

The sheriff straightened, hands trembling upon his reins. "If thou wouldst kill me, do not prolong the charade."

"I have never before killed a man from desire, sir sheriff, and I'll not forsake heaven for you. Henry, lead thou the sheriff's horse."

The party marched through the trees to camp, with the blindfolded sheriff in tow. After awhile, mixed with the speech of the leaves, odd snatches of conversation drifted toward the party. These cheerful, woodland voices grew louder and nearer, until the shouts of laughter were discernible from the calls of the deep-throated larks. Of a sudden they were upon it: the timeless camp of Sherwood.

Robin deposited the butcher's apron in the treasury, should he need it in the future. Meanwhile, the sheriff was given a show. The archery of the outlaws, after two years of practice, had advanced, and the band contrived to demonstrate this. A garland was placed upon a pair of stakes two hundred paces distant. If an arrow felled the garland whilst whizzing through it, the archer received a buffet from Little John. A few men found themselves motivated to improve. The sheriff so enjoyed the show he cheered aloud.

The games ended and the sheriff was shown to the table. Whilst the band alighted as charging bulls, each member in turn was introduced to the sheriff. His jaw bleached at Little John. Then Nottingham's protector looked down and saw his silver plate. When his own cook approached, carrying a platter of venison, he cried, "What is this, Robin Hood, that thou stealest from me — the High Sheriff of Nottingham? What have I done, that thou dost take my plate from mine home, and turn my servants against me? Today thou hast deceived me and taken me prisoner. Is *anything* too low for thee?"

To this Robin Hood answered never a word, yet Anne's voice was dangerously low. "Thou talkest as though thou wert too good to steal from. Dost thou not tax every penny from the poor to fill thine own purse? Didst thou not send John Little to capture Robin Hood? Didst thou not take Will Stutely and the widow's three sons prisoner? We have only revisited thine own deeds upon thine head. If thou wert ever an honest man, it would have been quite different for thee."

Seeing one hundred and more faces echo agreement, the sheriff busied himself with eating rather than rebuttal.

Such jests were told that soon the mood lightened. Songs were sung, and wine was drunk.

At last the sun waned, and the sheriff said he must take his leave. He mounted his horse, a number of the band trailing behind.

"If ye must go, sir sheriff," quoth Robin, "then ye must. I am sorry ye were vexed, but still, 'tis somewhat to think upon . . . One thing remains. All who feast with us must pay for their meat. I would fain not have you pay, for was my meat at your hand not free? Yet this noble company doth not share my sentiment."

The sheriff wasted no time but drew forth his purse and from it twenty pounds. "There ye are, my lads." He would have gone if Robin had not stayed him.

"Sir sheriff, the price at our little inn is four hundred pounds."

"I have not the sum with me yet, if thou wouldst accompany me back to Nottingham, I shall pay thee in full."

Robin laughed. "Do ye take me for a fool, lording? I enjoy the company of my thumbs, and would fain not be strung up by them. Did ye not come with five hundred pounds? Pay now else ill befall you."

The sheriff turned as white as his horse, giving his purse to Robin.

Handing it to Little John, Robin Hood spake to the sheriff. "My lord, how much money do ye carry?"

"Naught but the five hundred pounds in that pouch." The sheriff gazed mournfully at Little John, who was counting the money onto a cloak spread over the ground.

When finished, the giant spake. "The sheriff hath spoke truthfully. There are five hundred pounds within."

"Then we shall take but three hundred," quoth Robin.

Little John had separated the amount and returned the purse to his master, when Roger the cook approached with a clattering sack.

"Sir sheriff," quoth Robin, "for the past two years we have enjoyed your silver service. It is returned with our apologies, for it wrongfully departed from you."

Surrendering both plates and purse, Robin made ready to have the sheriff blindfolded.

Anne and Will Stutely came up.

"Master," Stutely began, looking to the sheriff with contempt, "Lady Anne and I have been at speech with the others. We feel the sheriff should take an oath that he'll no more hunt us but leave us in peace to live free in the forest."

"A right sound notion, friends. Well, my lord?" Robin again turned to the sheriff.

"Yes, yes, I swear by Saint Peter. Never shall I hunt you in the forest . . . yet let me catch you out of it." This last part the sheriff spake under his breath, unsettled by the sight of Will Stutely and the hatred in his eyes.

The twilight framed a grand sight: the High Sheriff of Nottingham blindfolded and clutching a sack of silver, being led through the forest by Robin Hood.

CHAPTER TEN
Plane

T HE WINTER CAME AND WENT. The prices upon the heads of the Sherwood men grew. Robin's alone was valued at five hundred pounds, an amount otherwise unheard of — unless one were purchasing cattle from a prodigal butcher.

Some nobles said this increase was useless, for the band must have been killed in the winter cold. Yet all the poor held that Robin's men were well. Long had they waited for one to ridicule the fierce forest laws that starved them. Not one peasant would consider their champions could be defeated by something so unromantic as a winter breeze.

The band left their moss cots under the stars to shelter in Barnesdale's caves, using deer pelts — the fur facing inward — for blankets, and every morn gathering 'round a bonfire to break their fast.

Whilst the outlaws rested themselves for more adventures, they heard many tales from Anne. One of their favourites ran thus:

"Come and listen, yeomen all, to hear how a nobleman hunts his deer, for he doth not track it quietly but maketh a grand show and ceremony of the thing.

"Baron Fitzwalter is a nobleman who enjoys the hunt. Though he doth not hunt by stalking, as do Sherwood's outlaws and its poachers, neither doth he prefer the *par force* hunting so popular with many men of his rank. Whilst he hunts *par force* from time to time, he much prefers to hunt using bow and stable.

"Upon the baron's land stands a park where he might hunt deer at his pleasure. Enclosed by a ditch and an oaken paling, it can channel deer toward their ends very neatly and hath two deer-leaps, where the beasts might jump inside without chance of again escaping. Now is a fortnight before Lent is due to begin and the season for hunting hinds.

"Upon this particular day, the baron hath with him some huntsmen, one of whom is the father of our own Will Stutely. Also accompanying the baron are his fifteen-year-old daughter, Marian; his squire, Robert; and our good Will Stutely himself. All are dressed in green, so as to blend with the trees and not alarm the deer.

"The baron is anxious to hunt, this day above all others, because he hath recently been given an alaunt by the Earl of Chester. The dog hails from Spain, whence all the finest of its breed are come. His body is shaped like a greyhound's, yet the head spans broad and short, each ear trimmed to a point, and with more muscle upon his bones. His coat is smooth and white, swathes of black about his ears and tail. The dog hath already been favoured with a heavy, studded collar. He is named Percival for, like his brethren, he is dim-witted and bold.

"Baron Fitzwalter's other alaunts know well how to use their strength to grip a deer better than three greyhounds together, and to bring low even the swiftest great hart so that the huntsmen may catch up and slay the beast. Upon occasion, even these well-trained dogs become overzealous, and run down oxen or other kept animals. The baron holds high hopes for Percival, who is muzzled and led alone by a fewterer, not to be released until the prey is close at hand.

"All have heard mass, and swallowed a hasty mouthful of bread, including Percival, at least as regards the latter. Before even the dawn hath parted its heavy eyelids, all ride high in their saddles, Percival striding alongside upon his leash. They know where the deer reside this morning, for the beasts have been spied out in advance.

"Robert, Marian, and young Will Stutely dismount, leaving their horses alongside the cart that will come later to take up the deer slain. Not far on they come upon the herd. Deer, being timorous, are more likely to trust to four-legged creatures than to two-legged ones, despite the great folly this can entail. Therefore, Percival, the fewterer, and our three youths conceal themselves by stepping lightly with the mounted hunters, using the horses to hide from the herd's view as they cross downwind in front of them all. The youths stop one by one at their trysting trees.

"Though one might expect to find Baron Fitzwalter amongst the archers, he instead prefers to ride his horse in driving the deer. Being a man of energy, he favours such a pursuit above the patience required of an archer whilst hunting.

"Now the riders circle upwind, moving with all subtlety so as not to startle the deer before wishing to do so. Having gotten upwind bit by bit, with plenty of stops for their horses to take a swallow of grass, that they might seem less of a sight to remark, the riders creep nearer the herd.

"Our three archers wait all this time at the foot of a wooded valley, never speaking a word lest it trickle into the ear of one of the deer above and cause them to climb out at the valley's sides, rather than be driven down it. A handful of huntsmen form the stable, lining the valley's top ridges, that they might shout and startle any rogue deer back down to the archers. These latter remain motionless with their backs to their trysting trees. Too great a movement may also cause the deer to veer away and be lost. Their bows they hold at half draw, straining the muscles in their backs, between the blades of their shoulders, the twisted green silk of the strings cutting Robert's and Marian's fingers, Will Stutely's flax bowstring cutting his, as they keep as still as they can, feeling the moments stretch longer for not knowing when the last will come. Marian, in the middle, stands farther down the valley than her two companions. Nearly a stone's throw spans between one archer and the next, for the wood is open, though not as open as it might be. The fewterer keeps a little ways behind the archers, ready with the alaunt. To pass the time, Marian, Robert, and Stutely watch for signs of how the wind passes through the leaves and grass, noting how this must guide the direction of the deer they hope soon to see, and how they must aim, for the barbs of their arrowheads measure four fingers' width, and so sway their path under the wind's influence.

"At last comes the blast of a horn. The archers' blood pumps harder, though they dare not chance a move otherwise. Marian strains to mark the direction of Stutely's gaze, for his ears are keen, and he can trace better than any the notes' path through the trees, as they follow the herd in flight.

"Hoof beats sound. Fast upon them the cries of 'Hey!' and 'Ware!' from the stable. The thump of blood in the archers' ears rivals the pound of hooves.

"A stag gallops in sight, ahead of the others. He passes between Robert and Marian. They must leave him go, for in the fermisoun season only hinds may be slain.

"The hinds descend. The first breaks toward Marian's right. She leaves it for Stutely, as to shoot right she must swing all her body, whilst to shoot left he need only shift his bow arm. Stutely does not aim far enough ahead of the hind, and his arrow passes behind the beast by the time it reaches her path. The shaft rams into a trunk only two trees apart from Marian's trysting tree, with a sound heard even amidst the stampede.

"Marian aims for the middle of a hind's chest, as 'tis still far away and so not moving by as quickly as the one Stutely had sought to fell. She looses.

"The hind stumbles, falling amidst the others, who leap over her.

"Robert hath shot two hinds. Marian takes aim again, fighting the thrill in her heart, to keep her hands steady.

"The arrow flies into the hind's chest, yet not in the middle so as to split its heart. It bleeds, but still it runs.

"Baron Fitzwalter and the other riders can now be seen behind the herd. Three long notes sound, giving the signal for Percival's uncoupling. The baron leans forward, his face alight, to see what his new alaunt can do.

"The fewterer slips off the dog's leash and muzzle. Percival does not abide a moment, but leaps at the hind Marian had wounded, snapping at its blood-dappled fur, ploughing into it and dragging it down.

"The hind screams before Percival silences it.

"The baron cheers. Yet it is only half a cheer.

"He hath ridden amongst the fleeing herd for a better look at his beast's skill. A hart running with the hinds lowers its horned head, charging the baron's horse. The points of its massive antlers pierce blood from the horse and from the baron. His cry shifts to one of surprised pain.

"'Father!' The word is hardly from Marian's lips when a mass of white fur streaks through her vision.

"Percival parts the herd as though he were Moses' rod. The hart sees, and lowers its head, running to meet the alaunt.

"Percival slips aside, gracefully dodging. The hart waits and, not feeling an impact, raises its head and races off between Marian and Robert. They can do nothing but watch it go, for to kill the murderous beast now is not permitted.

"A horse screams. Robert and Marian turn back to see.

"Percival hath leapt upon the baron's mount. The horse's hooves shift all about as it staggers, trying to resist being dragged down by the alaunt. The dog, stupid and vicious, smells the blood brought forth by the hart's antlers and thinks only of killing.

"The baron shouts at the dog, as do the other riders. Still it bites and claws at the panicking horse. Baron Fitzwalter exerts all his strength to keep his mount, for it will trample him if he leaves its back.

"The alaunt's claws rake the baron's leg where the blood already flows. Baron Fitzwalter cries out, and Marian screams. The frenzied dog sees its master as prey. Men from the stable come running and the riders continue to shout, but none can approach the alaunt without risking death for themselves. Baron Fitzwalter slashes at Percival with a hunting knife, but the dog is quick to avoid the blade, and the horse's strength is fast failing as blood pours down its side.

"The deer have all passed. Marian runs up the slope.

"An arrow cuts the dog's spine with a sound that cracks off the trees. Trapped in the bone, the shaft sticks out like a spike.

"The alaunt slows its attack, though only by a fraction.

"Marian halts, glancing back at Robert in time to see him nock his second shaft, his face strained as she hath never seen it before. The arrow leaps.

"The alaunt falls to the ground, dead.

"Baron Fitzwalter's horse cries out. Its legs buckle.

"Marian runs again, coming upon her father as he staggers up, having just avoided the horse's weight crushing his uninjured leg. He leans upon the dying beast, as it shudders to rise beside the sprawled body of Percival.

"'Fetch the cart to carry my lord back to the castle,' Stutely's father shouts to one of the mounted huntsmen, leaping down to support the baron.

"Marian embraces her father upon his uninjured side.

"'My brave girl,' he kisses her head, 'running to rescue me when none dared come near.' He raises his voice to old Stutely. 'See for certain that the dog is dead, and put the horse out of pain.'

"Robert hath run up, Will Stutely behind him. They stare at the blackened, flattened grass, and the scene upon it. Robert is panting. 'I am sorry, sir.'

"'Sorry?'

"'For shooting thine horse, sir. I tried only to shoot the dog, but that did not stop him.'

"'Percival had killed the horse before thine arrow. We were in such a tangle, I am fortunate, Robert, that thou didst not shoot me.'

"Robert remains silent, which is hardly like him.

"'I loved that horse and that dog, yet if thou hadst not shot the alaunt likely it would have turned upon Marian as she neared. It is worth a horse and a dog; it would have been worth my leg.'

"Marian turns her head against her father's shoulder, and finds Robert's eyes already upon her. They exchange a long look as old Stutely slits the horse's throat.

"'I fear I shall have to wait at least one season before being able to hunt again.'

"The cart trundles into the clearing. Those deer killed must be left for later. The baron hath more immediate need of the cart, thankfully, due to a youth whose skill could hardly be replicated by a man twice his age in the calmest of circumstances. This is how a nobleman doth hunt, with a grand show."

Chapter Eleven
Ash

SPRING ARRIVED AND THE BAND returned to Sherwood's walls. They lived well off the sheriff's money.

It was an indolent afternoon, with most outlaws extended upon the sward. Some sang, others jested. Contentment rested upon all, with most willing to sleep the day into dusk.

Robin lounged under the greenwood tree. Of a sudden, he bolted up. "Fye! 'Tis the month for wages, and we have no cloth of Lincoln green in our stores. Little John, busk thee to Ancaster to buy the material. Bide here whilst I retrieve the money."

Robin made his way through the few yards of brush between the camp clearing and the treasury cave. He set aside the camouflage branches, turned the key kept about his neck in the lock, and opened the oaken door. Stepping sideways, the Hood entered the narrow cave and took up a sack of silver. Many bags of coins loitered about. Trunks contained the clothes of friar and monk, peasant and pilgrim, engrosser and attendant, tinker and tanner, esquire and lord, along with a pile of silk handkerchiefs, a pouch of rings, and a few golden chains. These last were customarily sold. Half the treasury stores were dispersed to the poor. So thankful were these folk that they provided food and shelter for outlaws pursued by foresters, or far from camp at night.

Returning, Robin handed Little John the purse. "Fare thee well, Little John, and keep clear of mischief."

Little John started upon his journey, right foot foremost.

Birds flitted from tree to tree, the scent of flowers and thyme upon their wings. The dirt danced a crackling jig beneath the giant's feet, and the staff he held felt cool against his palm. Oak leaves pounced about, making shadows with the sunlight. Sky arced in all directions, so clear a blue that one could see the stars.

Soon the path split, leading Little John away from Ancaster to the Blue Boar Inn, for the birds now carried the aroma of ale's song and laughter.

The next morn, Little John was early upon his way, breakfast safe inside him. At first he intended to make up lost time, yet leisure took hold again before long. He ambled off the path upon some half-formed fancy.

Wending past flowers and ferns, he came to a clearing. Here, Little John was jerked from his dream world to his body upon realizing himself no longer alone.

A man — a tanner from the look and smell of him — had entered the clearing at the opposite end.

Having been so rudely yanked from his own thoughts, the tanner scoffed. "Well, well, thou art a pretty piece of fluff, I daresay."

"Who dost thou call fluff, vagabond?" growled Little John, in an equally foul temper. "Canst thou not see that here stand

I, the man of us, with staff in hand? Thine arm is so weak thou dost strap thy staff to thy back."

"Fye! One who dawdles in the forest, instead of doing man's work is hardly better than a fellow who sweats for his bread!"

"Come forward, knave, and we shall see how thou dost sweat!"

⊕ ⊕ ⊕

Word entered Robin's ear of how Little John had lazed at the Blue Boar. Since returning from the sheriff's, the giant had passed up duty for pleasure, gaining fat about his joints, and losing the quickness in his step. Robin had chided him, though it did little good. Little John was still as willing to please, only his effort was dampened.

Robin Hood set off to remind the giant of his errand in Ancaster. Hurrying along the road, the outlaw's irritation was fed by the words he thought of to scold his lieutenant.

Now Robin could hear the thuddings of a quarterstaff bout, and thought to see what was afoot. It sounded as if half a dozen men fought in yonder clearing. Lying upon his stomach, Robin peered through the leaves that he might observe. He found Little John and the tanner bashing right mightily.

Robin said to his mind, 'Truly, Little John is more evenly matched than ever I thought to find him.'

The two warriors went back and forth, up and down. Both were tiring, yet Little John took the worst of it. Each time he struck, his chest heaved for the effort.

The tanner caught him in the side. The giant wheezed as all his air rushed away. The tanner thwacked him upon the ribs, making the spot tender. Little John clenched his teeth, yet the third blow made him yelp. He tumbled to his knees. The tanner brought his staff down upon the giant's shoulder, causing him to sink closer to the ground.

"Hold!" cried Little John, when he saw the staff raised again. "I yield me. Hold."

"Dost thou agree that I am the man of us two?"

"Aye."

"Who is the fluff, then?"

"That am I and praise to thy skill at the quarterstaff — now let me up!"

"Very well, and thou mayest thank the saints that I show mercy."

As Little John rose to his feet, Robin came stumbling from the brush, caught in fits of merriment.

"Oh, John," he managed to say, "never hast thou yielded thyself so before — *praising* thy conqueror. Thou didst stand as if stone and watch the staff descend."

Little John's nettle was up and his side sore. He told Robin plainly that he found no humour in the situation.

After another outburst, Robin replied, "Do not fret, lad. I came to thrash thee for not doing as I commanded, yet this fine fellow hath beaten me to it. What be thy name, good tanner?"

The tanner had stood with a sullen air, wondering at the newcomer. "My name is Arthur a Bland, and I am come from Blyth to the Nottingham market, where I have sold my calf skins."

"Welcome, then. Men do call me Robin Hood, and this is my right-hand man Little John, thy boon companion."

"Oh, master," the tanner gasped, "I have heard of you. If I had known — mine apologies, good John."

The giant did not respond.

"Come now," quoth Robin, "do not act so high, for it doth ill befit thee. This man hath saved thee from me, and thou shouldst be grateful. Arthur, thou hast proved thyself a right fair hand at the quarterstaff. Wilt thou join my band?"

"Marry, mine heart leaps for the chance, good master. I shall be loyal to you 'til the end of my days — ye have the word of Arthur a Bland."

"I thank thee, Arthur. Thou art a good fellow and true. My thanks for finding Little John." Robin turned to the giant. "Did I not send thee to Ancaster, and yet thou hast spent the night at the Blue Boar?"

"I am sorry, master," said Little John, submissive in manner and meek in speech. "I would have gone to Ancaster straight away, yet it looked like rain."

"Then Arthur and I shall accompany thee part way, for next perchance it may threaten to snow."

Little John felt stung yet spake nothing. He wished the ordeal over, and further comment would prolong his master's chiding.

The sun warmed their faces, heating the breezes that would have chilled them. As the day wore on the party waxed thirsty. They stopped to drink from a blethering brook and sit awhile in the shade.

The three's minds wandered back and forth. Robin peered within the valley they rested upon the cusp of, and smiled. "Ho lads! See this fancy traipsing fellow come tripping o'er the lea?"

A youth of eighteen sniffed a rose as he walked through the valley. A white feather streamed from his wide, scarlet hat. Beneath a faint beard, a musing look bathed his slender face. Light hair curled upon his shoulders. Lace lined his collar and cuffs. His scarlet surcoat boasted gold stitching, and he wore silk scarlet hose. His shoon tapered into points, and a jewelled sheath swallowed his sword.

"It wounds the eye to see riches flaunted," quoth Robin. "Such a pretty creature would faint at the sight of a quarterstaff."

"But master," said Little John, "see how he carries his shoulders back and his arms bent stiff? I wot he is a tougher bird than he would have us believe."

Arthur a Bland nodded.

"I shall meet him and we shall see who hath guessed his true colours." Robin stepped into the road.

It took the stranger a fair time to reach the outlaw. He came glancing now at the sky, now at the ground, now at the hedgerow lining the path. Ever and anon he would sniff at his rose, never showing sign of seeing Robin.

When at last he came close enough, the outlaw called, "Hold there, fair friend."

The stranger spake in a soft, gentle voice. "Greetings, sir. Please, relieve thy mind of troubles by telling them to me."

"I tell thee plainly, the sight of a traipsing boy spending lavishly of honest men's gains sickens me to the soul. Hand over thy purse that the proper tax may be extracted."

The young man inclined his head sadly. "I fear I must continue my journey, friend, for my business is urgent. I give thee good den; mayhap thou wilt find better luck with the next traipsing boy to happen along."

Robin blocked the road with his staff. "Thou wilt pay or have a right sound beating." He twirled the weapon above his head until the air whistled.

The stranger tossed his rose aside and drew his sword.

"Put up thy sword, fellow," quoth Robin. "My staff is such that thou couldst not stand against it. Cut thyself a weapon in yon thicket."

The stranger eyed Robin's staff, sheathed his sword, and commenced sizing up the thicket's trees. Finding a sapling fitting his purpose, the man in scarlet set his heel to the ground and lifted the tree — roots and all — in a single heave.

Little John and the tanner watched unnoticed in the shade, feeling their hearts chirrup. Robin kept his ground whilst the stranger approached, trimming branches with his sword, as if naught had happened.

When finished, the stranger put his sword in its place. "Dost thou truly wish to fight, good fellow? Thy pate is too pretty a one to bruise."

"Thou shouldst worry for thine own pate," Robin returned.

The first to strike was the outlaw, scoring a crack to the other's ribs. The stranger came back with a mighty blow, yet Robin ducked beneath. Even whilst the wind sang above his head, the outlaw dealt another belt to the side.

Many times the stranger gave wallops that would strike Robin dead, yet the outlaw danced out of harm's way again, thwacking his opponent's ribs.

The stranger thundered a blow down upon Robin that vibrated the outlaw's weapon so he could no longer hold it. Dropping the staff, Robin himself was not far behind. A clout fell upon his shoulders, causing him to drop as if dead. Again and again the stranger smote him, until he could barely breathe.

Little John broke cover and ran to his master's side, calling, "Hold, hold! Strike him no more!" Arthur a Bland ran after the giant, and the stranger looked up.

Little John knelt and helped Robin to his feet.

The outlaw spake through clenched teeth. "Well, lad, thou hast beaten me fairly. What be thy name?"

"William of Gamewell," the stranger answered, his eyebrow raised. "I am travelling to Sherwood Forest to abide with mine uncle."

Robin squinted at the stranger, as if noticing him for the first time. "Will Gamewell? Aye, I should have recognized thee from thy pretty clothes. Dost thou remember me, lad?"

After closer examination Will spake. "Can this be Robin Hood? Truly, I did not know thee — art thou a'right?"

Robin straightened at a snicker from Little John. "Nay, lad, I am well. Though I tell thee thou art the strongest man I have ever crossed."

Will laughed. "Strength hath its downfalls, Uncle. These muscles have made me slow as oxen. Besides, that was the reason I sought thee. I am on the run from the law."

Now Robin laughed. "Dawdling as thou wert? I spied a snail overtake thee."

"Speed in accomplishing a task only causeth matters to go awry," Will returned.

"How wert thou outlawed, friend?" asked Little John.

"'Tis a sad tale. Regretfully, I have killed someone."

"Did he threaten to rob thee upon the highroad?" The giant smirked.

"Nay, he was my father's steward and a right naughty fellow. One day he had the misfortune to insult my father within mine earshot. I gave him a box o' th' ear. He fell, ne'er arising. They say I broke his neck. Mother bid me go to Sherwood. As it seemeth, Uncle, thou hast found me first."

"Yea," replied Little John, "our master hath a knack for finding people. Especially those holding talent with the quarterstaff."

"That is enough, Little John," quoth Robin, his sore limbs shortening his temper.

The giant would have ceased, yet in his ears rang his master's chidings of that morn and the two years past. "But master, thou dost love a merry jest. Hast thou not made many a clever remark upon the fat about my joints?"

"I have said enough."

"And was I right in seeking shelter from the rain last night?"

"Fye! Thou wert right to shelter thyself in the Tower of London for aught I care!"

"Then that score is settled also. For myself, I have neither seen thee plunged to the dirt nor beaten black by this good fellow." Little John spake with so sober a face that snickers were heard from the two standing by.

Robin turned to Will and spake. "Many will be looking for thee, lad. We must e'en change thy name. I christen thee Will Scarlet, for never before hath a man sought to flout the law in such colours."

After a brief discussion, it was decided to journey to Ancaster another day; for Will could be spotted a mile away, and Robin and Little John had wounds to nurse.

◦•◦•◦

There is little rest for those seeking it. The men waxed hungry, stopping to buy bread and cheese. At the roadside they chewed their meal. Will told of Robin's mother. She was well and in good spirits, cared for by her eldest son, who would be wed in summer. Then Will, whose voice shone soft as a rabbit's fur, took up a tune.

> Now listen thou to this fine tale
> Of love I sing to thee.
> For 'tis a pretty little tale,
> And hath sweet melody.
>
> One day there roved a fairy small
> In amongst the flowers,
> When all a sudden came a voice
> With wond'rous magic pow'rs.
>
> It sang so prettily and soft,
> As his own ears did hear,
> Yet she who sang so prettily
> Did look so very queer.
>
> Short was the maid, and oh so small,
> Came only to the side
> Of every full grown man and oh!
> This thought did cause her sighs.

"Come with me now," the fairy said,
"For I do love thee so,
"And care I not one little bit
"That thou art small and low."

Away, away those two did flee,
Flying across the lea
Upon the fairy's wings of gold,
With feelings oh so deep.

The song was a trifle childish, yet all agreed Will sang fair. After mentioning a cough he had been suffering, Little John trolled:

Go down to the valley,
Lover mine.
(Down to the valley)
Where thou wilt find
(Deep in the valley)
What thou didst leave behind . . .

"Look there," quoth Robin, pointing. A short man with black hair and a scrunched face trudged toward them under a heavy sack.

"He is scarcely worth interrupting a song for," grumbled the giant.

"Nay, Little John, 'tis naught to be sore at," replied his master. "He is a miller; I have seen him about. Ho! what say ye to having a jest with this fellow? Let us forth as common thieves seeking to rob him. Then we shall take him to feast at camp."

"I have no want for another beating this day," quoth Little John.

"Seest thou how small he be? And are there not four of us?" Smiles appeared, and the giant felt his face redden.

When the miller neared, the four highwaymen leapt from the undergrowth, giving the little man a start that nearly caused him to drop his sack of flour.

Robin spake. "Hold there, friend. It doth seem thy load be a heavy one. Mayhap we can assist by lightening thy purse."

"Midge the Miller's son can carry a heavier load than lazy bandits. This is Robin Hood's territory, and if he found you robbing an honest craftsman, he should beat you blue and black." The miller glared at Robin, who only laughed.

"I and my men are a fair match for Robin Hood. A midge thou truly art, and not much a man to see. I tell thee again, hand over thy coins else ill befall thee."

The twirling of the thief's staff unnerved the miller. "I have no money about me."

Robin's eye roved. "Thy bag of flour," quoth he at last, "mayhap there be a penny or two in the bottom."

The miller unslung the bag from his shoulder and dug 'round in the flour. As the curious yeomen peered inside the bag, the miller flung two great handfuls of flour in their faces.

Staggering about in the road, the four yeomen tried to clear their eyes and noses. Tears streamed down to blind them, and they could hardly breathe, for flour had entered their mouths as well, making them roar.

After a moment of shock at his own courage, the miller began beating the four with his staff, flailing as one gone mad. He threw more flour. "Varlets! Ye demanded coins — I intend to pay in full!"

Robin fumbled to find his silver horn. When the three notes came echoing from tree to tree a group of the Hood's men, led by Anne and Will Stutely, flew toward the alarm. They were confronted with quite a scene.

There stood five men white from head to foot (for flour had fallen back upon the miller, too). Hardly a blade of grass within five yards was not sprinkled as if with snow. All movement ceased when the outlaws in green appeared. It was as if the fairies of spring and winter met and knew not what to think of each other.

"What is this, master?" Will Stutely asked, staring 'round with round eyes.

"Christmas come early, perhaps," quoth Anne, striding toward the miller. She smiled as she passed the other four. "Greetings, friend. I am Anne o' th' Hood. I presume thou hast a reason for beating these men."

Startled, the miller's son answered, "They sought to rob me, milady. I told them this was Robin Hood's territory . . . they only laughed."

"Thou hast defended Robin's land bravely, and I am sure he fain would thank thee."

"Truly, milady, 'twould be my pleasure."

Smiling ever wider, Anne announced, as a herald might proclaim King Henry, "May I present the King of Outlaws, the Prince of Thieves, and the Lord of all Sherwood and Barnesdale: Robin Hood." She swept her arm to indicate Robin, who stood holding his bruised sides and coughing.

The miller's son tiptoed forward. "Forgive me, master. Had I known 'twas you, I would have given all my money without opposition."

Robin was forced then to explain how he had thought to play a jest upon the miller and gotten himself a beating instead. Then Little John, despite his earlier promise, told how he and the tanner had fought, and also of Robin's battle with Will Scarlet. When the men laughed, Robin grew snippish, refusing help to brush off his clothes.

Anne met Will Scarlet gladly, and allowed the miller into the band when he inquired, giving Robin time to be ashamed, of which he took full advantage. His pride had been wrenched from him, though he had had more than a helping of it before.

When all were prepared to leave for camp, Anne sought out her husband. Sauntering over to Robin she whispered, as if relating a humorous secret, "I tell thee, love, the men of this country follow thee 'round as ducklings do their mother. Just *think* what troubles they should plunge into if thou didst not lead them so cunningly. I can see this day being a good deal worse for them."

This smoothed rough feelings, and they all turned toward the shelter of the greenwood.

⋄⋄⋄

Robin Hood, with Little John, Will Scarlet, and Midge the Miller's son (who, in jest, had now changed his name to Much) awaited some guest by the roadside for the midday meal. Church bells crowed that mass had ended. The outlaws were banned from such services.

Little John worried over his master's health, knowing Robin often neglected his well-being for the sake of adventure or charity. "Master, 'tis growing late. If thou wouldst eat, it would do thee good."

"'Tis inhospitable to begin the feast ere thy guest arrives. I return to camp; bring a guest with all speed." Robin disappeared amidst the leaves.

Within the hour came a horse's clopping hooves. The rider was a knight, yet his clothes were torn and stained. His head drooped to his chest, his arms hung limp, and one foot swung outside its stirrup. His horse chose its own way. When Little John took the bridle, neither beast nor man twitched an eye.

"Good day, sir knight," quoth the giant.

The chest filled, bobbing the knight's head. His voice slid out in a sigh. "Is it?"

"Come. My master hath fasted these six hours awaiting you."

They led the knight through the forest without blindfolding him, for the fellow looked not to notice where he travelled.

Entering the clearing, the knight only peered up when Robin spake, and then only slightly.

"Greetings, sir knight," quoth Robin. "This noble company hath awaited your coming most eagerly. Come eat, lording, lest the meal grow cold."

The knight dismounted and sat with the outlaws. His company joked, and bread and meat warmed his tongue, but the knight ate little and said less.

When the meal ended, Robin spake. "Sir knight, ye go your way and we go ours. Therefore, we must settle the score, for 'tis not the custom for yeoman to pay for knight. I reckon you at two hundred pounds; is it not so, my men?"

A cheer of agreement sounded.

The knight only looked sad. "All I have in the world, master, are the ten pounds I carry. Thou art welcome to them."

"Search him, Little John," quoth Robin, unsure what to think of this melancholy gentleman. "If he carries the amount of which he spake, then we shall take not so much as a groat."

Laying a cloak upon the ground, Little John counted but ten pounds.

Robin said, "Ye have spoke soothly, sir knight, yet how hath one of your high rank become so low as to have only ten pounds?"

"My name is Sir Richard. I lived in Castle Lea with my liege lady and our children. Many pledged me their true friendship, yet when hard times came I found myself alone. Mine only son was right good at the joust and entered a competition. He inadvertently slew his opponent in the fray and was outlawed. I sold my possessions to pay for his pardon. I have mortgaged mine home to St. Mary's Abbey and, unless I pay six hundred pounds this very day, mine house and lands are forfeit. I was journeying to ask an extension, yet the brothers are not known for their mercy." It exhausted his energy to end the story.

"I have heard of you, Sir Richard," quoth Robin, half to himself. "Ye are a noble knight and never despoiled another whilst gaining your position. We shall give you the coins to repay your debt." Never had the outlaws aided a gentleman before. Yet Robin never judged a man by his status but by his honesty.

Sunshine beamed from Sir Richard's face and did not seem like to stop. "Thanks to thee, master! My wife will be very happy, and so am I."

"Little John, go thou to the treasury to fetch the money, and five yards of blue silk for the Lady at the Lea. Then gather a score of men and escort Sir Richard, lest less honest thieves attack and despoil him." Robin knew the abbot of St. Mary's had taken the giant's lands away before Little John had turned outlaw, and expected buried feelings might be freed if the giant showed what he had made of himself.

The knight responded, "I promise by the fair hand of the Virgin Mary to aid thee, Robin of the Hood, whenever thou mayest have need of me. Hold no doubt."

"Good sir," quoth Robin, smiling at the name of the Virgin, "ye are a man after mine own heart. Godspeed."

⊕⊕⊕

St. Mary's Abbey was celebrating, for hair nor hide had been seen of Sir Richard. Clergymen and nobles gathered to divide the knight's lands, eager to devour what biscuits they could from Sir Richard's crumbs. The men sat at table in the abbey's guesthouse. The walls were simply stone, giving no hint of warmth or of being home to anything but the wind whistling through the casements.

"The castle should belong to the most worthy of us," quoth the Bishop of Hereford.

"Indeed." Baron Fitzwalter, wearing his crest, twisted his fingers beneath the table, for being in such company irked him. "Would not ye agree, sir sheriff?"

Swallowing a lump of white bread, the Sheriff of Nottingham nodded.

"Whosoever receiveth the house must pay land rents to us," the Abbot of St. Mary's reminded them. Fur lined his holy robes. His bald pate reflected no sun.

Sir Richard burst into the room, followed by three stout fellows in Lincoln green.

"Reynold Greenleaf!" cried the sheriff, sputtering wine.

Little John smiled. "Greetings, sir sheriff. I trust thou hast found a suitable replacement for me?" Turning to Baron Fitzwalter, he said, "Sir, I tell you truly, your worthy daughter is safe and contented. My master loves her dearer than his own heart."

Sir Richard knelt before the abbot. "Sir, have pity upon my misfortune, and give me another month to pay."

The abbot cast dark eyes upon him. "If thou hast not the money, thy lands are mine."

"Please, sir! Can ye not see a man upon his knees? By all the saints, have mercy."

"No saint in heaven can save thee, Sir Richard. Give me the money now or take thy leave." The abbot's lips curled, for he knew the knight could not pay. Thoughts of the crops he would gain filled his head, and he gloated to envision the land rents from his future tenants.

Sir Richard sprang to his feet. He flung a pouch upon the table, the sound beating the walls of the stone room. Silver coins spilled. None of the rich men could avert their eyes.

Sir Richard left the abbey. He went to his wife, and they journeyed home to Castle Lea. The outlaws escorted them before returning home themselves to a fortress far grander than any made by man.

CHAPTER TWELVE
Boxwood

WILL STUTELY LED HIS USUAL party, sixteen in all. They spied foresters to avoid, laymen to aid, and noblemen to rob. Walking a little-used path, a boy of seventeen appeared, who had the look of former richness. The lute upon his back showed that he had been a bard in a lord's household. Tears slipped down his face. His right arm hung limp in its rags, like a leaf skittering in the breeze. His left trailed a noose along the path.

The sight of the rope silenced the outlaws' chatter.

Will Stutely's throat drew in upon itself. Stepping forward, he spake. "Ho there, lad! 'Tis a pretty string thou holdest. Hast thine horse run off?"

The boy's voice was sweet, yet choked with thorns. "Not a horse, sir, but my love. The string is for my neck, for the thing is too short for my liking."

"And dost thy love approve thy neck's length? Methinks she hath left thee, for the rope, it speaks to me. Surely she is a sorry love if she left thee for a longer-necked man."

The boy faced Stutely with flames in his eyes, quivering with the heat. "How darest thou!" His voice shuddered so fiercely he could hardly control it. "Thou knowest her not, thou rogue! What dust for brains hast thou, to call so wonderful and pure a creature traitor to my face? I might like company upon my dying day — bear that well in thy mind." The boy spun away.

Stutely stood in surprise, yet his tongue recovered soon enough. "I am sorry, lad, to tease thee in thy strife. Marry, come with us and swallow a last meal. Death is not an appointment for which to be on time."

The lad consented, a simple, sad look upon his face, even when they reached the outlaws' camp and Robin and Anne Hood approached him.

"What wandering minstrel is this?" asked Robin jovially.

"Allan a Dale," with a slight bow.

"Now I know thee," quoth one of Stutely's party. "He is a famous songster, master. I heard him sing like honey."

Allan's face remained stone-set. His gangly figure flapped even in the still air.

"What dost thou do in Sherwood, lad," quoth Robin, "when thieves and outlaws run amok?"

"Perhaps to be beaten and robbed before I die." Allan smiled faintly. "I am come to hang myself, for my lady love marries another two days hence."

Tears welled in the lad's eyes. Anne led him to the side clearing where Robin attended to private matters. Little John and Will Scarlet were called, and Stutely followed. These five stood silent whilst the minstrel divulged his story.

"I have been a lord's bard since age fifteen. My master is an old man, and recently betrothed to the only daughter of a poor baron, whose lands he covets. From the instant I saw her, she has shone in mine heart with a passion. When I got up my courage and told her, she said . . . " He choked. "Perfect angel said she loved me too. Mine heart leapt as her hand touched mine . . . " And so forth.

Little John and Stutely looked both patient and impatient at intervals, hoping the boy would come to his point before his teeth fell out in old age.

"When last we met, my lord found us. He hath sent me away and now my fair Edith will wed him and I shall never see her again and my life is forfeit and we shall be eternally unhappy and so I hang myself."

Bidding him wait and congregating in a circle, the outlaws consulted.

Anne whispered, "Surely we can help this lad."

"There be not much we can do," said Little John.

Stutely rubbed his neck. "Perhaps he could join us, but I think he would rather have himself killed."

Quoth Anne, "'Tis not only the boy, but his sweetheart. An' she doth love him, she is as much despaired as he."

"Would she have the courage to say 'nay,' I wonder." All turned to Scarlet, for his quiet speech often made others listen more attentively. "If she bends to the whim of her father and this lord, could she deny them both?"

"There is naught to be ashamed of in helping a free man live a free life," quoth Robin. "Yet if that be our goal, we shall want a plan." Stepping forward, he addressed the minstrel. "Thou sayest the wedding doth take place in two days. Hast thou a notion at which church?"

"Aye," Allan answered. "'Tis a small chapel not far from here. The Bishop of Hereford is to perform the ceremony. Few will attend." Though he tried to banish hope from his face, his eyes betrayed him.

"We shall need another priest," Robin murmured. "I fear the clergy would rather be slain than do me favours."

Allan jumped up, the broadest smile lighting his face. "Then I am to be married, sir?"

"An' thou dost wish it."

Allan yipped and skipped about and would have hugged them all if they had not stepped back to look upon him as one gone mad. The noise could be heard from the camp, and Much the Miller's son poked his head through the brush. "What goes on, master?"

"We shall have a wedding two days hence — spread the word."

"Uncle," quoth Will Scarlet, his quiet voice strangely audible over Allan's noise, "there liveth a hermit not more than a day's journey from here. The Friar of Fountain Dale would perform the nuptials for no price, being true to the Church of Christ. He is a lively, jolly sort, I remember me."

"Will, thou, Little John, and Stutely accompany me to meet this priest. We shall stay with the friar tonight, an' he will have us, and hurry back tomorrow afternoon. Anne dearest, wouldst thou look to our guest? He should be no trouble, for an' he doth continue to jump about, he will be too tired to fuss."

Anne loosed a deep breath, knowing she would miss an adventure. "Have no fear, my love. Only, have a care for the future before plunging into one of thy scrapes." She kissed

Robin's jaw and set to unriling Allan. Meanwhile, those chosen for the journey donned coats of mail and fetched swords, bows and quivers.

They set out, coming within half a mile of the abbey by the feasting hour. To accompany their passage birds, invisible amidst the leaves, whistled songs. The outlaws' footsteps kept the beat, whilst rustling leaves created music of their own.

The others waxed tired, so Robin bid them rest whilst he scouted ahead, leaving his bow and quiver.

Coming to the edge of a brook, the outlaw kept behind the briar bushes, for upstream sat a friar, his back against a tree. A sword hilt nuzzled his side, and his simple, grey robe could not conceal evidence of girth. He was chewing pigeon pie and gulping ale.

The friar plunged his hand into the sticky depths of the pastry, pulling out a dripping chunk of it. Robin stepped from his cover as the friar lifted the pottle of ale to his lips. When he saw Robin approaching, he replaced the jug in a ring in the grass.

"Ho there, friar," called Robin. "I have travelled far this day. What good fortune 'tis a churchman I stumble upon! Prythee share thy drink with me."

The friar handed over his pottle. He was a hermit, used to having a whole meal to himself. Whilst Robin drank deeply, the friar looked on with a mixture of malice and imploring.

When the outlaw had done, he handed back what ale was left and asked, "I am seeking Fountain Dale. Dost thou know how far it lies?"

"None too far past the opposite bank, thou rogue."

The outlaw grinned, having found someone willing to play. "Why dost thou assume me a rogue?"

"Thou hast the look of one. All smirks and greed for honest men's ale. I have seen many a one such as thou art."

"Doth it not say, 'Do not judge, lest you be judged'?"

The friar's eyes narrowed into shining slits. "What dost thou know of Scripture? Thou hast not been to mass in years, I wot."

"True, yet 'twas not by choice, for the law demands that when a man is outlawed, he be also excommunicated."

"Hah!" cried the friar, flying to his feet. "I knew thou wert a villain the moment I clapped eyes upon thee."

It was then the outlaw had one of his famous ideas that often landed him into his even more famous scrapes. "Please, sir, I ask a favour of thee. As a member of the clergy hast thou not vowed to help thy fellow man? As thou canst see, I am wearing fine cloth — not so fine as most, yet more so than thine — and also a good broad sword. Also thou canst see that no bridge crosses this stream. I implore thee to keep thy priestly duties in mind and carry a poor sinner to the other side."

The churchman's eyes adopted a merry twinkle. "Gladly, lad, gladly."

Gathering up his skirts to show his breeks, the friar walked to the stream bank and bent his back to Robin. Then, as if remembering something, he straightened.

"Lad," quoth he, "e'en if thou dost ride upon my back, thy sword may get wet. I shall carry it under mine arm along with mine own."

Robin removed his sword and scabbard, handing them to the friar and climbing upon the broad back. Stepping into the stream, the friar crossed the slippery bottom with ease.

When they neared the other side, Robin leapt ashore. Quoth the friar, "Now, 'Do unto others as thou wouldst have others do unto thee.' Since I have two swords and thou hast none, carry me upon *thy* back, for I would rejoin my repast."

Robin stood with his mouth open, finding his plaything had turned upon him, as kittens do when they scratch. Then he bent forward to carry the friar back.

The water bit Robin's legs, and though his Lincoln green usually proved enough to warm him, it could not protect against the damp cold that now flooded up to his waist. He slipped, skidding that way and this, under the corpulence of the churchman.

The friar had tucked both swords under his arm and, though the outlaw had been surprised, he was no fool. Reaching land, Robin deftly twitched the weapons into his own hand as the friar dismounted.

"Now," gasped the outlaw, out of breath, "it doth seem the situation hath reversed itself."

The friar peered sceptically toward him. "If thou wouldst return me my sword, good sir, I would be glad to journey with thee once more."

So Robin returned the friar's sword, again climbing upon his back. A third time, they ventured into the stream.

When they reached midway, the friar stopped. "Methinks," quoth he, "this is as far as I shall take thee. Now go thy way, and I shall go mine." He let go of Robin's legs, bucking the outlaw overhead into the water.

Whilst the friar returned to his pie, Robin sat sputtering in the cold currents, sore from the streambed stones that had caught him. He waded through the swirling water, drawing his sword. "Prepare to fight."

The friar stood, and the two battled along the shore, their blades shrieking and throwing sparks. Fifteen minutes they fought, and each man's anger drowned in admiration for his foe's skills.

"Thou art well-skilled," Robin called. "Shall we declare a draw? I take pleasure in this sparing, yet my business urges me onward."

"Nay," quoth the friar. "I do not cease to fight until my foe giveth over, e'en should it take 'til nightfall."

"At least allow me a moment to wind mine horn in admiration for thee." Robin clapped the instrument to his lips, blowing three loud blasts.

"Thou art skilled as well as I," quoth the friar, watching narrowly. "Here's to thee." Pulling a whistle from his robes, he gave three chirps as loud as Robin's.

As Little John and the others reached the edge of the brush behind their master, three giant dogs splashed across the stream toward them. Fortunately for Robin his feet were light. He scrambled into the branches of a nearby tree before the frothing beasts could reach him.

Little John and Stutely pulled their bows. Both arrows were loosed yet, faster than the eye could see, the two targeted animals dodged aside, catching the shafts in their mouths, and crunching them to splinters.

The two archers nearly toppled then and there, and likely would have been killed where they stood had not Will Scarlet stepped forward.

"Ho! What is this? Stop your charging. Down, down! Down! I say."

At the sound of his voice, coarse when he yelled, the dogs dug in their heels and drooped, shuffling over to sniff at Scarlet's feet.

"Attack, mongrels!" yelped the friar.

"It would seem thy fair beasts are not the raging lions thou wishest them to be," quoth Scarlet in his usual, quiet voice.

"Yea, truly, yet who art thou to transform them?"

"I was Will of Gamewell, now Will Scarlet, an outlaw in Robin Hood's merry band."

Robin thumped to the ground the same moment the friar cried out: "Will Gamewell! I thought not to see thee again! Where is thy master? Truly, his head was worth full seven hundred pound the last I heard."

Will chuckled. "Why, he is that wet bird thy dogs did tree."

The friar turned to Robin (who was giving his smirking cousin a thou-wouldst-do-better-not-to-talk-to-Anne-quite-so-oft look) and said, "Sir, if I had known 'twas thee, I would have done thy bidding gladly. Even Friar Tuck of Fountain Dale knows the ballads of Robin Hood. No manner of hermitage can protect against them."

"Uncle," quoth Will, "here is the friar thou seekest."

"Truly, friar," quoth Little John, jumping in with a merry word, "I am glad, for these beasts seemed invincible. I thank all heaven Scarlet is a friend between us."

"We would," Robin said to Friar Tuck, "ask two favours of thee. Will tells us thou art a true man of the cloth, not the like of those who choose money as their god. Firstly, I pray thee to give us shelter this night, if thou dost have the room. Secondly, to perform a wedding two days hence."

Tuck responded, "The first I shall, of course. The second, I suspect, hath a story behind it, which I shall be glad to hear. I have not meat in my stores, though there is cheese and bread in plenty, and what remains of a pigeon pie. Ye all are welcome. A shallower crossing lurks downstream. Come."

The outlaws had a real roof over their heads that night, and food other than what the forest provided. There lay an earthy smell over the friar's dwelling, which was not altogether alien, and they slept well in the confined cell.

Back in Sherwood the rest of the band were having a time of gaining sleep, for Allan a Dale could not settle himself, nor could he strum his lute softly. Off key and in darkness, he finally dropped into dreams.

⊕⊕⊕

Next morn, Robin and the others awoke and ate before the friar had finished complaining over the time of day. The party arrived at camp in late afternoon, receiving a disgruntled welcome, for Allan was fraying everyone's nerves.

"Thank goodness." Anne approached them, her face paler than usual. "Allan is driving everyone from their minds. Between his jabbering and the way he plucks at his lute, we are ready to beat him. Greetings, friar."

"Hallo, child," Tuck returned, cheeks quivering, for Anne's temper was beginning to show.

"Barely five hours' sleep and constant prattling upon this girl's beauty and charm and grace and kindness and frailty and courage, and the list goes on so long as it is not halted by an irritated woodsman. Praise heaven 'tis only thirteen hours 'til sunrise, and we can be off!"

"Thou hast thought this through," quoth Robin.

"If I did not allow my mind to wander whilst that boy nattered, I should not have kept my sanity."

Robin glanced her over. "Thou dost not look all sane, love."

"Thou wantest to keep Allan company? So be it."

Robin kissed Anne's forehead and cast her a look of apology, though unable to keep the smile entirely from his face. He beckoned the friar to follow. They two approached Allan telling his story to a pair of drowsy outlaws, who looked grateful to escape to the trees.

"Lad," quoth Robin, "here is Friar Tuck. He will perform thy wedding ceremony."

Allan jumped up, wringing the friar's hand so that both their bodies quaked. "How glad I am to see thee! My love will be equally pleased. Thou wert probably ever so busy — I thank thee from the very heights of mine heart! However can I repay — "

◈◈◈

Allan's lute was confiscated, and he was ordered to sleep, upon penalty of being left behind the next day. The outlaws welcomed sleep soon after their supper, though first they listened to a short tale told by Anne as an attempt to lull the young minstrel, for he seemed like to hold a loudly sighing vigil through the night, so anxious was he for the morrow.

"This is the story of two children," Anne commenced, "a girl and a boy who lived long ago, before the time of Charlemagne. This tale I learned in my father's hall from a well-travelled minstrel, though yeomen such as we are now do not often hear tales of this sort.

"The pagan King Fenix ruled in Spain and sailed to Galicia, killing the Christian pilgrims at St. James' shrine. Amongst those slain was an old French knight, travelling with his daughter. She was a widow and with child. King Fenix captured her as a slave for his queen, who was also with child. They gave birth upon the selfsame day, the queen to a son named Floris, the knight's daughter to a girl named Blancheflour. The Christian woman raised both children until they were seven, so that they were always together.

"Floris was summoned before his father, who said he would be sent to learn his letters, as all men must.

"Floris replied, 'I cannot go to school without Blancheflour.'

"Thus they went together, learning Latin and writing, and their great wit was a wonder, bested only by their great love. The king grieved as he saw how much Floris loved Blancheflour, when soon they might be of an age to wed. King Fenix told his wife he planned to kill Blancheflour, so that Floris might soon forget her and marry sensibly. The queen persuaded her husband that it would be more honourable to give the girl in marriage to someone else.

"Floris was sent to his aunt, yet he thought always upon Blancheflour, for love was his heart root. He lived a fortnight feeling one day as long as three, awaiting Blancheflour's arrival, as promised by his father. When she did not come, Floris ceased to take meat and drink.

"Learning of this, the king called for Blancheflour's head, but the queen again intervened, persuading him with much difficulty that, by selling the girl to a rich merchant of Babylon, he would not only be rid of her but would gain a profit. Thus was Blancheflour bought for twenty marks of red gold, and a richly made cup.

"The merchant sailed the girl to Babylon and sold her to the emir for seven times her weight in gold. The emir thought to make her queen, and placed her in his harem.

"Floris returned home, asking her mother where Blancheflour might be. Forced by the king, the woman replied that her daughter had died for love of him, and Floris swooned away. He awoke weeping and sighing, and the queen led him to the false tomb his father had built, where he swooned thrice more. Floris drew a knife, saying, 'Upon one day born we were. If death were dealt aright, we would be dead both upon one night.'

"The queen fell upon him, wrestling away the knife that would have pierced his heart. She ran to the king, telling him that, if he did not allow Floris to marry Blancheflour, their only child would die.

"Hearing the truth, Floris immediately prepared to search out Blancheflour. His father gave him the richly made cup and men, money, and horses, so he would appear to be a merchant. His mother gave him a ring from off her finger, saying it could save him from burning, drowning, and injury from iron and steel, and that because of it he would have whatever he willed.

"Floris' search brought him to Babylon, where he learned that the emir had bought his sweetheart. Yet Babylon's wall stood seventy miles around, with an hundred towers. One tower stood a thousand fathoms tall and an hundred wide, atop it a lantern like a sun in the night. Two dozen maidens lived within, served only by eunuchs. Any other man seeking entry would be beaten and castrated. Thus, Floris planned to enter by wit rather than by force.

"He adopted a disguise, approaching the tower as though he were a stonemason, saying he wished to study the build of the thing to replicate it in his homeland. The porter responded by challenging him to chess. They played for money, Floris bringing with him twice as much the second day. Upon the third day he brought the richly made cup, and gave it to the porter, saying it suited him. From that time, the porter became Floris' man.

"Hiding Floris in a great basket of flowers, the porter smuggled him inside. A maiden named Clarice, a great friend to Blancheflour, set about sorting the flowers and, seeing Floris within, she screamed.

"The other maidens came running. Clarice, piecing together from Blancheflour's confidences what she had discovered, recognized Floris as though she had beheld him before. When the other maidens asked what had startled her so, Clarice replied that a butterfly had flitted out of the flowers, and she dreaded such unpredictable creatures. The maidens laughed and departed, but Clarice bid Blancheflour stay to see a certain flower.

"Blancheflour replied with sighing. 'The emir would have me to wife. Yet that day will never be that men will reproach me for being untrue in love. Now I have lost sweet Floris, no other man will have bliss of me.'

"Floris jumped up from the basket. Blancheflour changed hue. They hurried together without a word, embracing and touching lips a long while that they thought only short.

"Clarice led them to a bed, drawing a curtain around it. Floris, though pagan, gave thanks to God's Son for reuniting him with his love after so long and painful a parting.

"That morning the duty fell to Clarice and Blancheflour to serve the emir, the one bringing a cloth and basin of water, the other a comb and mirror. When Blancheflour did not appear, the emir asked after her, and Clarice replied that she was not come yet because she had knelt all night in prayer for him. The emir sent his chamberlain to seek her. The chamberlain reported back that there was not one in Blancheflour's bed, but two. The emir caught up his sword, finding Floris and Blancheflour asleep. They awoke with the blade drawn over their heads.

"The sweethearts begged mercy, and the emir spared their lives until his barons could be called to sit in judgment.

"Before all the kings and dukes in his hall, the emir arose in wrath. He told how he had bought Blancheflour to be his queen, and how she had betrayed him. The barons then said it was only right to hear out the accused.

"Two Saracens came to fetch Floris and Blancheflour. He said to her: 'Sweetheart, we cannot be saved. Twice I should rightly die, one for myself, another for thee, for this death thou hast for me.' He drew his mother's ring from his finger, saying it would save her life. Blancheflour refused it, for she would not see him die. They thrust it back and forth until it dropped to the floor.

"They entered the hall weeping. To see such fair youths sorrow so, the barons were minded to set them free. This angered the emir so he ordered the lovers bound and cast into the fire.

"Floris begged the emir to spare Blancheflour, and he would lose his life if willed to. Blancheflour claimed all the guilt for herself.

"Near mad with rage the emir raised his sword, impatient for their deaths.

"Blancheflour stretched forth her neck. Floris pulled her back and stretched forth his own. Blancheflour again presented her neck for the blade.

"Eyes filled with tears all about the hall. The emir remembered how dearly he had loved the maiden. His sword fell to the ground.

"Floris saw his chance and told how he was born a king's son, upon the same day as Blancheflour, how they had loved one another and been foully parted, how he had devised entry into the impenetrable tower — that the emir might secure it better in future.

"The emir freed the lovers, knighting Floris. They went straight to the church, where Floris and Blancheflour were wed with the queen's ring, which one of the dukes had found. Through Blancheflour's counsel, the emir married Clarice, and there was great feasting.

"Not long after, Floris heard tidings that his father had died, and his own barons wanted him at home. Thus Floris and Blancheflour returned and were crowned, turning their realm to Christianity. Now ends this tale of how after travail comes relief. May God grant us the same." Anne eyed Allan.

"For 'tis no use worrying, whatever the trials to come. One must merely keep wit and heart at the ready."

⊖⊖⊖

At dawn, the outlaws splashed their faces and donned coats of mail. Each caught up their weapon of choice: longbows, quarterstaffs, or broadswords.

The church chosen for the wedding was made of brown Derbyshire stone. Oak trees bowed over the roof, tickling with their leaves. But a score of men would escort the wedding procession, so Robin divided his forces into two groups: those with swords and staffs to secure the wedding parties, those with bows to provide cover from the surrounding flora. They were to slay no one. Even after nine years of outlawry, Robin wished his men to share none of the grief that came with committing murder.

The outlaws arrived as the bishop drew up at the church. He and his seven attendants used ten mounts, two of them pack horses laden with chests. The beasts were tied and left to mill about, sampling the tall grasses.

Robin wore a gaily coloured motley of patches and rags, two bright red circles painted upon his face. He and Friar Tuck approached the church door.

"What dost thou here?" quoth the Bishop of Hereford.

"My lord," returned the friar, "I am Tuck. I am come to behold today's union, for it is a goodly sight."

"And who is *that*?" The bishop cocked his head toward Robin, who bowed with great flare.

"We met upon the way, sir. This minstrel boasts the power to cause the bride to love her husband. From the way he talks, he could out-sing a siren."

"Sing somewhat," commanded the bishop, squinting like a cat amongst his silken robes and the layers of gold chains encircling his neck.

"I defy your order. I sing only for the bride and groom."

"Scoundrel!" shouted the bishop. "How durst thou to speak to me in that manner? Following this wedding, I shall see thee whipped, stand sure of it!"

They heard hooves upon the earthen veins running through the forest. The groom's party arrived. The old lord sat curled in his saddle. Just as Allan had said, twenty armed men rode with him, staying close even as they dismounted to the greensward. Some guests accompanied them.

They had not long to tarry before the bride appeared. In the trees, Little John held Allan, so the latter would not break cover and run to her. With her rode two maidens and an older man: her father. Edith sat atop a white palfrey, her blue dress hanging lightly in folds around her, making her appear quite delicate. Her cheeks were streaked where tears had wound their paths and, though her stoic countenance remained intact, her shoulders drooped, sometimes giving a shudder. The bride's party dismounted before the church.

Three horn blasts echoed into the trees and through the church doors.

A sea of outlaws in Lincoln green burst out with raised swords and staffs. The groom's men-at-arms drew their swords but found themselves outnumbered with blades at their throats. They were bound, along with the bishop and his attendants. The guests crowded together in fright.

Robin motioned the archers from their trees.

The old groom lashed his teeth like tiny black whips. "Foresters, what right have ye to attack us? This is Allan a Dale's doing!"

"Nay, 'tis mine."

The groom twisted his neck. "*Who art thou*, minstrel?"

Robin laughed, bowing as deeply as his muscles permitted. "I am no minstrel, but an outlaw, and these are my men. My name, an' ye ask it, is Robin Hood."

Little John had let go of Allan, and now took hold of the groom.

"I have done you no harm, sir." He tried to pull back, yet Little John gripped him firm. He knew the reputation of the outlaw before him and, as did most of the wealthy, disregarded what he had heard of Robin's mercy, concentrating upon his having shed blood.

"Do ye deny intending to wed yon lady, knowing she loves another?"

The groom felt his life slipping away, for to his ears the outlaw's accusation sounded as death creeping upon him.

Allan had stepped forward, sidling up to the bride. Edith spun, smiling, and they stood holding hands.

Quoth Robin, "I trust ye do not object to proceeding with the ceremony, Allan a Dale assuming your place?"

The groom hesitated, hoping he need not answer, yet as the woodsmen waited he embarrassed himself by a dogged nod.

Little John called the banns and, if three times were not enough, he bellowed seven. Friar Tuck climbed the steps into the church's south porch. Allan and Edith stood before him. The maidens, fearful at first, saw there was no danger and took their places, as did the bride's father, with a stony look upon his face. The guests stood by the bound churchmen and men-at-arms, and hardly knew what to think.

All advanced well until Tuck asked if anyone objected. It seemed as if no one would say a word, but then the bride's father burst out, "Nay, I can keep silent no longer. Dost thou hate me, my child? Dost thou not care what happens to me? I, who raised thee when thy mother, God rest her soul, passed from us when thou wert but small? All I have ever asked of thee is to marry this lord. And with all respect, he will die soon. Let him spend his remaining time in happiness. What is one or two years? Perhaps five? Then thou wilt inherit a share of his riches."

Edith's eyes filled with tears. She looked down to hide them, her mouth twisting.

Anne approached her father. "Could I speak with you, sir?" She walked with the old baron around the church's corner, where none might hear them. "Sir, see ye not what ye do?"

"What right hast thou to lecture me? A runaway, exile to the depths of shadows. Whose head is forfeit, and — "

"Shut your mouth, sir. This is your daughter's day, not mine. Nor yours either. By scolding her ye only complicate her decision, for either she marries Allan and is miserable upon your account, or else she marries that lord and is miserable for Allan. If ye truly want what is best for her, tell her to choose the way she wishes and give her your blessing, even if her choice is to marry no man. Whatever her decision, I shall see she is provided for."

The baron regarded Anne, and something seemed to pass between them. He returned, lugging his feet. "Edith," said he quietly, "I spake harshly. I love my daughter amidst all trials — choose thine own way." These words may seem malformed upon paper, for they came awkwardly from his mouth.

Edith stood, frozen and in amaze. "I would marry Allan," quoth she at last.

"My blessings, then." The baron smiled as though he did not feel so happy as he tried to be. He willed himself look glad for his daughter's sake. After a nod to Friar Tuck, the ceremony concluded. Then all entered the church to hear mass.

⊕⊕⊕

Though the guests and the bride's father arrived home in good time, the rest of the wedding party remained away all night. Next morn, a search party was sent to the chapel. They found the old groom perched in a tree, where he had spent the night. The organist and his assistant were locked in a room, with men-at-arms in the choir loft, bell tower, even a pair squeezed inside the organ itself. The Bishop of Hereford and his attendants were crammed into the confessional, though not on the priests' side. Everything sat otherwise in its proper place.

After the mass, the outlaws had taken the bishop out to his horses.

"Methinks, my lord," quoth Robin, "that your pack animals be too heavy-laden for a man of the cloth. How rich are your tenants that they can spare so much?"

"Nay," replied the bishop, his mind more often upon his money than upon any other thing, "my rents are but meagre. These two chests are none of mine. I merely transport them, as a messenger with a document. Do not disturb them lest thy soul be imperilled."

"Surely, there be no harm in looking, my lord." Robin strode to the lead animal, extracting a roll of parchment from its saddlebag. This he handed to Anne and bid her read aloud.

"The first chest containeth three bales of silk cloth for the Chapel of St. Mary."

The outlaw nodded. "That we shall leave, for it doth belong to the Virgin."

The second wooden chest bore an enormous padlock and girded edges.

"This belongs to the Bishop of Hereford," Anne read.

Robin turned to the churchman. "Did ye not tell me, my lord, that none of your burden was your own? Lying becomes you not. Have ye the key to this chest?"

"Truly I do not," replied the bishop. "Thou mightest then let it be."

"Have no fear; we have our own ways of opening locks. My cousin ranks as expert at the job. Will."

Scarlet stepped forth. He was the strongest in the band for, though Little John stood tallest, the giant was rather thin for his height and, though stronger of arm than the average, not as powerful as young Gamewell.

Will drew his sword. He dealt three clamorous blows with the pommel, and the lock shattered. Kneeling beside the chest, he removed the lid. A flow of starlight spread trinkling over the ground.

Little John bent down to count it. He whistled through his teeth. "Twelve hundred pounds, master," he breathed. "Truly, I have never seen so much together in all my life before."

This was an untold of sum. A peasant earned a single pound in a year, and here were rents from more than a thousand.

"That is mine income," cried the bishop. "Its rightful place is with me."

"If these are your rents," quoth Robin, "then ye are more a thief than any of us. We steal without lies, whilst ye seek the same end by more devious means. However, methinks I know the true purpose of this. For we lent a knight six hundred pounds to pay his debts, and God hath sent this treasure to repay us."

"Only six hundred?" The bishop looked hopeful. "Then the other six hundred are for me."

"It doth appear so," quoth Robin, "for if we took our payment twice, we could no longer call ourselves honest men, could we?"

"Indeed not." Hereford's face shone ruddy with cheer.

The outlaw clapped his hands together. "It is decided, then. We shall take only six hundred pounds for ourselves, and the rest we shall donate to charity. Does that sound well to your mind, sir bishop?"

The bishop uttered no word but watched as his great fortune was divided and taken off.

"Now, my lord," grinned the outlaw, "ye must make confession, that the Lord may forgive you for lying to us."

When the bishop was freed from his cramped quarters and asked why his horses had come home without riders, he would only reply, "Robin Hood hath caused the bride to love her husband."

❧❧❧

If the minstrel went to his father-in-law's house, the old groom could make trouble for Edith and her father, so Allan insisted upon staying with the outlaws, and Edith insisted upon staying with Allan. The pair grew at home with the band, and Allan calmed himself considerably now he had his wife. His voice was sweet, as was his temperament, and so he was allowed to stay upon the condition he no longer strum his lute into the small hours of the morning. Soon Robin was bidding his dinner guests to, "Come and sit under the great greenwood tree. For our minstrel hath been composing all manner of songs and will feel glad of a fresh audience."

Through Allan many stories came out: of how Robin and Anne had married, of Little John's time living under the sheriff's roof, and — much to the Hood's dismay — of the day he had met Will Scarlet and Much the Miller's son. Allan also composed a tale of how Robin had been earl over Huntington, which was not true, but Allan said minstrels were entitled to "a little creative meddling." Allan's creative meddling extended even to not referring to Anne as of the Hood, as she preferred to be called, but — in some ballads that have been lost through time — as Anne o' th' Woods, which he said gave the audience more variety of names, as well as rhyming with "Hood." Even Sir Richard's plight was put to a tune.

PART THREE

CHAPTER THIRTEEN
Chestnut

T HE MEN OF SHERWOOD LOUNGED under their trysting tree with never a care, some jesting, others dozing. Robin Hood and Little John conversed.

"The company was merry last night at the Blue Boar," quoth Robin.

"Aye," returned Little John, "especially the barefoot friar. That man's free life be the best this world can offer."

"The beggar, I thought, led the merrier life; though his lot often be braggarts."

"Yet the friar hath a simple life, as St. Francis hath said, wandering where he pleases."

A thought awakened in Robin's mind. "Why not have a wager? We each shall dress for the part we deem best and see who spends the better day of it."

Little John agreed, and they went to the treasure store.

Within one trunk they found the habit and rosary beads of a barefoot friar, yet nothing resembling a beggar's clothes.

When Little John appeared wearing the habit, laughter burst amongst the band. Leaves rustled with the sound.

The giant's hem, instead of rustling about his ankles, barely touched his knees.

"Anne," called Robin, seeing her sojourning past. "My love, which life dost thou think the merrier, that of a barefoot friar or that of a beggar?"

Peering at Little John, she responded, "Neither. I hold that the life of a Sherwood outlaw is merriest. To prove this, I shall spend the day as such. So whilst ye are both tired and hungry, with the sun blazing your backs and the path scorching your feet to blisters, think of me, for I shall be dozing in the forest's shade." Kissing Robin, she ambled toward the greenwood tree.

The two men set off, one north, the other south.

Little John strolled, singing to his footsteps. Noontide nearing, he met no one. The sun baked the path dusty and dry. Only his legs escaped the oven of the dark habit. Turning 'round a curve, he found a shaded grove with an inn tucked in the corner. The weathered sign proclaimed this haven the Blue Oak, and it seemed as if the giant had entered a new world.

Sitting in the green grass outside the door were two beggars and a palmer, basking in each other's company.

"Come join us, friar," called one beggar, "for thou art a merry sight indeed."

Little John sat, and was soon laughing and jesting over a barrel of ale.

"Friar," quoth the palmer genially, "thou hast a fair voice. Why not sing us a ditty whilst we pass the day upon the greensward?"

"Yea, truly," replied the giant, "for thou hast bought me drink when I was athirst, just as our good Saviour commanded." Hawing to clear his throat, he began.

When thou see'st the hunter,
Oh sweet turtle dove,
Beware, beware, for thy meat so fair
Be what of thee he loves.
So linger no longer by the nest,
For the hunter is about.
And forever be wary
(Sweet dove be wary)
For thy mate doth love thee dear.

At perch or . . .

A ruckus arose within the Blue Oak, and Little John ceased his singing, half in annoyance, half in curiosity. Three angry voices came muffled through the door. Two holy brothers emerged, slamming the oaken slab in their wake.

"Such a lot of money for the simplest things! *One meal* at such a price!" cried the first.

"Wholly do I agree with thee, Artemis," replied the second. Then, to those assembled outside the door, "Why do ye laze about with an entire day of work to be done? And thou, brother friar, hast thou no concept of thy vows, that thou dost shirk thine holy duty to sit idle and drinking?"

Little John heaved to his feet. "I shall go with you, my brothers, an' ye may show me good behaviour for a priest."

"Nay." The monk retreated as his eyes grew wide. "We ride horses, and they cannot carry one so large as thee."

"No fear," replied the giant. "I am well able to keep pace with those of four legs."

The two brothers kept silent whilst the landlord brought their horses. The beggars and palmer smiled at the churchmen, and bid them good journey.

Before setting off, Artemis cautioned, "We travel far, to Fountains Abbey in Yorkshire. 'Twould tax thee to spend the day running betwixt two beasts in the hot sun."

"No worries, brothers. I mind not your company." The giant strode in between the horses, standing and stretching his legs.

The monks mounted and set off. They waited for Little John to give up, but he did not. The giant could jog 'til it turned too dark to see where his feet struck.

The two churchmen grew increasingly irritated. Both were habituated to having their way, and neither was fond of such undignified company as Little John.

At last the second monk burst forth. "Thou rogue! Why plague us? We asked not for thy fellowship."

"How now," quoth the giant, "what manner is this for Christian men? Is this how ye teach me improvement? Truly, ye need more guidance than I, and ye be in luck, for I myself am a teacher much renowned."

So saying, he laid hold of both their bridle reins, jerking the horses to halt.

"Let go, fellow!" quoth Artemis. "Let us go our way and thou goest thine."

"Yet I have grown attached to you. However, if ye wish to part, then I shall not force you to remain."

Both monks relaxed.

"Yet ere I go . . . "

Up they straightened.

"Please hearken to me, brothers, for I am but a poor, wandering friar, and your silken saddle blankets bespeak you well off. Have ye any coins about? But a penny would fill my stomach with bread."

"Nay, fellow, that we have not," quoth the second monk.

"And thou neither?"

Brother Artemis shook his head.

"Thou swearest upon thine holy word that neither hath coin between ye?"

"Not a farthing," quoth Artemis.

"Then down with me in the road, brothers. Upon your knees. We shall pray heaven to send us money for our journeys."

Before either could protest, Little John had yanked the monks from their horses, forcing the men to their knees in that dusty road under that hot sun.

"Oh Lord Jesus who died upon the tree," Little John began, "we humbly call upon Thee, we three, that Thou mayest send us money for bread, lest we shrivel away to naught. I pray Thee to send each of these brothers ten shillings, lest they become too greedy. Anything more I shall know be meant for my wretched, sinful self. By Thine own holy, everlasting name. Amen."

The monks sprang up, batting the dust from their clothes.

Little John stood to his full height. "What have ye in your purses, fair friends?"

Each brother put his hand into his purse, yet drew forth nothing.

"What!" cried the giant. "Are your purses empty indeed? We must pray a second time to prove our faithfulness."

He forced them to their knees once more and prayed again to the Holy Son.

When they stood to check their purses, again the monks showed nothing.

"Perhaps the coins hide in a seam, and so ye cannot find them, brothers." Little John thrust his hand into the purse of one, then the other. When the money he found was counted, it totalled ninety-seven marks. "See!" quoth Little John. "I knew there would be something. And now I must leave you, for the day grows late." He gathered the coins in his own purse, leaving only one pound for the monks.

Whistling his way back to Sherwood Forest, the giant soon came upon three flower-scented lasses. In her arms each carried a basket of eggs, which she was taking home from market.

"Ho there, fair ladies, why burden yourselves? Come, hand me your baskets and I shall carry them."

At first the maidens looked untrusting, yet after holding a short conference they decided Little John seemed trustworthy enough, being dressed as a friar.

"But how wilt thou carry all three?" asked one lass, her hair russet, like the skin of a winter apple.

"Simple," replied the giant, gently taking the basket offered him. "I tie my rosary to the handle of this, and sling it 'round my neck so it hangs over my back. Then I take one basket in either hand."

The group started for a village near the forest outskirts. They chatted, and soon grew a great liking for one another.

When they neared the village, Little John bid them stop, for he had no wish to go into town, where a king's forester might recognize him. He gave each lass a peck o' the cheek as he handed back her basket.

Continuing along the road, the lasses spied after him. Quoth the redhead, "'Tis a shame such a kind and handsome lad be a clergyman."

"Yea," quoth another, "truly he is a lusty lad."

The third agreed, and they were soon gone from sight.

⟤⟤⟤

As Robin travelled south upon the road toward Huntington, he passed lasses and farmers' wives journeying to market and greeted them with merry words. At nearly noontide, he happened across a beggar.

"Ho there, friend! What tidings hast thou?"

The beggar used blackened nails to scratch between the hairs of his light brown beard. "The sky be clear and the birds sing. Is it not so with thee?"

"Aye," laughed Robin.

"May I ask, fellow, what thou art about?"

"I am about to collapse from hunger, for I have eaten naught since dawn. I ask thee, good fellow, and tell true for I am a dying man, hast thou any food about thee?"

"I do not carry much," replied the beggar, "for when mine hunger is sharpest what I do have be the more savoury. I have not sipped a drop of ale in a sennight. After finding a pigeon pie cooling upon a windowsill, I thought to find the owner before some rogue stole it. Alas! the landlord mistook me for that rogue and banned me from his inn. He sells the finest ale this country hath to offer. I find myself longing for a dram, 'gainst my will."

Robin did not believe his innocence, for many beggars found awaiting donations dull and stole what they craved. "If thou wouldst share what is in thy bags of bread with me, then I shall fetch two skins of the ale thou dost covet."

The beggar all but jigged. "Aye marry, 'tis a bargain. Bring three skins, fellow, for my thirst pricks as sharply as thine hunger." The beggar laid his patched cloak of black, blue, and red upon the ground and spread upon that the contents of his bags.

When Robin returned, his lips drifted apart, for the beggar had laid out a feast of boiled eggs, bread in three loaves, six hunks of goat cheese, half a pigeon pie, both a chicken's drumsticks, and several small roasted birds. In the centre resided a side of dried salmon, and Robin's mouth watered at the sight.

The beggar shrugged. "It appears I have more than customary."

Robin smiled and sat upon the ground, placing the skins upon the cloak. "I hope thou wilt not hold to ceremony."

"Nay," returned the beggar, clutching one of the skins. "At times like these one harbours no need for such things."

Both fell to. Soon hardly anything remained either to drink or eat. They reclined upon their elbows until Robin broke silence.

"Friend, I have a matter I would fain discuss with thee."

The beggar showed himself wary, yet neither spake nor moved.

"I bear affection for thy way of life, and if thou exchangest clothes with me, I offer thee five shillings."

When the beggar spake it was in a serious tone. "It doth require years of apprenticeship to properly perform the job. Besides, the Beggars' Guild would reject thee — thou art too old. Not everyone can be a beggar. The country would be overrun, for our way of life is fine. Nay, I shall not yield my clothes."

"I tell thee, fellow, if thou wouldst not give them when I ask, then I shall take them. It would be wise, methinks, an' thou wouldst accept the five shillings rather than the tail end of my staff."

Quoth the beggar, "I have cracked many heads playing at quarterstaff. But for the ale thou hast given me, I would add thy pretty pate to my list."

"If it be the only way to persuade thee, then I must. Though I doubt my pate will be the one cracked." Robin got up, and without another word they set to.

Robin ducked the beggar's first blow, tripping him with a stroke behind the knees. The beggar's staff flew from his hand and, once he regained his feet, he spake. "Never have I been triumphed over so easily. I accept thine offer upon the condition thou takest only my clothes, and let me keep whatever else I have. This including food and money."

"By all means," quoth Robin.

Taking a small knife from inside his cloak, the beggar cut along a seam. From within he drew out twenty pounds.

Robin's mouth hung open a second time.

The beggar smiled. "I warrant thou didst not expect such a sum."

"Truly, I did not," quoth the outlaw, "and but for my promise I would relieve thee of it for, unless I mistake, thou didst not come by it honestly, as with the pigeon pie."

The two exchanged clothes, and Robin gave the beggar five shillings, though the latter was already too rich for a man of his trade.

Continuing on, Robin passed few people as the sun grew hot. Anne's words echoed back to him and his lips pressed into a smile. Once, a stray dog came up to him and sniffed about, yet it made no snorts as dogs are like to do when sniffing a beggar, for Robin was clean, and honest in his way.

He came upon three beggars finishing malmsey and a meal by the roadside. The blind man had a blindfold hanging about his neck, though his eyes seemed as keen as any. The second fellow, with a scar upon his jaw, talked loudly to him. The third man kept a crutch by his side, though his legs looked strong as he rose to meet Robin.

"Greetings, brother," quoth he. "Come sit with us."

"Hallo, brothers," returned Robin.

The scarred man hardly glanced at him, but continued to speak to the blind man. "And so I left my father's farm and became a beggar, for a scar in this profession makes the day flow by easily and, unlike threshing crops, begging is unlikely to earn me any further marks."

"What do ye this day?" Robin asked.

"We journey to Lincoln Town," quoth the lame beggar, passing the skin of malmsey, "there to deposit our spoils in the Beggars' Guild treasury."

"Hush now!" quipped the blind man. Then to Robin he spake. "We would not doubt thee, brother, yet ours is a mission of grave importance. We are near to Sherwood Forest, and if Robin Hood knew the sum, we might not hope to come out alive, for he is crafty and dislikes our trade."

"He is a fair archer," quoth Robin, "yet I wot I could send a shaft as true as his."

"Thou art a sore braggart, from my view," spake up the scarred man. "Thou hast no bow. What kind of beggar art thou, anyhow? An Abraham-man? Clapper-dudgeon? Dommerer? Jurkman?"

Robin looked 'round the group in frank amazement. "What dost thou speak of, brother?"

"Hah!" cried the scarred man, for he had been suspicious of the clean face and smooth hair. Robin looked too honest to be a beggar. "I thought thou wert masquerading. There are many who seek an easy living, yet be not qualified. He hath heard too much, brothers. Let us dispose of him."

All three jumped to their feet, catching up their staffs. Robin saw they would kill him, for being near Sherwood put them upon edge.

Grasping his staff and dancing so he had his back against an oak, he called upon them to attack. The scarred man put all his weight into a blow that sent him spinning when Robin dodged and knocked out his wind with a thrump to the back.

Next came the blind man, who got a rap upon the head; Robin leaped forward, striking down the beggar, even as he flew.

"Mercy!" cried the lame man. "Mercy for the malmsey I gave thee. Please, sir, lay not thine hand against me."

He looked so pitiful the outlaw conceded. "I shall not hurt thee, fellow, if thou givest me the money thou didst speak of before."

"But sir . . . "

"Now, I say, for I am Robin Hood."

If the lame beggar looked as though he would faint before, he seemed like to die now. Kneeling by the scarred man, he unstrung a pouch from his comrade's neck and handed it to Robin.

Opening it, the outlaw's mouth fell wide for a third time. Robin stared as silver coins flowed over the purse's lip. He plunked himself upon the ground to count the sum. The lame beggar wandered about, wringing his hands as he went.

A low whistle skidded between the outlaw's teeth, and the beggar sidled up to see.

"Never did I know," quoth Robin, more to himself than the lame man, "that the Beggars' Guild took such coin to their treasury. Two hundred pounds and more, sirrah! I shall keep this, for those who are truly in need of charity."

Slinging the purse about his neck, Robin arose, catching up his staff. To the lame beggar he spake. "Thou art none too bad a fellow and could find better work if thou didst wish. The lands surrounding Sherwood mark a dangerous place for thy profession. Journey not into the den of thine enemy. Tell all that if Robin Hood catches beggars nigh Sherwood again, he shall beat and strip them as he hath done today."

Before, the beggar had not fully believed this was Robin Hood, yet the threat held such feeling that his doubts would not sustain him. Ere he could reply, Robin turned his back and set off toward the forest trees.

Robin saw, riding along the forest's perimeter as if gathering courage to plunge in, a wrinkled old man upon a fine, dark horse. Strolling over, the outlaw placed his hand upon the bridle rein.

"What dost thou, beggar," cried the man, "to stop me, a corn engrosser, upon the king's highway — and upon the outskirts of Sherwood, forsooth! Dost thou not know of Robin Hood's dislike for thy trade?"

"Dost thou not know his dislike for thine? To raise the price of corn by withholding it until famine prices are reached is depraved. Only profit concernest thee."

The man inhaled sharply.

"It seems to me," quoth Robin, "that if we venture through Sherwood together we may end better off. Brothers are we, to be in this plight, and brothers are we in taking from the poor — so many would say. Come, brother — together we be stronger."

The corn engrosser considered and, deciding Robin spake soothly, they took the road into the forest together. At first the outlaw sang, and blithely enough, yet the corn engrosser bid him be silent, lest Robin Hood should hear.

"I only act my part," explained the outlaw. He again took hold of the bridle rein and, looking 'round, spake in hushed tones. "I appear as a beggar, yet wot I am as rich a man as thou art." He showed the contents of the purse about his neck. "I wear this garb to fool those who would seek me. Yet judging that Robin Hood likes a beggar no more than a rich man, 'twould seem my disguise be in error."

"Stow thy purse inside thy tunic, fool! Thou dost not find me flaunting my coins where anyone may see."

"Where dost thou carry them?" asked Robin, eyes wide.

Considering a moment, the engrosser spake in so low a voice that Robin neared to seize the words. "I have as much money by me as thou dost, and Robin Hood, crafty as he may be, will never find it."

"How dost thou conceal it?"

Looking 'round as Robin had done, lest the other had missed something, the corn engrosser spake in a voice lower than before. "These wooden clogs I wear — when I have them off, I lift a door in the heel. Within hides a hoard of coins, wrapped in sheep's wool, so as not to betray their merry jinglings."

Robin laughed, nearly scaring the corn engrosser out of his precious shoon.

"Quieten, thou rogue! Wouldst thou lead Robin Hood straight to us?"

"There is no danger in that, for I am he. Now off with thy shoon, for I have taken a fancy to them. Thou mayest have mine in return."

His jaw muscles bulging, the corn engrosser slipped his shoon from his feet. They thumped to the ground.

Still clinging to the bridle rein, Robin lifted them, removing his own shoon and handing them to the corn engrosser. The outlaw's feet could not fit into the pointed toes of the clogs, and so he entered the woods with his feet wrapped in rags ripped from his cloak. The corn engrosser was left to ponder in the road, watching the trees bow to their king as night's shadows crept beneath them.

A. E. CHANDLER

Back at camp, Robin Hood and Little John told of their adventures. Some of the band held that their master had had the merrier time, whilst others sided with Little John. However, all agreed with Anne, that the best life to lead belonged to an outlaw of Sherwood Forest.

Chapter Fourteen
Linden

Friar Tuck had returned to his hermitage a few days after Allan and Edith's wedding. He had felt tempted to stay, and the outlaws required a priest, yet his dogs had whimpered for home.

That morn, Friar Tuck was praying in his chapel when in burst a man clothed in horse skin. The hide smelled rank with weather and rot. Its mane and tail intact, two bloody holes showed where the beast's eyes had been gouged out. The man's face did not show beneath, cloaked in a shadow so black his voice seemed to call from the pit as he barked, "Robin Hood — or I kill another dog."

Fear froze the friar's heart, melting it away. Peering past the figure in his doorway, Tuck saw a mound of brown fur upon the step. He dared not blink lest tears jostle loose. His mouth lolled open, as if he were choked by a hangman's noose.

"*Where is Robin Hood?*" The man shrieked as if demon possessed.

"I-in Sherwood."

"I know that, thou bloody cur!"

Tuck raised his eyes. "I have told thee true. Now go thy way with God's blessing, and leave me to attend the corpse of my dog."

The man posed as if to speak, but paused. "Very well. Like as not thou art as useless as thou art fat."

The friar followed his guest over the threshold. Coming to the dog's body, the man ground his heel into the animal's ribs until a crack issued, echoing inside the church. Tuck pushed the man from his dog.

The man hurled around. He gashed Tuck's cheek with a dagger. "Thou art fortunate I do not exact my revenge more fully." He turned and ambled away, disappearing into the dark folds between the trees. The reek of rotting flesh died with him.

Minutes passed. When Tuck moved, blood was soaking down his chest. He cleaned his wound with water, binding it as best he could.

Beauty lay upon the step where the man in horse skin had cut her throat. Tuck bent to rub behind her ears, feeling the warmth of her fur. "Poor girl. Thou didst think he would pat thine head and scratch thy neck. He hath scratched thy neck at that."

Burying Beauty occupied the friar's mind so fully, it was afternoon when he thought of his other two dogs.

When he called, only Tricket came. Tuck found Sweetheart's body in the undergrowth, grasses and thistles wrapped around the dog's legs, as if claiming her for burial.

Not until evening did the friar's head clear so he realized what was afoot. That the man in horse skin — whosoever he was — sought to kill Robin Hood.

Tuck dared not leave his chapel, lest the man watched amongst the briars. He did not wish to send his last dog, either, yet he feared for the outlaws. Scribbling a note in Latin, he tucked the parchment in Tricket's collar and sent him out the back.

⊕⊕⊕

In the early morning a howl was heard, and all the outlaws grasped their weapons, thinking the king's men had discovered them.

Henry o' Lincoln chuckled. "No fear, lads. 'Tis one of the friar's dogs."

Tricket pranced from the shadows to Will Scarlet, rubbing against his legs.

"What urgent business, pray tell, hast thou upon such an hour?" Will stooped to pat the beast's neck. "A message? Thou art in certain a clever dog, sir, to communicate in missives." He unfolded the parchment as Tricket walked 'round him, pushing against Will's legs all the time. "And in the language of priests, forsooth. Thy master hath taught thee prettily."

Trailed by many of the band, Will stepped near the cooking fire, reading so all could hear. "'A man dressed in the hide of a horse seeks master Robin of Sherwood. Be advised this fellow is dangerous, having killed two of my dogs. The third I entrust to outlaws. God's blessings, Friar Tuck.'"

Neither Robin nor Little John were on hand to heed this warning. The band being divided after their previous contest, the two had this time forthed as foresters, to see who might have the merrier day, parting before the sun arrived.

It would do no one good if all the band searched and ended up shot. All patrols from the farthest reaches of Sherwood were recalled, spotting nothing of their leader, or Little John as they returned. Anne sent Stutely to the Blue Boar with a message for Edgar to make known that a man dressed in horsehide hunted Robin Hood. Every mouth spake word. The hollowness in Anne's stomach consumed her. She wrapped her arms 'round her middle, face and hands pale as parchment. The band waxed anxious. It was common knowledge amongst outlaws who of their profession wore a horse's skin.

Little John journeyed for the Fox and Glove Inn, where he thought to serve ale to the king's men. The outlaws rarely came to this part of the forest, yet the giant craved to win the bet against his master.

Coming to a clearing, Little John's fingers twitched as if loosing an arrow. Here was the Sheriff of Nottingham, with a full score of men, preparing to hang a youth of sixteen years.

A cloud shadowed the giant's mind. The only thought to penetrate ran, 'See the sheriff upon horseback? Thou canst send an arrow into him before anyone knows thou art here. Thou wilt be a hero, John. Thou wilt win the wager!' The giant strung his massive bow and made ready to shoot, kissing his arrow.

The sheriff stood in his stirrups, pointing and calling some instruction to his men. Little John's arrow flew, lodging in the sheriff's rear end. The giant drew another shaft from his arrow bag.

The sheriff's men spied him. They charged.

Little John nocked the arrow, pulled back the string.

The men raced nearer, sweat coiling their bodies.

As the giant pulled the bowstring, the yew snapped. The bow fell in two jagged ends, the arrow dropping.

Fifteen of the sheriff's men jumped upon Little John, beating him with the pommels of their swords. A bloody outlaw was dragged before the sheriff.

Nottingham's protector stood, supported between two of his men, whilst a third extracted the arrow (which made the sheriff yip) and wrapped the wound.

"Reynold Greenleaf," quoth the sheriff, his face a cloudy hue. "Again thou dost wrong me."

"I only sought to free the boy," Little John grumbled, glancing at the trembling youth. The boy's thin wrists were bound with thick rope, and his lively blue eyes betrayed terror.

"That I much doubt." The sheriff's voice flowed from his throat like a threadbare cloth. "Bind him, men, and let us twist him a noose, sin' he hankers for one. But wait awhile, for I feel faint. The Herefordshire man will soon have slain the master and, with this rogue gone, the rest will be flushed out."

Little John clapped his gaze upon the sheriff. "What sayest thou of my master?"

"Only that soon he will be dead. Come, men, perhaps some wine may cork my pain."

The two men-at arms-aided the sheriff back to the inn, whilst the rest brought Little John, the youth, and the sheriff's horse. The two dead men cast their eyes about, seeking less for a rescue, than for a last look upon life.

⊰⊱⊰

Not far from the Fox and Glove, Robin was walking blithely when he came upon a strange tableau. A three-legged monster leaned against a tree, its long face draped in shadow. A sword hung by the creature's side; pronged daggers glittered upon its belt.

Coming closer, Robin found that the figure was a man dressed in a horse skin, its tail the third leg. "Hilloa, man. Wherefore art thou in the greenwood and in such strange garb, forsooth?"

"I cut this skin from a live horse. Its owner refused me shelter, and I took the hide to keep dry. I say this so thou knowest I am not a man to cross."

Robin's stomach tightened, for he knew well who stood before him, yet he tried to keep his voice free. "Such a sour mood! Do thou tell me thy business and mayhap I can aid thee, for I know this forest as well as I know how to shoot."

"Thou canst not shoot so well as Robin Hood, and it is him I seek."

"Why seek Robin Hood? Dost thou know him?"

"I do not. Yet the Bishop of Hereford doth. Robin Hood humiliated him. Anger still boils the bishop's veins so his skin ripples with the pulse of it. He reasons to cast off his rage by removing its instigator."

"Then thou meanest to kill Robin Hood?"

"Aye. The bishop hath given me charter to slay the fiend for a fair sum, though not the seven hundred fifty pounds the king offers. I am to sever Hood's head for the bishop's hall. If thou knowest the fiend's camp, announce it."

Robin eyed the man, noting his cracked knuckles, and the black scab blooming beneath his jaw. "I shall show him to thee for two things: a chance to prove my worth at the bow, which thou dost doubt, and also thy name."

"My name is Guy of Guisbourne, an outlaw from Herefordshire."

"Of course. I have heard of thee, that thou hast killed a dozen peasants, even women."

"More than a dozen, to be sure."

"Thou didst once burn a hut that denied thee pleasure, causing a child to miss her life in the flame."

"Aye. 'Tis better to deal with peasants, for they can be taught to fear. Robin Hood harasses the rich and see how the bishop deals with him. I shall shoot with thee. 'Twill warm my blood for the hunt." Guisbourne cleared his throat with a snarl and propelled himself upright. "Show me the target. I would kill before nightfall."

Robin carved a wand from a tree limb, keeping his gaze down to hide his temper. He set two wands twelve-score paces down the path.

When he walked back to Guisbourne, the scoundrel spake. "Art thou daft, man? Not even the doomed Robin Hood could split yon sticks."

"Hah! Nottinghamshire men are archers born." Robin turned, and before one could say, "Huzzah for Barnesdale's king," his shaft had flown with its brother, splitting both wands in twain.

"Well shot," quoth Guisbourne, his brow peeling into thoughtfulness. "Mayhap thou canst shoot as well as Robin Hood."

"I should not be surprised, braggart, for he and I are one."

Robin's sword blocked what would have been a death blow before sliding completely from his scabbard. This battle was to the grave.

They plunged off the path and into the trees. Their feet pounded grass and clovers lifeless. The air whistled with blows; crashes shook the leaves as steel banged around both bodies. Dead blood already stained the assassin's blade.

Robin gained the upper ground by bounding upon a tree stump. Guisbourne's next blow battered his balance. He fell upon his back.

Seeing his chance, Guisbourne leapt to the stump. He plunged his sword at Robin's heart.

Robin caught the blade in his bare hand, steering it into the turf by his head. Hand bleeding, he got to his feet. Guisbourne yanked free his weapon.

Robin ducked the next blow. Rounding to Guisbourne's left side, he thrust his sword in, so deeply that the point emerged under the fiend's right arm.

Guy of Guisbourne screamed, his voice stabbing the forest like a dagger. The sound peeled away and died within him. His mouth hung open, a dark pit.

Robin withdrew his sword. The corpse thumped to the greensward. Blood scented the ground like rancid meat, soaking into the dirt, that it might be remembered no more.

Robin set his sword against a tree and tore a strip from his tunic to bind his hand. He stared at the body, watching the blood ebb. Feeling his stomach convulse, the outlaw turned his back and set about cleaning his sword. He streaked Guisbourne's blood upon the greensward and saw it melt away. "Would God men might forget how to butcher one another."

His mind revived. "This scoundrel did say the Bishop of Hereford sent him. I should not feel surprised if the sheriff be near. Little John had craved adventure from the Fox and Glove Inn. I must find him. There I shall need a disguise."

Stripping the horsehide from Guisbourne's body, he strapped on the fiend's sword, carrying his own as well as the two bows, two arrow bags, and his silver horn.

Before departing, Robin told his opponent, "I hope thou mindest not mine omitting to bury thee, but by filling the birds' stomachs thou shalt do some good."

He was nearly across the clearing under the Fox and Glove when Little John appeared in the doorway. For a moment, Robin felt relieved. Then he saw the giant's hands were bound, and behind stood the sheriff with a score of armoured men.

The sheriff stepped around the giant. "Ah, Guy of Guisbourne, thine horsehide coat is ripped and bloody. Am I to presume thou hast met with Robin Hood?"

"Presume what ye wish," quoth the outlaw in a gruff voice, not unlike Guisbourne's.

"Is he slain?" asked the sheriff, fairly clapping his hands.

"That outlaw will no more plague the land."

The sheriff cried for joy whilst Little John bellowed, "A thousand plagues upon thee, Guy of Guisbourne! Thou hast slain the best man England ever knew! Now, coward, kill me and be done!"

Little John's fellow captive gazed about. The youth knew Guisbourne's reputation, and Robin Hood's. Feeling a heat brew inside him, he shouted, "And kill me, too."

The sheriff ignored his prisoners. "Tell me, Guisbourne, what was thy price?"

"Nevermind it, for I should like nothing better than to grant these vagabonds their appeals. Bring them nearer the trees, lads, that their comrades might find their bodies."

"Thou art a fool, Guisbourne," quoth the sheriff, loathe to let Little John slip from him. He ground his teeth so they scraped like nails. "Thou couldst have taken silver, or pardon. Do as he commands, my men."

The procession headed for the woods' edge, led by the grim figure in horse skin.

"That one." Robin pointed to a tree by a thicket, and the two captives were shoved before it.

The sheriff's men tossed nooses over the tree's thickest branch, placing one snug around the youth's neck. They had to poke the giant with their daggers so he would stoop to wear his rope.

"Stand back, now," quoth the outlaw. "I shall give them the last rites." He set the bow, arrows, and sword of Robin Hood near the prisoners' feet, secretly drawing a dagger and approaching Little John.

"Thou cursed beast!" howled the giant, straining at his noose. He could smell the rotting flesh of the horsehide. "If mine hands were not tied I would ask no weapon but choke away thy life."

The answer came in a whisper. "Peace, friend Little John. Hold thou still whilst I cut thy bonds. When I say, take my bow."

The giant's eyes flushed with tears, and he cocked his head as if to clear water from his ears. "Master . . . "

The ropes fell. "Now go!"

Before the sheriff's men knew what he was about, Little John had nocked an arrow. "None move, or I vow on the greenwood tree that the sheriff shall die!"

Robin, stepping over to the youth, removed the horse skin, and flung Guisbourne's sword to the ground. He turned upon the sheriff, brow clouding as he yelled, "Thy man is slain! His corpse lies within the forest walls where thou shalt never find it. Let this teach thee that Robin o' th' Hood, King of Sherwood and Barnesdale, can more than match thee or any man."

He cut the youth's bonds, and the three disappeared through the greenwood's gates, where few are fair to go.

⊸⊸⊸

The party was sorely fussed over back at camp, for all had felt ill at ease.

The youth saved from hanging bore a story. Trained as a wrestler, he had felled many veterans in the ring. When his family could no longer support him, he sought his fortune in the world. Yet he had not heard from his family in months, and knew not where they had gone. That morning he had found a deer slain near the forest. Hungry, he set up a fire to eat all he could. The sheriff and his men, upon their way to the Fox and Glove, had caught him.

As the lad had no place else, he joined the band. Thus the great wrestler David of Doncaster turned outlaw.

CHAPTER FIFTEEN
Laurel

NOW STAYING PERMANENTLY WITH THE band, Friar Tuck wrote a letter to the Archbishop of Canterbury, England's highest ranking man of God, of the Bishop of Hereford's dealings with the poor, Edith a Dale, and the vile Guy of Guisbourne. Tuck then laid Guisbourne's character against Robin's, concluding that the bishop preferred unrepentant murderers to forest thieves.

The letter seemed a benefit, so Robin Hood undertook its delivery. His band would not let him go alone, however, with the bishop in London and coddling a grudge. Donning palmer's cloaks and bringing food, coin, and weapons, Robin, with Anne, Little John, and Will Scarlet, started off, saying they would return in a few days' time. Will Stutely was left in charge.

Canterbury lay in Kent, a county bordering the Strait of Dover, which connected to the English Channel. They walked with wide gait and brisk pace, journeying day out and in, telling jests and remarking that the air was good and the scenery better. Hills of green and forest tumbled about the country, playing with sheep that hemmed tunes in the fields. The outlaws spent their nights at inns near Coventry, Abingdon, Woking, Maidstone and, finally, Canterbury. This route avoided London and the king. By the king's own seal they were outlaws, now the most infamous four in merry England.

They stopped at an inn near the city's edge, a place with a roof to let in the rain, and the smell of ale and cheese in the walls.

"Ho, innkeeper!" called Robin, setting himself upon a bench. "Four tankards of ale."

When the barmaid delivered, Robin bid her tell them the news. She stood a buxom lass, her thick copper hair bursting over her shoulders.

"Oh! matter o' fact, there's a tale wendin' 'round that Robin Hood hisself may be about." She lowered her voice to a whisper. "The queen 'erself sent word to Sherwood Forest by 'er page Richard Partington and the famous William Stutely, who was a'most 'anged a few years back, says 'is master had gone to Canterbury Town with a message to th' archbishop! Partington rode through 'ere this morn upon the search."

The four passed looks between them.

"What business can our queen have with an outlaw?" asked Robin.

The barmaid grinned, showing teeth spaced so far apart a coin could be rolled between them. "Oh, she told good King Henry she'd find archers to beat 'is. 'E's a-braggin' all over London 'is archers are tip-top. There's tell the queen will pay Robin Hood th' money she wins. I says 'tis a ruse t' lure Robin

Hood, and many agrees wi' me. If I was a' outlaw, I'd never let others spy my face anywheres, let alone London!"

The innkeeper called the maid back to her work.

"We must find the queen's page," quoth Robin.

"We ought to deliver the letter and return to Sherwood quiet as monks," quoth Anne.

"Yet why should the queen seek us now?" Will asked. "Mayhap she meaneth no ill, wishing us to shoot for her honour."

"Mayhap she asks to lull us off guard."

"I shall hear the queen's page before reaching a decision," quoth Robin. "Meantime, ye must look to the friar's letter. Is that fair to thy mind, Little John?"

"Aye, master." The giant exchanged a look with Anne.

By asking those upon the streets, they found the page outside Canterbury Cathedral. He had been within asking their whereabouts. A great stone wall surrounded the cathedral and its lawns. Studded doors of thick wood girded the entrance, adorned by a crest with four faces turned left. Pilgrims clogged the entry yet, if one ventured close enough, one could glimpse the cathedral beyond, its grey glass windows each dwarfing a house in height. Here was one of the greatest Gothic churches in all Europe. Built in the shape of a cross, peaks upon the cathedral's towers spiked the sky, as though replaying the instance at Babylon. The three elbowed inside to deliver Tuck's letter, Will and Little John planning to distract whilst Anne placed it in the archbishop's path.

Hood tugged over his face, Robin approached the page. "Ho there, ye pretty boy."

The lad, though not keen of stature, was dainty and highbred. Diamonds of gold stitching orbited his plum-coloured hat. His cornflower hair rode in waves, held in a bundle by a dark blue ribbon detailed with golden thread. Cloth blew in puffs about his waist. His face flushed with youth and the urgency of his message, from a queen to a king.

"Sir," quoth the page, "what wouldst ye have?"

"The message ye bear, and I would have it in a more private place."

"Sir." The boy's face was a lantern as he grinned. "Are ye truly Robin Hood?"

"Only as long as the queen holds an outlaw in her favour."

Slipping to an alcove in the wall where none might overhear, the boy introduced himself.

"Sir, I am Richard Partington, royal page to Queen Eleanor of Provence. As a show of good will, she gives you this ring of red gold."

Robin kissed the ring before slipping it upon his smallest finger. "By this I know that our queen means naught of harm. Prythee, lad, speak the message."

The page bowed, a stunted gesture between the folds of stone. "Her graciousness Queen Eleanor of England requests the outlaw Robin Hood shoot at Finsbury Field against the best archers of noble King Henry's guard tomorrow day. She bids you come to London Town and, if ye wish, to bring your yeomen."

"Once my companions return, sir, we shall away with you to London. Never would I refuse our queen so simple a pleasure."

203

The page smiled, bowing again. "I thank you, sir, and likewise doth our queen. Worry not for your safety, for the queen will protect you."

Three palmers emerged from the cathedral. Stepping from the alcove, Robin introduced them to Richard Partington.

"We must hurry, sir," quoth the page after Robin had done, "if we would make London by suppertide."

Robin held out his hand to his friends. "See, as a sign of good will the queen hath given a ring from her very finger."

Anne stood by, keeping a concerned frown from her face, whilst Little John and Will Scarlet admired the ring.

They made London by dark the next day. The city air smelled heavy with smoke and refuse. They waded through muddy streets to the bank of the Thames. Here stood the Tower. Built nearly two hundred years before by William the Conqueror, it was the first stone castle constructed in England. King Henry had whitewashed and surrounded it with towers connected by stout walls. The Conqueror's White Tower keep stood square and massive, its walls fifteen feet thick, a square turret at three corners, a round turret at the fourth.

Richard Partington conducted the outlaws to their rooms. The Tower was a royal residence, where the king entertained guests, and where he kept gifts from foreign kings: a camel, buffaloes, three leopards from Emperor Frederick II, a bear from Norway and, from Louis IX of France, a lion and the first elephant seen west of the Alps. The Tower was also a prison. If the queen's pleasure turned, the outlaws could find themselves in a chamber with bars instead of beds.

Next morning, the four were summoned to the queen's apartments. Having bathed in hot water, they combed their hair, and donned their suits of Lincoln green, leaving the palmers' cloaks behind.

They crossed to Lanthorn Tower, waiting outside the bower to see the queen. Robin paced about, staring at the stone carvings. Will Scarlet sat stiff. Little John hunched over his crossed arms, hoping to blend in by shrinking. Anne kept her gaze along the corridors, watching the men-at-arms.

When at last the doors opened, Richard Partington announced them, and they walked a long red carpet, Robin and Anne Hood half a step before the others.

Surrounded by attendants, the queen perched upon a raised dais, her pale hands settled in her lap. Half concealed by her silk robe, bejewelled with circlets, pointed the toes of golden slippers. A sweet smile sat upon her lips, two more in her eyes.

Having pushed back their hoods, the outlaws bowed.

"Art thou the renowned archer Robert Hood, formerly of Huntington?" Queen Eleanor's voice flowed like birds' song.

Robin stepped forward, bending upon one knee. "That am I, gracious queen."

"Who are these with thee, sir outlaw?"

"My queen," Robin arose, "may it please you to meet my nephew, Will Scarlet of Gamewell; my right-hand man, Little John; and my dear wife Anne, eldest daughter of Baron Fitzwalter."

The queen greeted each in turn, surprised at their knowledge of courtesy, having expected outlaws to speak only in oaths. She held an interest in forest life and was eager to hear all she could, so Robin and his companions told of their adventures.

Wind through the window brought noise from the crowds outside, a reminder of the contest.

"Robert Hood," quoth Eleanor, "wilt thou do thy best for my sake?"

The outlaw bowed. "Yea, my queen. I vow to do you credit or pay your loss to the king myself."

The queen bent her head a small ways to conceal a smile. "An arduous vow, for the wager waits at three hundred tuns of Rhenish wine, three hundred tuns of ale, and three hundred of the fattest harts running Dallen Lea."

"I have given my word, my queen, and shall pay an' I fail."

"I know thou wilt try thy best, sir outlaw." The queen exited, seeming to float without her golden slippers stepping a pace.

At Finsbury Field, Eleanor sat upon a covered dais, in a throne covered with fine cloths. Behind stood noblemen and ladies, all in their brightest clothing. Beside her sat the king, a thickset man of medium height, with one drooping eyelid beneath his narrow forehead. To him she spake. "Mine archers have arrived, sir. Is your wager yet fair?"

"Of course," quoth the king. "I would set my three men against an army of archers. They are the best of my guard and can never be beaten."

The queen looked 'round at those upon the dais. "Edward, my son, will ye take my part in this?"

Prince Edward was a tall man, nigh two fingers' breadth taller than Robin. His fine and long limbs were ideal for wielding a sword upon horseback and, though he was but thirty, he had fought in many battles. Dark hair swam in waves above his broad forehead, and the droop in his left eyelid echoed his father's. "I shall take your part, Mother, that is," he replied, with a lisp that did not detract from his eloquence, "if my father permits."

King Henry nodded consent.

"And thou, Sir Robert Lea?" the queen asked the knight beside her son.

The young man bowed. "My father Sir Richard ever taught me to defer to a lady."

Eleanor smiled. "Sir Bishop of Hereford, wilt thou take my part also?"

"I prefer the king's side," replied the bishop. He squinted short-sightedly at the field, his vision growing darker with age.

"Come now, sir bishop, surely ye would not refuse a lady?" The voice came from before the dais, where stood three men clad in Lincoln green and a woman draped in a brown mantle.

"Dear king," quoth Eleanor, "these are mine archers: Locksley that spake, the lady his wife, the yellow-haired fellow his nephew, and the tall one a nail-maker's son. They travel from the north country."

"Since ye will not take the queen's part," quoth Robin to the bishop, "will ye wager with me?"

The bishop smiled, revealing that some of his teeth had rattled loose from their sockets. "Here is my purse, fellow. It holdeth an hundred pound."

"So be it." Robin bowed to the queen, king, and prince before leading his friends to the field.

Scarlet's lips drew together in a smile. He stayed by the dais to watch the other three shoot, his soft voice carrying to those above. "I know who this money must win."

The king harboured three favourites amongst his yeomen: Gilbert of the White Hand, considered best of the guard; Tepus, the king's bow bearer; and Clifton of Buckinghamshire.

When these three arrived upon the field, the court and common folk gave up a cheer. The yeomen approached the dais and King Henry spake low, yet a few heard his words and the malice that soaked them, "Do your best, for he who wins will choose his prize. Do not make me a fool."

A herald with a grey beard sparse as a spider's web proclaimed, "The competition will be one to one, with three shafts to each man."

A coin was tossed, and the lot fell to the king's archers. Clifton stepped to the mark, nineteen-score yards from the target.

For his first shot, Clifton lodged an arrow in the second ring from the clout. Pulling more carefully, he caught the target just inside the centre ring, and the third shaft entered beside the second.

He stepped back, wagging his head smugly at the crowd's cheer. Anne took his place.

She shot quickly. Her first arrow landed in the ring next to the clout. This was fair shooting, yet nothing exceptional compared to the king's guard.

The second shot lodged halfway between the clout's edge and its centre. All remained silent, for the next shot decided the winner.

Slower this time, Anne pulled the bowstring, careful not to let it creep, only taking it fully to her ear when she felt sure of her mark.

The shaft alighted less than a finger's breadth from the target's centre.

Clifton hung his head, dashed, refusing to lift his eyes, even when Anne spake to him. The king's two other archers shuffled with widened eyes, vowing not to be careless.

Queen Eleanor clapped, a smile curving the corners of her dainty lips, a sly look about her eyes. "Mine archers are more seemly than ye think, my dear."

Spake the king: "Mayhap, yet I doubt not that they are beaten."

Tepus shot his first arrow, which lodged in the clout. He pulled back the string a second time, hurling the shaft beside its brother.

Birds overhead circled and chirped, hoping for crumbs, yet no one paid mind, engrossed in the shooting.

Tepus stood tense as his third arrow flew. It landed in the clout, yet only just.

Little John approached the mark. His bow was as long as his body and as strong. Few men had the muscle to pull it fully. Many felt amazed when the giant eased the string to his ear.

Spinning toward the target, the arrow clove between Tepus' first shots.

Little John nocked the smoothest arrow from the bag at his belt, running its length along the bow. Springing forth, the arrow landed three finger's breadth from the target's very centre.

All rested upon the third flight, and the giant kissed the head of his arrow before sending it.

Affection gave no luck. A wind gusted the arrow to the second ring.

The crowd cheered, not wanting country woodsmen to outshoot London archers.

King Henry laughed with his subjects. "Ye are tied, Eleanor, soon to be beaten."

The queen replied nothing.

"Not so cocky, my lady? No man ever hath outshot Gilbert of the White Hand. He is best of all my guard."

"And my man is best in all the world."

Gilbert came to his mark, standing with heels aligned. Carefully, frowning with the effort, he aimed and sent his shaft a mere hand's breadth from centre clout.

The crowd could not forebear to cheer. Though there had flown fairer shots, this one was made by a king's archer.

More cheering was heard when the second arrow sheathed itself but *two fingers* from centre.

Gilbert set his final arrow at the brace height with all care. At this, his last chance, he used his utmost skill, holding the arrow upon the string a long while, his elbow never creeping.

He let go, revealing all his careful aim. The arrow lighted in the clout's very centre.

"Hah!" crowed the king, amidst a deafening roar, "Gilbert hath won, and fairly. No man alive can better that shot! Why, he would have to cleave Gilbert's shaft in two!"

The queen knotted her fingers. All rested upon Robin Hood.

He strode to the mark, showing no dread. Gilbert stayed close to watch, and Robin spake to him as he shot. "Truly, lad, thou art a great archer and more suited to woodland than city. These streets are less forgiving than soft greensward and, unlike trees, stone walls hide all sunlight. Thou couldst live a free life under Sherwood's protection, never wanting for sweet venison. Indeed, thou wouldst have fifteen marks a year, three green suits, and nine-score merry comrades." Robin finished shooting, all eyes bounding between the target and the man in Lincoln green.

His first arrow had split Gilbert's shaft (which had lodged dead centre), his second arrow had split the first, and his third had split the second. Never had anyone seen the like. They were too surprised to cheer.

"Sir," quoth Gilbert, "truly, thou art no ordinary man to shoot in this wise."

Robin laughed. "Mayhap I am more legend than man."

The herald proclaimed triumph for the queen's archers, bidding them approach the dais.

As they came, Eleanor turned to Henry. "My lord, there is something I would ask of you."

"Ye would have more even after winning our wager? What is your wish, dear wife?"

"That mine archers have your leave for forty days to come and go in peace."

The king thought this a strange request, yet gave the queen what she asked. "Thou, Locksley," he cried when the archers approached, "the flower of archery. Thou art welcome in my guard."

Robin bowed, his blue eyes dancing. "I thank you, my king, yet regret I must decline."

"Decline thy sovereign lord?"

"Regretfully. Your archers are fine fellows, and would not accept an outlaw in their ranks."

"An outlaw?!" yelled Henry, his neck red.

Robin bowed again. "Yes, my king. As the queen hath told you, my name is Locksley. At least, that is a pet name from my wife. To most, I am Robin Hood."

The Bishop of Hereford cried, "Sire, bind and hang him — do not allow the demon to escape!"

"What authority hast thou to order me?" A rage fell upon the king, yet it was already with the bishop, who at the same time shivered in a fit of fear.

"Sire, forgive me, yet this roguish knave hath imprisoned me in a confessional and stolen my twelve hundred pounds!"

Eleanor smiled, cooing, "And now another hundred."

"Sir bishop," quoth Robin, "in recompense, I offer half your silver again."

"Nay," said Little John. "Master, it may not be, for half we gave to the poor, and half be in our treasury."

"Gracious king," called Robin Hood to Henry, "an' it please you, we came to shoot for our fair queen's honour. We do not wish to vex you, only to perform our duty as men and woman of England."

The king slouched in silence, not having thought an outlaw, an enemy to all, could be loyal to country or sovereign.

The bishop piped in. "Hang them, my king, for they are notorious wrong-doers, and slippery. Ye will have never a chance as good as this."

The king remained still, yet his eyes flicked over Robin Hood, resting when they came to the outlaw's eyes. Robin looked back upon the king, full in the face, an act in itself of impudence.

Noise swished forth and back through the crowd. They had heard Robin's name and now stared in amazement, wondering if it could truly be him.

Placing her hand upon the king's, Eleanor spake softly. "My dear, remember your promise to these men and myself. They have free pardon these forty days. Ye cannot take them without breaking your royal word, and all would deride you for such a dishonourable deed."

Moving with the deliberation of a tortoise, King Henry nodded to the herald to distribute the prizes.

Anne's prize was ten tuns of Rhenish wine, of which she let anyone present and thirsty take drink.

Tepus accepted his prize of three-score fallow deer with pleasure and humbleness. Little John, though bitter over losing, regretted not the prize for, he said, what good would it do him to shoot the deer upon Dallen Field, when he had all he could want betwixt the trees of Sherwood.

Robin's prize consisted of a silver horn, fifty pounds, and a robe of rich ermine. The robe he gave to the queen, to thank her for her kindness. When she offered a portion of what she had won of the king, Robin refused it, saying all was fairly hers, and he would never take aught from a lady.

King Henry did not watch the archers collect their prizes. He hurtled away to brood in his chambers.

The Bishop of Hereford saw a chance for revenge, and followed across the field behind the dais. "My king, if I may ask, why not take the fiend?"

"I did promise the queen," grunted King Henry.

"Aah," the bishop continued, as a serpent slips through the grass, "yet here is the most cunning thief in England. If *I* were king, I should not let a foolish promise, made in a moment to a woman who cares not for justice — nor the great law of our country — silence a lesson that has needed teaching these nine years past."

The king saw truth in what the bishop said, not because there was any but because he wished to see. By the time he reached his chamber, he had decided.

Henry charged Sir Robert Lea with gathering men to capture Robin Hood. This troubled the knight for, having heard Henry's promise to the queen, he did not like to see it broken. To save the honour of his sovereign, for honour weighs more than life, Sir Robert went to the queen and told her all.

Thanking him, Eleanor sent Richard Partington to warn the outlaws. He found them amidst a crowd of spectators storming praise and admiration, eager to see the famous outlaws, and mayhap have words with them. Dodging elbows, and tripping over feet, Richard Partington was pummelled full sore. Several times he lost sight of Robin and floundered amongst the crowd. At last he reached the outlaws.

"Sir page," quoth Robin, "were it not for you we might never have come. Accept our thanks, and tell the same to the queen."

"Sir outlaw," returned the page, "there be no time — the king sends armed men, that ye might be hanged. Hurry to your forest stronghold, for there ye will be the safer."

"We thank you yet again, lad. Farewell." The outlaw squeezed Partington's wrist and slipped away with his companions.

Thus it was that Robin Hood, Little John, and Anne o' th' Woods proved their worth upon Finsbury Field.

❧❧❧

Mere moments passed before the king's men appeared to arrest the queen's archers. Finding them gone, the men reported back to the king, and again the Bishop of Hereford oozed treachery.

"Sire," quoth he, "your pride is hurt the more. If ye leave the business, word will spread of the useless breaking of your promise to the queen, and the people will grumble against you. Yet if ye had somewhat to offer them — to wit, Robin Hood — they should rather praise you instead."

"The knave must be in Bedfordshire by now," returned the king.

"He is not yet in the forest, my king. Intercept him before he reaches Sherwood. Send men along the roads and persistence will reward you."

Meantime, Robin and the others had stopped for the night at a small inn approaching Wembley. They sat at a table of blackened wood and called upon the landlord for food and drink.

"'Tis best to go not by the main roads," quoth Anne.

"I agree." Will spread his thin fingers to stretch them. "We must tread carefully, having angered the king."

"Aye." Little John ripped meat from the bone, his mouth already half full.

Robin spake. "An' ye will it so, we shall. Yet it is unlikely the king will follow us so long. We need not hasten."

A barmaid brought them more food. Little John inquired as to her health. Neither Anne nor Will ate much, their gullets filled with the sense that something unforeseen was about to make itself known.

This came to pass when the landlord approached Robin, saying a page atop a white horse would speak with him outside. Robin went out, finding Richard Partington.

"Greetings, sir page. Have ye come to dine with us?"

"Nay, master Hood," quoth Partington, his face flushed. "I warn you against one thousand men and more, led by the Bishop of Hereford, that the king hath ordered to drag you back to London for execution. The queen doth bid you flee to Sherwood fast as ye may — they come along this very road."

"Ye save my life a second time this day," quoth Robin. "Next we meet I shall repay you."

The page turned his horse, spurring it back toward London.

Robin returned inside. "We must away to St. Albans," he told the others, paying the innkeeper.

Once upon the highway, and well away from the town, Robin bid them halt and told all. "We shall not go to St. Albans, as the innkeeper thinks. Ye will take the forest paths to the east and Sherwood, whilst I go to the west and circle back by northern roads. 'Tis myself the king wants, and ye will be the less in danger. Never waste a moment."

He said farewell to each, determined to ignore that this could be the last they were together. The others knew this as well and, whilst tears twinkled in Little John's eyes, they flowed freely from Anne's. Robin embraced her until his own eyes watered. Kissing her he left quickly, that the others might not see him cry so.

Little John, Will, and Anne travelled by Bishop's Stortford in the northeast, then to Biggleswade in Bedfordshire, and Huntingdon upon the Great Ouse River, Stamford farther north, Grantham in Lincolnshire, and into Sherwood's realm.

At camp, Will Stutely greeted them with arms flung wide. When the pleasantries ceased, he asked, "Where be our good master?"

Anne took him by the shoulder. "He hath not yet returned?"

"We have not heard from you for two weeks and more. Word spread of your triumph in London, and then the king sent men to block all paths into the forest."

Anne seemed not to hear. "Will — where is Robin Hood?"

The forester looked flustered, as though speaking with a wall pressing the tip of his nose. "I . . . I do not know."

CHAPTER SIXTEEN
Maple

ANNE STOOD UPON THE STREAM bank behind the camp, gazing into the water. It was streaked with the colours of storm clouds. The water's chortle washed into her ears. Today its tone sounded like mocking voices, as from the crowds that gathered at Nottingham to hurl dirt and rotted food at men being hanged.

"Hey."

Anne's breath choked her as she turned. "Stutely, thy feet are too quiet."

"Oft I tell them so, yet they make no reply."

Anne turned back to stare in the stream.

In his right hand, Stutely held a knife. In his left, he carried an apple. He nicked the apple, and it coughed. "He is well, my lady."

"Thou hadst news?"

"No, yet my master is a charmed man. God doth love him too greatly to allow him death." Will slid his knife under the apple's skin, swirling the blade so the peel spiralled off.

"God will save his soul. I worry for his body."

"My master is clever and, should it come to a fight, he will win."

Anne's head tilted to one side, and Stutely saw the stream reflected in her eyes. "Dost thou recall when we were children, Will? We would find a rabbit in the woods, and he would have to creep nearer to it than the rest of us. We would race through the fields, and he would have to run farther, to see past the next hill."

"Aye. When we were ten and climbing trees, I reached the second-highest limb, but dared go no higher for fear the next would break. Yet Robin went ahead."

"And nearly split his head falling through the branches to the ground."

Will grinned. "Yet not a scratch to show."

"Now, when all men are fighting, he must follow that adventure. He acts as though nearly dying would make him immortal. Yet no man, however great, is immortal."

"Ye would have him weaving tapestries all day?" Will kept his head down.

"I would have him sensible. Then perhaps he would not have the king's men keeping him from us."

"'Tis no fault of my master's that the king be so enraged. Ye speak unfairly, my lady."

Anne turned to Stutely, her face dripping as if she had washed it in the stream. "Have I not a right to speak so? I can have no life without him. Robin knows this, and still he takes such risks as would make a fool blush. And thou *art* blushing, Struts." She gave a small smile.

Stutely blushed deeper and held out his apple.

Anne shook her head and returned to watching the stream.

⌀·⌀·⌀

The next morning found a yeoman, all in Lincoln green, walking the countryside from Dudley. He seemed not to have a care in the world, and any lass who saw him had a merry greeting. The woodland air made him smile, for with every step he came closer to home and friends.

An hour or so before noontide, the yeoman spotted a stream, such as he could easily jump. Covered upon either side by dense thickets, it crossed the trail he walked.

He bent, scooping water in his hands, when something brushed his ear.

Robin ran headlong into the thicket, never stopping to see who had sought to slay him with the grey goose shaft.

Another arrow, followed by a shout of, "Thou canst not outrun the king, Robin Hood," was hurled at his back, yet neither death nor threat of it reached Robin as he flew.

He was three days from Sherwood Forest and fortunate his feet were better suited to the greensward than those of his pursuers.

He ran even when he could no longer hear the crashing, ill-laden footfalls of those behind him. In sooth, before he stopped, Robin had gone a mile.

He came to rest in a patch of grass, thanking God to be alive.

Catching breath, he spake to himself. "That be the closest thou hast come to an end yet, lad. Thou shouldst look over thy shoulder ere drinking."

Along the road came a man clothed in coarse wool, as much patches as clothing covering his body. His grubby hands were hard-skinned from honest labour. Duncan the Cobbler, from

Derbyshire, returned from selling a pair of shoon to a rich farmer in the north, making a profit of which he was much proud.

Robin noted this man carried a fat capon and a pottle of ale. 'Twas nearly noon and food was first upon the outlaw's mind. "Ho there, friend! Bide here awhile for I have a proposition."

The cobbler halted, gawking so that Robin thought if the man was the intellectual as he looked, there should prove no trouble in prying some merry jest from him.

"Friend," quoth Robin, "thou lookest to have an eye for bargains — wouldst thou give me thy clothes for mine? Thou wouldst have ten shillings for thy trouble."

"My clothes are ragged. Why wouldst thou want them?"

"To be an honest cobbler is my wish." Robin gazed at the sky. "Thou wouldst not deny a fellow his dream, friend?"

The cobbler stared, his mind working as bread flows. He cried out, "Duncan the Cobbler was never one to refuse a good bargain, nor a man his dream — come, friend, I do as thou sayest!"

So Robin gave him the money, donning the cobbler's garb, and Duncan bedecked himself with the hood, tunic, surcoat, and hose of Lincoln green.

Laying his weapons to ground, Robin laughed at seeing the cobbler look himself over. "Truly, friend, thou art well-suited in green."

"Come, fellow." Duncan sat down. "'Tis nigh the hour of meat and, as I see thou hast none, thou wilt dine with me."

For this kindness Robin felt grateful. Though there was little fare, the two ate heartily and were soon contented with the weights in their stomachs. They stretched upon the grass in silence.

A half dozen of the king's men crested the hill, shining in coats of linked mail.

Nearing, each drew his sword, and the lead fellow shouted as he seized the baffled cobbler by the nape of his brand new hood, "Hah! We have caught thee, Robin Hood."

The cobbler stood aghast. Robin, fearful for his life, spake first. "I didst think he was a naughty fellow, yet can this vagabond be that famous fellow?"

The armoured man sneered. "Aye, the most cunning, and crafty of outlaws. He is cocky as well. So cocky as to slight good King Henry. The Bishop of Hereford will see thee hanged," quoth he to Duncan, "and right speedily."

This frightened the cobbler past words, and all he could do was stutter.

"Poor fellow," quoth Robin, appearing a fool with a blank face. "Ye scatter his wits as so many seeds for the birds. He knoweth not whether he goes or comes."

Truly Duncan did not for, as he stared at the king's men, and then at the man who wore his own clothes, he began to wonder with a mind clouded by surprise and fear if he were not the outlaw of whom the soldiers spake.

So with his hands tied behind his back, and six of the king's men leading him by a rope 'round his chest, Duncan the Cobbler was heard to call, "If the king orders it, I shall go, yet I warn you — ye have laid hands upon the stoutest outlaw in all Sherwood!"

☙❦❧

Robin laughed at the thought of the bishop's face when Duncan was brought before him, knowing the cobbler would come to no harm, and thanking God his life had been spared again, for truly Duncan had performed the work of an angel. As it was getting later, Robin kept good pace that he might reach some town by nightfall.

With the sun half set, Robin felt glad to see the light of an inn ahead, for he was nigh exhaustion. He asked no food or drink, only a bed and, stripping off his cobbler's garb, fell to sleeping with main and might.

This was a small inn with but three rooms. Four of the king's men shared two beds, with Robin in the third. A summer storm lurked in the breeze, with many a burst of dry lightning. The village possessed no other inn and not for miles could another be found. With the storm at his back, a friar in flowing silken robes came riding up to the old inn door, and called for the stableboy to feed his donkey.

Entering, he ordered the best food and drink, and sat before the fire cackling in a stone pit in the room's centre. He complained of all he received, calling the ale bitter and the meat foul. Still he ate with such an appetite that only crumbs and a small pool of gravy remained once he had done.

Calling the landlord, he quoth, "Thy stores are pathetic, and I marvel I have not turned green and fallen dead. Thou canst be thankful I was so hungered, else not a drop of that poison thou callest ale would have passed my lips. Now, as I am doubtless the highest guest thou hast ever housed, I expect my room should reflect this. If not, no more than a farthing wilt thou receive from me, and that a gift of charity for, by my troth, thy fare doth not deserve it."

The friar was none pleased to find himself bedding with a common shoemaker, and complained so heartily that the landlord proclaimed if he spake one other ill word, he should sleep in the stable like the cow he was, and mayhap that would teach him to be more Christlike, for Our Saviour minded not to be born amidst hay.

The friar consented to be shown his room by the landlord, who left him at the door with a candle stub.

The walls and floor seemed covered in pitch. The friar held his candle aloft, that he might better see the man with whom he was to bed. Robin did not stir. The friar was put more at ease by this cobbler's cleanness and smooth hair.

Undressing, the newcomer laid his shaven head upon a pillow, and Robin rolled to make room, still unwaking.

Soon as the sun showed sign of rising, the outlaw was full wide awakened. The threatening storm had passed in the night.

Suddenly aware of another's breath sounding beside him, the outlaw beheld a tonsure, and so knew he beheld a clergyman. Easing from the bed, Robin stood with his head cocked, thinking of the danger if this friar recognized him. Then he struck a plan.

Donning the friar's silken robes, he graciously left the cobbler's garb behind, though there was a temptation to take that as well. Stealthily as a panther, he went out, drawing the hood over his face. He paid the innkeeper double his score, and the man's feelings were put at ease, for the friar's speech had upset him against all who ask a favour, and then take kindness for meanness.

When the stableboy saw the friar come from the inn, he asked whether the churchman would like his donkey. Robin answered yes, mounted the beast, and rode off.

Now the friar, as he was wont to do, did not awake 'til eight hours into the day and, when he found his clothes gone as well as his purse, yowled with a rage that made the landlord and the other guests rush in.

"No cobbler was that, *sir*," croaked he to those in the doorway, "but a *thief* with whom thou madest me bed. He hath stolen my clothes, and eke my purse. What now am I to wear? These shorn rags, that those I pass may call me 'Patches'? Nay, say I — fetch him here at once!" The friar crossed his arms o'er his chest to demand obedience, though he had naught but what God gave him by way of clothing.

The king's four men exchanged glances. He who led took a sly step forward and spake to the reddening friar. "Tell me, gossip, hast thou travelled far these past few days?"

"A friar such as myself would not live in so meagre a place as this, fool!"

"And thou sayest thou hast the garb of a cobbler?"

"Scaramouch! Art thou deaf as well as daft?"

With mounting gusto, the king's man asked, "Didst thou not get this clothing from a shoemaker that was taken before the Bishop of Hereford as Robin Hood? And art *thou* not Robin Hood thyself?"

The friar started, showing his bare crown and insisting himself a holy man.

The king's men would have none of this. They questioned the landlord who, though he did not say false, said nothing to deter the soldiers' assumptions, silently blessing the masquerading shoemaker.

Throwing the cobbler's apron over the friar's head, the king's men led off their captive without further words, not heeding the man's pleas or threats. The landlord watched the friar bounce away, bound and thrown over the backside of a soldier's horse, his own backside shining in the sun.

⟡⟡⟡

By now the Bishop of Hereford was in a rage and nothing impressed by the king's men, who brought him every man they crossed upon the highway.

Notice was given that Robin Hood had disguised himself in rich friar's robes, and the outlaw skated into direr straits. Had he not been near enough Sir Richard at the Lea's house to reach it by noontide, he would surely have been captured.

Sir Richard, helped by Robin Hood the year before, welcomed the outlaw despite danger from King Henry. The castle could withstand attack, though not such as the king could give. He had the power to surround small Castle Lea in an endless siege, from which no friend could or would come to deliver it. Trapped inside with dwindling supplies, the defenders might not even see an assault, for the king would have no need to risk his men. Either starvation would drive the castle to surrender or someone within would turn traitor when facing such a death.

In the great hall of Castle Lea, Robin Hood met the master of the house. Those two only were present, lest a treacherous ear should hear them.

"What needest thou," quoth Sir Richard, "that I might return thy kindness?"

Robin's features waxed solemn. "I trust you have heard of my plight. I cannot return to Sherwood, and the king's men linger at all turns."

"Thou couldst remain here," mused the knight. "Though soon enough someone will think of searching this place."

"Aye. It would seem that, an' I cannot reach my stronghold of Sherwood, and all England is upturned, London be the only place that I can hie."

Sir Richard thought a moment. "That is perhaps more true than thou dost intend. If thou wouldst reach London alive, disguise thyself as my retainer and journey with me. Without the queen's aid, I doubt thou wilt see thy wife, and thy companions again. Deliver thyself to her mercy. Only she might persuade the king for thy life, for women know best how to influence their husbands."

Seeing no better option, Robin agreed, and the next day Sir Richard led four-score men toward London.

Days later, the queen strolled in her garden amidst the yew hedges when it was announced that Richard Partington escorted a guest, seeking her upon a vital matter. The queen set her face as the page approached with a knight's retainer.

The man knelt before her. "My queen, I have come to beg your grace, for the king doth seek to slay me and hath severed me from my companions."

"Robin Hood!" Queen Eleanor cried. "Why dost thou come to the king's stronghold? This is a madness."

"Verily, for I am enough endangered. I have come, as I said, begging your grace to persuade the king to let me return home in peace."

The queen turned away. Pausing a moment, she then left the garden. Robin waited upon the rocky path, remembering softer ground beneath his feet and wilder limbs about him.

At long last she returned, with the look of one who has laboriously won an argument: nettled, yet exhausted.

With her walked a knight. He stood taller than Robin, yet not so tall as Little John, and he dwarfed Eleanor. A solemn look, such as Robin was not used to, beset his face. "The king allows thy return to Sherwood under mine escort. Thou dost owe thy life to the queen, for she disputed heartily. Further, thou canst be thankful our gracious king be honourable, and keeps to that which he hath promised. He congratulates thy boldness in coming to the pit of the raging lion. But, outlaw, be advised by me that boldness nigh slipped the noose 'round thy neck. Thou shouldst be less bold and more honest. Though a king to thine outlaws, thou art no more than a traitor to the nobles of London."

For the queen's sake, Robin held his temper. He earnestly thanked Eleanor, and set off for Sherwood Forest.

⊕⊕⊕

Riding for Nottinghamshire, they passed many of the king's men. Some looked longingly at Robin Hood, imagining they drove a sword through his hide, yet by the king's command they could not touch him, and this galled.

Once upon Sherwood's borders, Robin dismounted his horse and spake to the knight. "I thank you for all ye have done, though I know ye like me not. I would tell you, for it hath troubled me these days past, that I am as honest a man as I can be and have never disobeyed the laws of chivalry. Therefore, be not so hasty to judge."

"No one will trouble thee." Turning his horse's head south, and taking the reins of the other, the knight retorted, "A woman hath saved thy life and one day a woman will take it." His voice, like his horse's cry, did not penetrate inside the forest.

⊹⊹⊹

No more could the outlaws of Sherwood and Barnesdale be called merry. Too many days had fled without word of their master. The men performed their duties without vigour.

They had endured a scare two days before, when Anne collapsed in the middle of camp. She had not slept for five days, eaten of three, or had aught to drink since noon the day before. She felt too troubled by Robin's absence to have a mind for such things.

The band was anxious for news, as the soldiers surrounding the forest were all but dispersed, and none could say whether Robin Hood was taken.

In the late afternoon, a rustling in the brush near the outlaws' table roused the band. The bushes there grew thick, and no one simply wandering through the forest would chance that way.

Some men had their swords or another weapon ready, for though only one set of footsteps could be heard, an ambush might be near, the king tired of searching for the lion when he could have the pride. Or perhaps the foresters, no longer besieging Sherwood alongside the king's men, were scouring the greenwood for the outlaws' camp, emboldened to seek glory.

A lone man appeared, dressed as a knight's retainer. He looked in his late twenties, and his blue eyes, though weary, showed gladness. When the man straightened, he stood a finger's breadth more than six feet tall and, for a moment, all remained still.

The man's gaze fell upon Anne. She hurried to embrace him, her eyes flooding. Many of the band felt tears, and soon he was so closely surrounded by the cheering yeomen that he could barely breathe.

"Methinks," quoth he, "I stood in less danger of strangling in the courts of London."

A great feast was held, the like of which Sherwood had ne'er seen, and adventures were recounted. The merry men now felt all stood right in the world, for Robin Hood had returned.

PART FOUR

CHAPTER SEVENTEEN
Thorn

T HE WORDS OF THE KNIGHT stayed with Robin, both for their severity, and for the adventures and mishaps of the king's chase. During a year's time the outlaws did not step outside the woods where they dwelt.

In caves the outlaws passed their winters, all but cut off from the rest of England. Thus it was not until spring that the sad report reached them. Due to weakness in her old age, and illness from the cold, Agatha, Countess of Huntington, mother to Earl David of Huntington, Lady Margaret of Gamewell, and the infamous outlaw Robin Hood, had passed on to heaven.

The news vexed Robin full sore, and for days he would not speak, save to Anne. He ate and slept little.

Anne passed into a clearing, barely as far across as the height of a man. She sat down next to Robin, who was bent over, resting his arms upon his crooked knees, and his head upon his arms so his face stayed hidden. She kissed his hair, behind his ear. "My love, it pains me to see thee thus, even two months after hearing of thy mother."

"Then thou shouldst not seek me out." Robin's left hand reached beneath his right arm, closing around Anne's fingers. A great exhaustion hung in his voice.

She kissed him again. "What wouldst thou rather?"

Robin remained as he was a long while. "When my father died, my grief at his loss was matched only by my grief at returning home and being parted indefinitely from thee. I did not know how to bear it alone."

Anne pressed his hand.

"Now, my grief at my mother's loss is matched only by my grief at having been parted from her these ten years past, by mine own impulse and temper and pride. God knows I have pained her all my life with the dangers I have sought out, foremost amongst them mine outlawry."

"Then, to be rid of this burden, my love, thou must confess."

"I am banned by the church."

"By the law and the clergy."

"By the church."

"Thou hast committed no heresy; thou wert merely outlawed."

He lifted his head. "It is done."

"My love, dost thou not see thyself as thou art? Robin, thou art the outlaw who doth sit here defending the rule of the society that hath cast thee out, as hath been ever thy wont. Thou art the criminal who doth uphold justice better than the sheriff. Thou art the robber who can be more generous than the gentry. Thou art the excommunicant who doth show more devotion than the clergy. Thou dost preserve what they claim to love by being thine own hypocrite. Go to confess, whatever others call thee, and give thy burden to God."

Robin's face softened a little, and he kissed Anne's fingers. "Aye, my love."

He set out alone for St. Mary's Church in Nottingham, seeing for the first time since his mother's death how lively a green were the trees of the countryside.

Shrouded in a deep green mantle, a broadsword beneath his only weapon, he entered the city gates and made his way to High Pavement, where sat the parish church. Entering by the south porch, he stood in the nave, which was lined either side with aisles marked out by two rows of columns. There Robin heard a mass for the Father, another for the Son, a third for the Spirit. When all others had gone, he stayed kneeling upon the ground and praying. Sun flowed through coloured glass, tinting his face with yellowy green. The priest, seeing him, ventured nigh.

Though his praying hands obscured his face, Robin could not forebear tensing as the churchman approached, remembering the Bishop of Hereford and many others. Opening his eyes, Robin saw first the figures of Christ and His Apostles carved upon the rood screen, then shifted his shadowed gaze to the knobby knuckled man at his left.

"Thou lookest to have a difficulty," quoth the priest. "I have time to listen, if thou wouldst say what is in thy mind."

At first Robin was silent. Then, "I have not had confession for many a day. I have done much wrong in that time, yet I would have thy word as a true man of God that thou shalt not tell a soul, for my life doth depend upon that."

"I promise," the priest answered, snapping his tongue, for his mouth had gone dry. He sounded quite serious, strangely honest.

Robin shared all his troubles. Not only of his mother's death, but of murdering two men, marrying in secret, and all else. "My final sin that I can recall," spake he slowly, "is coming here, for I am an outlaw and so excommunicated."

"Why didst thou come?" asked the priest, stunned to find what this grieving man had done, who seemed so gentle and troubled. "Thou dost ask me to forgive thee, when thou dost rob great monks and bishops? I cannot see that it should matter to thee what an humble priest says."

"Great monks and bishops know more of wealth than they do of God, and they know nothing of people. Thou art a parish priest, sir. Thy business is not to make thy cathedral the richer, but to minister to the people amongst whom thou dost live. Thy life is nearer to that of our Saviour than are the lives of those who claim to spend their days and nights in prayer and fasting, when they lounge and feast."

"Thou shouldst not speak so of the regular clergy."

"I speak so of the corrupt — not of the secular clergy and not of the church."

The priest kept his gaze fast upon Robin. "Yet the church hath excommunicated thee. Thy sins cannot be removed."

"It is too heavy a burden for me to bear longer, and I come to beg God to forgive me of it."

The priest knew not what to say to so strained a plea, for if this man had been banned by the church . . . yet he could not turn his back, for the excommunication was only a result of the outlawry, and Holy Scripture itself taught that the Saviour wished all to come to Him and not be hindered. Thus the priest argued within himself. "Thou art forgiven," he uttered at last, "by God's grace and through the death and resurrection of our Holy Saviour, Who hath taken thy sins upon Himself that thou shouldst see heaven." And with a smile, "Thou hadst best be gone before thou art discovered."

Robin smiled in return, his heart light as the bird he was named for, knowing his past troubles forgotten and that to God it was as if he had never done aught wrong, for when repentant we are all forgiven, and through Christ's victory we are saved.

This is what caused Robin to rejoice as he strode through the forest, as did the knowledge that his mother now lived in holy paradise.

Even those whom men condemn, God stands willing to redeem.

❧•❧•❧

Robin Hood returned to his kingdom in the greenwood, believing all lay aright in the world. Though he still felt loss for his mother, he found comfort in her being reunited with his father and with his heavenly Father.

Although Robin glimpsed anew God's love, the rest of England seemed able only to see the devil. A murrain killed many cattle, impoverishing families the breadth of the country. Rain refused to water the crops. Rufford Abbey burned. An hour before Matins, when the land lay in darkness and the monks slept, a cord of lightning had gashed the sky. It struck the north transept, carried there people said, by the ill wind that comes from that direction. No rain fell to feed the ground, but fire sparked, destroying the transept before the monks were able to quench it. Those who lived throughout the county said that the lightning had been a judgment from God.

For eighteen years the monks of Rufford had been felling trees in Sherwood, where the abbey had stood for over a century. Thousands of oaks had fallen, with the monks claiming that a vaguely worded charter of King Henry gave them the right. The fire seemed to those living in the villages and towns nearby a verdict from heaven that the monks were taking what did not belong to them. This had ranked as the most discussed topic in the county. Until the wolf attack.

The beast had come down from the hills, seeking out a flock of sheep and doing what only a wolf would do. It had killed every sheep in the flock. Killed them for sheer spite, consuming only parts of two. And it had killed the young boy watching over the sheep. His father had discovered him lying in a field of blood.

The boy had been buried in the churchyard of St. Mary's of Edwinstowe, a village in Sherwood Forest. His grave lay to the south of the church, where its walls could shield him from the north wind.

The news of this destruction hung heavy upon the people of the forest, including its outlaws. Robin Hood had thus ordered his men to spread through the woods, each searching his own part, until the wolf was found and its threat put to rest.

⊕ ⊕ ⊕

Will Stutely had chosen for himself the part of the woods where he thought the beast most likely lurking. He had been a forester and the son of a huntsman, and he knew the lands of Sherwood better than even most others in Robin's band, from having patrolled and hunted in them so often. Still, he did not trust to his skill alone.

Stutely had shot a deer, severing its legs. The carcass he left in a clearing. Each leg he took in turn toward one of the cardinal directions, then dragged it back to the open ground surrounding the main carcass. During the night he camped well away from the spot, hoping the wolf would snare the scent and come to feed. With the first light Stutely slunk back to the clearing, careful to keep downwind. The wolf had not appeared.

He spent the day stalking through the forest, passing that night in the same way as the last. It was only upon the third day, wending amidst the trees, that he located the first sign of a wolf. The tracks stretched too big, too round, to be those of a dog. Even had anyone been brazen enough to bring a dog bearing all its claws into the forest, these were bigger and less pointed. Following the pawmarks, he soon found droppings to one side of them, showing that the wolf was male. The droppings contained sheep's wool.

Stutely strung his bow.

He crept along the tracks, losing them now and then to patches of grass or rocks, and having to cast about for a ways in order to find more. After an hour, he heard the leaves ahead moving.

It was not the movement of the wind through the trees but of something more solid. Stutely set an arrow upon his string. He bent his bow to half draw. When the time came to loose, the motion of it would not be as large or as long, and so have less chance of frightening off the quarry before the shaft could strike it.

As he neared, Stutely could discern that the movement he heard was not casual. Something swift, something large, raced through the trees. Too large to be a wolf.

He broke into a run to keep up.

Stutely's ears told him he ought to be upon it before his eyes could find anything. Three foresters darted past.

Stutely dipped behind a tree to avoid their seeing him. Then he turned upon his heel and followed after.

Dressed in green, they blended with the leaves, and he had to count them several times to be sure they were three. He also had to be wary, making as little noise as possible whilst speeding after them, lest their ears perceive him and he become their quarry. They must pursue the wolf yet, more than likely, they would stop to take a wolf's-head instead. Outlaws were given this nickname as they, like wolves, could be killed without penalty to the one who slew them. The thought flitted through Stutely's mind that there was something odd in a wolf's-head hunting a wolf. That fancy, coupled with a sense of pride that he could still be the one who reported to his master that *he* had killed the beast, rather than merely that it was dead, pushed Stutely to slip 'round ahead, though the effort took some time to bear fruit, the foresters ran so swiftly.

At first, having gotten in front, Stutely could spot no sign of a wolf. He cursed the foresters for losing sight of it, or chasing nothing but a phantom to begin with. Yet, raising his eyes, he saw something. At first he could not puzzle it, having been convinced absolutely that the foresters pursued a wolf, yet they were after a person.

His feet quickened with new life, fearing that this danger threatened one of his companions. Within a few paces, he could glimpse that the quarry was not one of Robin Hood's outlaws, but a woman with reddish-brown hair split into two braids.

Stutely hesitated a moment, yet he knew what Robin would say. Breaking his cover, leaping ferns, he tugged the woman's arm.

She tried to wrench away, eyes wide and wild.

"I swear by St. Mary, I am a friend." He steered her by the elbow.

They veered aside.

Stutely listened behind him. After a moment he heard the foresters veer as well. They were not merely following by momentum but tracking her.

His mind showed him a map of the forest. He flew by imagination through all the area nearby.

Stutely pulled the woman after him. He might take her through a briar or two, but the foresters would surely know of these and how to skirt them without losing pursuit, so they would not be scratched or spined at all.

The woman swatted at Stutely's hand upon her arm, panting, "It is open ground this way. They will see us and be able to shoot."

"Trust me, mistress." His heart quickened as they broke from the trees' cover. It might gain them some distance, if the foresters stopped to shoot, and distance they needed. As long as no arrows pierced their targets.

A shaft stuck in the ground by Stutely's foot. He sped up. The next tree line would hide them and it stood only fifty long yards away.

The woman shrieked.

Stutely glanced over, and saw her neck bleeding. The shaft had missed, but the edge of the broadhead had not. If one struck home, it would rip a hole into them so wide that they would bleed to death in moments.

They ran headlong into the trees. The woman tripped. He had to let go of her, nearly slamming into a trunk himself.

Stutely waded through the ferns to get back to her. "Come, come." Picking her up, he set off again running.

She was gasping, stumbling more.

"Nearly there." He could hear the foresters enter the trees behind them.

Her feet dragged still.

They reached a stream that curved through the forest with more turns than the wiliest snake.

"Careful." He slowed, splashing in up to his knees. If the smooth rocks caused her to slip, they might not have enough time.

A few yards downstream the heavy branches of an oak overhung the water.

"Can ye climb?"

The woman nodded.

"Forgive me." Stutely grasped her waist, hoisting her up toward the branch. He could not hear the foresters now, with the noise of the stream. Leaping up, he pulled himself into the leaves. The branches swelled wide enough to stride upon, and he walked the woman to the trunk, shielding her against it with the green covering his body. "Do not move a finger. Do not loose a sound."

He could hear them clearly now, even over the water's noise. The foresters had reached the stream bank.

"See, lads, they have delved into the stream, as though we were dogs and could lose their scents."

Stutely heard one forester splash through the stream to the far side where they were hiding.

"They did not go straight across."

"Did they travel upstream or down?"

"We must split ways to see."

"Very well, but let us be quick about it."

Two of the foresters went downstream, one upon either bank. The third headed upstream alone.

Stutely waited until he could no longer hear their footsteps. "Come, mistress. We must double back before they grow suspicious." He helped her down from the tree, across the stream, and back over the open ground as quickly as they could go, lest the foresters grew soon discouraged and doubled back themselves.

Once they were again covered by the forest, the woman spake. "I wish to return home."

"They know you."

"I was too far away when they first spotted me, and I never turned 'round as they chased after."

"Were ye gathering firewood, mistress?"

"I do not know your name."

"Will Stutely, of Robin Hood's band. One of his lieutenants."

"I thought his only lieutenant the giant, Little John."

Stutely huffed. "Ye are fortunate, mistress, that we patrol in search of the killer wolf, else I would not have been at hand to rescue you."

The woman's green eyes lit. "Are your outlaws hunting the wolf as well? An' ye kill it, ye must bring it to me at mine hut upon the edge of the forest, near Papplewick."

"Papplewick?" Stutely squinted. "Where the boy was killed?"

"Aye. His mother and I have been the thickest of friends since we were children. I could not imagine a worse thing to happen to her than this. Yet, I thought, an' I could find the wolf and kill it, I could use it to help others, and that seems the only comfort my friend is likely to receive."

"Wolves are amongst the worst of vermin, mistress. They cannot help anyone."

"Not so, sir. The dried liver of a wolf, when rendered as a powder, can cure complaints of the liver in men. Also, a wolf's right forefoot can cure pain in the chest, or swelling in the jaw of a boar with a broken tusk."

"Ye are a healer, mistress?"

"My name is Aveline, Master Stutely."

He gave a small smile at the epithet. "I, too, grew up with firm friends, and poaching hath only ever brought them trouble. Once I return you to your home, Mistress Aveline, ye ought to stay there. Leave the poaching to the outlaws."

Aveline returned his smile. "I did not receive my trouble from poaching, sir, but because I came upon those foresters and their comrades felling trees."

Stutely frowned. "Foresters are entitled to fell some trees for their own use."

"Not as many as these foresters were taking."

"Mistress Aveline, an' ye would show me where ye saw this thing, I shall afterward escort you home, and consider myself well repaid for rescuing you."

"If that is your only wish, Master Stutely, I grant it you."

⊹⊹⊹

Robin was slipping through the trees as quietly as his feet could convey him when Stutely appeared in step behind.

"Master."

"Quieten. Thou mayest frighten the wolf if he be near."

"He is not near."

"Thou hast caught him, then?"

"Nay, master. I have travelled to Rufford Abbey."

"And left thy patrol?"

"Yesterday I came across three foresters chasing a woman and aided her in escaping them. Her crime was having seen them felling oaks. They have been at it some time, for there are stumps in the hundreds. I returned her home and have since discovered that the foresters have been spoiling the vert in exchange for silver from Rufford's monks."

Robin frowned. "God doth burn their abbey for stealing the king's trees, and they steal more to gain materials for rebuilding. There is no end to the hypocrisy of monks."

"They do not continue to thieve solely for materials, master, but also for money."

"They sell the wood?"

"I spake with the novice who assists the cellarer. He frequents the Black Swan pub in Edwinstowe. Many local merchants and gentry are eager enough for quality timber. The merchants sell it on at ever higher prices. The gentry build halls and barns. Even the sheriff hath purchased wood from the monks, to improve Nottingham's city walls and to construct houses that he can rent out at a profit to those unfortunate enough to have no place other to go. We cannot allow this to keep on."

Robin's gaze shot into Stutely. "Thou didst abandon thy post for two days, when there is a wolf killing children."

"I had to save the woman, master."

"Aye, and allow the wolf to escape because thou didst not think to tell any of us that thou wert obliged to escort her home. Is thy patrol vacant yet?"

Stutely's eyes dropped.

"Go, with all haste. No one else shall die in my forest."

"Master — "

Robin stepped forward, squeezing his shoulder and nodding.

Stutely set out, back for his patrol.

The sound of axes splintering wood cut through the forest, dashing jagged from off trunk to trunk. It echoed back through the trees, driving the birds from their nests, trembling the hares in their warrens. The hacking only ceased in reverence to a cracking, which ended in a muffled roar that seemed to shake everything.

The three foresters labouring to make these sounds hardly spake to one another. They voiced only the occasional necessity, such as to point out when a tree was near toppling. When one man ventured into the ferns to relieve himself, it was not such an occasion. He returned, his hood pulled up to shadow his face. His companions did not deign to notice, until he approached one of them, drawing his sword.

"Hugh!" The man leapt aside.

Robin pushed back his hood.

Anne bounded from the trees, sword in hand, cornering the other forester against a partially chopped trunk.

Will Scarlet strolled into view. Much the Miller's son trailed behind, with Little John dragging the forester who had gone to relieve himself.

"Brothers — " The forester began.

"If we are brothers, I must know thy name."

"I am called William a Trent."

"And I am called Robin Hood."

The forester seemed not to know what to answer.

"Thou didst make thine oath to protect the king's forest, and yet here thou art stealing his trees."

"I — we are merely obeying the king's own charter, which grants these trees to the abbey of Rufford."

"God Himself hath judged that a falsehood and hath struck Rufford Abbey with fire from heaven. Dost thou dispute with God?"

"No, Master Hood."

"Doth the abbey pay you well?"

"Ye must know, sir, that the king doth not pay us. We must e'en pay for our own stations. All the money we live upon comes from our enforcing the forest law."

Robin sheathed his sword. "Sin' ye were doing your duty only — as thou sayest — I am minded to leave you in peace. Upon the condition that ye take us with you to meet Rufford

Abbey's cellarer, to inform him that your work upon his behalf is ended."

"Yea, of course."

"Do not think to return to your old work. My men, my spies, will keep watch. An' I find one of you again violating the vert, ye will find a broadhead between your ribs."

"Sir — "

"Ye did think to do the same to the woman who discovered you. I shall be listening to hear whether any ill befalls her, most attentively."

"Aye."

"Lastly, thou sayest that ye do not dispute with God. Then ye will have no qualms over delivering Him the tithe upon your wages from this trade. I rather think a tithe of half your wages would be a small enough show of devotion."

The forester gritted his teeth, but nodded. "Shall we pay this tithe through you, sir?"

"Nay. Give it to the priest at St. Mary's Nottingham within the fortnight. An' I hear any of you have not honoured this bargain, I shall come to make a tithe of the whole."

The forester's throat tightened so that he did not answer.

"Now, let us away to see the cellarer's accounts and find what ye owe."

⊕ ⊕ ⊕

The church at Rufford Abbey followed the pattern of many churches, shaped as a cross, its head pointing east to face Christ at His next coming. Tucked beneath the southern arm of this cross spanned the cloister, a square courtyard surrounded by monastic buildings, such as the chapter house where the monks held their meetings, the dorter where they slept, and the frater where they ate. The cloister's western side held a second dorter and frater for the lay monks who laboured upon the monastery's lands, whilst the southern side was for the choir monks, who tended to the prayers and the church. William a Trent led Robin Hood and Will Scarlet, their faces shadowed by their hoods, to the arched entry in the western cloister wall. Anne, Little John, and Much guarded the other two foresters where they could see the entry, yet the linden trees covered them from its view.

The porter emerged, greeting William a Trent, and conducting the trio under the stone arch, unlocking a door embedded in its side. The three woodsmen stepped within, pausing to let the daylight fade from their eyes. Proceeding, they found themselves in a long, crowded chamber. Barrels and sacks, filled with all manner of drink and food, piled up to the curling ceiling. Its edges sprouted from corbels along the walls, and a row of octagonal pillars down the room's middle. What light there was had to travel a long way through Rufford's thick walls, in windowed tunnels of tanned stone.

A monk appeared, as though coalescing from the dust that cluttered the air. His habit was a coarse white and his tonsured head bulged as if it belonged to a man twice his size, though he boasted no small figure.

"Good afternoon, cellarer," called William a Trent.

"What dost thou do here?" demanded the monk. "Thou canst not have cut as many trees as I specified before now."

"Indeed not. I would see your account book."

"Thou canst not read."

"Yet ye can read it to me and tell how much tithing my brothers and I owe to the church."

The monk stared a moment, huffing, as though astonished and determined to conceal it. "I can deduct your tithe from your next payment."

"Nay, for we must tithe to the parish church of St. Mary in Nottingham."

"To what end? Leave your tithe to me, an' ye would make one."

"Nay." Robin stepped forward. "Thou dost steal the trees of the king's vert to sell for thine own profit. We shall see the account book ourselves, to be sure of the figures."

The great head purpled. "Thou callest me a *thief and a liar*?"

"Thine order was meant to be poor, and it hath become rich; it was meant to labour, without servants, and it hath recruited lay brothers to perform your toil; it was meant to exist sealed away from the world's sins, and now it sends ships all over the world to trade, as though monks were merchants. Thou lovest money better than any merchant, and I would as soon see a tithe set into the hands of a Jewish money lender as into thine."

"Who art thou, a yeoman of the forest, to speak to me so?"

Revealing his face, "I am Robin Hood, king of this forest, and a truer servant to King Henry and our Lady than thou hast ever been. Now, I would view thine account book."

"I am not minded to assist an outlaw."

"Cellarer, dost thou see here my cousin, Will Scarlet? Knowest thou that he was outlawed for breaking the neck of a sharp-tongued steward by a single blow to the head? An' I had as large a head as thine, I should be more wary."

Will drew back his own hood, trickling his gaze along the head and neck of the monk without any seeming speck of concern.

The monk hesitated a moment, before grumbling something too low for the woodsmen to hear and shuffling off through the barrels and sacks. Will followed after, both of them vanishing down a row stacked nigh unto the ceiling. A few moments later they reappeared, Will again following the monk, yet this time with a small book in his hands. The monk came to a halt before Robin Hood, and Scarlet spake without looking up. "He kept it tucked between two sacks of barley, Uncle. 'Twould seem he wisheth it kept secret even from his abbot and prior."

"I would know what each of the foresters hath been paid, what moneys have been given to the abbey, and what this cellarer hath taken for himself."

The great head purpled further. "Thou didst say thy wish was to know what the foresters should tithe."

"Aye, and they are tithing half their earnings. Surely it would ill-beseem monks to allow yeomen of the forest to show greater devotion than themselves."

"Thou wouldst rob monks, and the Virgin Mary herself."

"I merely propose to move our Lady's silver from her abbey to her church, and truly I believe she will have the greater use of it by such a transfer. Thou wilt keep the oaks thou hast taken to rebuild thy transept, and if God should see fit to strike this with lightning, as He did before, then none will have cause to speak against His judgment."

"I have the figures, Uncle. Truly, our cellarer is a most meticulous fellow, where finances are involved, if not scruples. It doth seem he hath kept all profits of the timber sales for himself."

"No doubt they are hid in this chamber, just as was the account book."

The cellarer stiffened, but said nothing.

Robin's expression relaxed somewhat. "Doth not the Bible say that, should a man's hand cause him to sin, he ought to cut it off, for it is better to enter the kingdom of heaven with one hand than to suffer in hell with both? That is why a thief's hand is severed from his body, is it not?"

The monk's hands withdrew into their wide sleeves.

"Have no fear, cellarer. We would hardly shed thy blood in our Lady's abbey. Yet, as I told thee, my cousin hath been blessed with a wonderful strength, and he can crush every bone in thine hands, one after another, until all the sin has sprinkled out from them in a powder. Will."

Scarlet set the account book upon the nearest barrel, stepping toward the monk.

The cellarer tried to back away.

Scarlet caught him by the elbow, pulling him close and fishing his hand from his sleeve, holding it fast. "Where is thy silver, sweet fellow? Though a thick coating of flesh doth cover thine hands, I can feel thy bones like brittle twigs beneath."

William a Trent turned his face away.

The cellarer's eyes darted. "Three rows upon the right, there sits a sack marked with white chalk that is full of silver."

Robin went to fetch it, hearing the coins jangle before he even opened the bag to inspect its innards. "And where is the rest, cellarer?"

The monk's eyes darted every which way. "That is the sum of mine earnings."

"A man who hides his wealth so, and apart from his account book, doth not conceal it all in one place."

Will squeezed the monk's hand. "Come, friend, the truth tasteth so much sweeter than a lie."

The cellarer's mouth gaped as though he would sing out in pain. "Two rows in the opposite direction, upon the left, and the devil take you."

Robin found a sack identical to the first. "Very good. Bind and gag our monk, Will, and be sure to bring along the account book. Surely 'twill be of more use to us than to a man who hath lost all his fortune. Such a man might seek to destroy it, yet it must still be of interest to some who can make sense of such figures."

The monk submitted to being bound, but purpled so that he looked nearly black, the rolls in his brow nigh as thick as his fingers.

"Leave him in one of the rows where he hid his sacks," quoth Robin. "'Twould ill-beseem his fellows to find him over-soon when he hath so many sins to meditate upon."

Will Scarlet smiled, doing as his uncle had bidden.

֎֎֎

Aveline awoke soon after dawn. Rising and dressing, she crossed from her bed to the hearth in the centre of her small, two-bay house, lifting the ceramic lid covering the fire by its strap. She fed handfuls of straws and twigs onto the coals, urging flames to rise, inhaling the scents of the herbs hanging from her rafters.

Taking up a pail, Aveline opened the door to walk to the stream, where she could wash her hands and face, and fetch water for the day's cooking.

Before her door sprawled an old, thin wolf, an arrow buried deep in a pit of congealed blood between its ribs.

Aveline skimmed her fingertips along the arrow's fletching, smiling to herself. "Thou hast met with Will Stutely," quoth she, "and now thou shalt do some good."

Chapter Eighteen
Beech

It BEFELL UPON WHITSUNTIDE, EARLY in a May morning, the sun up shining fair, that Robin Hood donned his deep-green mantle.

"This is a merry morning," quoth Little John. "A more merry man than I am lives not in Christianity. Pluck up thine heart, master."

"It is a fortnight," quoth Robin, "since I warned the foresters to make their tithe to St. Mary's in Nottingham. I must away to be sure it is done."

Then spake Much the Miller's son. "Take twelve of your wight yeomen, well weaponed, by your side."

Robin smiled. "Of all my merry men, by my faith I shall have none, but mine own dear wife shall I take."

Anne donned her brown mantle and off they set.

In summer, when the woods are bright, and leaves grow large and long, it is full merry in the forest to hear the birds' song, to see the deer draw to the dale, and leave the hills high, to shadow them in the leaves green, 'neath the greenwood trees.

When they reached the tree line, not far from Nottingham's walls, Robin spake. "We part here, dearest. Abide, an' thou dost list, and I shall return in one or two hours' time."

"Thou didst say thy wish was for my company," quoth Anne.

"I have had it and shall again, yet Nottingham is too dangerous for thee."

"I have accompanied thee to Canterbury and to London. There is no reason for me to hold back at Nottingham."

"My love," Robin kissed her forehead, "thou wert saved at London because I parted from thee. I would not see thee once more in danger."

"Thou wert nearly killed fleeing London alone, caring not a wit for thine own safety. I have been outlawed with thee nigh ten years; I do not fear Nottingham."

"I asked thee to remain in the forest whilst we rescued Will Stutely, and I ask thee again now."

"Thou didst set aside this needless trepidation for my protection long ago."

"Being hunted by the king hath caused me to take it up again, where towns are concerned. Wait here for me, or else journey back to camp. Please, love, I cannot endanger a lady upon a journey made for the sake of our Lady."

Anne stared, her jaw set. "Go alone upon thy masculine errand, then, as thou art no fit company. I shall be in the forest, challenging all comers upon the highway, for I am fit for any danger outlawry can offer." She strode into the trees and out of sight.

Robin entered the gates of Nottingham, and made his way to St. Mary's Church, where it sat across High Pavement from the shire hall. Outside this latter, grim building hung a pair of nooses, the rotting corpses of hanged thieves eroding with time and the weather, providing food for the birds. Robin mounted the stairs to the churchyard, which stood higher than the streets surrounding it by holding so many remains of the faithful, who would wake again once Christ returned.

Entering by the south porch, Robin passed through the peaked stone doorway, beneath the lion's face carved at its top with eyes rolled upward to heaven. The doors themselves showed images from Scripture, and that upon the right stood open to all comers. Inside, Robin put back his hood out of respect and knelt down to pray before the rood. He prayed for the safety of his wife and his men, and for his sister and brother, that they might bear up well beneath their mother's loss.

Though Robin would have garnered more attention from those others in the church had he been so callous as to keep up his hood, the attention he gained from lowering it was ill indeed.

֍ ֍ ֍

The great-headed monk, Rufford Abbey's cellarer, knelt behind one of the nave's stout Norman pillars. Having spoke with William a Trent, he had learned of Robin Hood's intention to confirm the foresters' tithe and had come upon the day appointed to see whether the outlaw would keep his word. The monk recognized Robin upon the instant and, once sure of the outlaw being absorbed in prayer, he stole toward the south porch.

Out at the door he ran, across High Pavement to find the sheriff sitting at the head of a long hall. Ignoring the others gathered to voice their business, Rufford's cellarer bustled straight to the sheriff's side. "Rise up, thou proud sheriff, busk thee and prepare. I have spied the king's felon — for sooth he is in this town. This traitor's name is Robin Hood and he stands at his mass. He robbed me of more than an hundred pound — it shall never go out of my mind. The fault is thine should ever he from us pass."

The sheriff bounded to his feet at Robin's name. He ordered every city gate closed and barred. Then he called for every mother's son under his command to march with him to the church.

⊖⊖⊖

Robin had been meanwhile recognized by another. The parish priest approached, glancing into the outlaw's eyes as he passed and continuing into the south transept. A moment later, Robin rose and followed.

"I had hoped thou wouldst not make this a habit," the priest murmured.

"'Twas not mine intention. Hath William a Trent and his two companions come to tithe?"

The priest looked surprised. "Aye, and more than a tenth have they given, unless they be knights and I stood unaware."

"The next time thou dost pass through the greenwood, stop at the Blue Boar Inn, and I shall see that thou art given the rest. Having received it, keep it well hidden, for I know well that the monks of Lenton take the lion's share of thy church's offerings."

"I cannot accept stolen moneys."

Robin looked grave. "They are the Virgin's. I am honour-bound to return them to her."

The priest nodded. "If it be so then I shall come for them, but please go thou hence with all haste. I would not have thee discovered here."

Robin turned, walking out to the nave and down the southern aisle toward the porch.

In at the door thrust the sheriff's men. Each one clasped a cudgel.

Robin halted in his tracks. His heart thundered, and he paled.

The sheriff, clad in mail and a steel cap, pushed through to the head of his men-at-arms. "There he stands!"

"Ye cannot arrest me. We stand in St. Mary's church."

"Should we stand in Canterbury Cathedral, I would see thee at the end of a rope."

"Sheriff, to force me from this place would mean excommunication for thyself and thy men."

"Thou shouldst have spared the bishops, if thou didst wish to call upon their protection." The sheriff waved his men forward.

From beneath his cloak, Robin took out his sword, where it hung down by his knee. Raising it aloft, he ran at where the sheriff's men stood thickest.

The men-at-arms drew back. The next moment they regained their courage, striking out at him from all sides. The sheriff shrank away. Robin swiped, only grazing his mail.

Such a confusion of blows arose that the sheriff's men seemed to strike one another more than their foe.

Robin wrought gashes in a dozen men. Blood oozed down, clotting mail. Battered, his ears ringing, Robin pushed forward again to swing at the sheriff.

As he raised his sword, a stout cudgel arced down, smashing the blade's middle. The sword shattered in half.

Robin's eyes widened. He pushed, trying to wade through the men-at-arms back toward the rood screen. "Mild Mary grant me sanctuary!"

A blow thudded across his shoulders. His vision misted and his hearing fizzled. He stumbled, his head disappearing below view.

"Sir sheriff!" The priest ran forward. "Sir sheriff, this must cease! This man hath called upon the holy Virgin in her own house. He cannot be harmed!"

"Seize him! Take him, and bind him fast!" The sheriff emerged again at the head of his men. "I have, priest, no intention of shedding this man's blood in God's house. Yet thou didst see him draw his sword and rush upon my men, who only defended themselves. Outlaws do not respect the church."

"I have witnessed all," the priest replied, his jaw stiff as he stared at the sheriff.

"This man is the king's felon. I shall take him to the shire hall, which is his proper place. Believe me, I never wished him killed here. Mine only wish is that the king's justice be fulfilled with a public hanging."

"This man hath claimed sanctuary."

"He is excommunicated."

"Sir sheriff — "

"Take him to the shire hall, men. I assure thee, priest, the king and all his bishops have prayed for this outcome. 'Tis best left to them." The sheriff turned to follow his men.

The priest watched after.

Robin was yanked and dragged across High Pavement. He could hardly feel the ground beneath his feet for the throbbing in his ribs and back, arms and head. Passing from the daylight into the shire hall, he thought he might have lost consciousness, all became so black. Then he heard the voice of the monk.

"That is him! Ye have him!"

"That we do," quoth the sheriff, "and nevermore will he be out of our grasp. Nottingham's gates will remain barred until he is hanged, and he will be hanged as soon as this is made known to the king. Until then, I shall keep him in the oubliette."

Robin felt himself shoved in the direction of the sheriff's retreating footsteps. These footsteps did not merely proceed forward, but down.

Nottingham stood upon a vast number of caves, hollowed deep in the sandstone. They had been used for centuries, without ever yielding up all of their secrets, for the next generations forget where their ancestors once slept. The caves beneath the shire hall ran far deeper than the building itself stretched high. Robin was taken through many chambers and tunnels, over uneven ground, but always farther and farther down. Men cried out as they passed, calling for mercy or food. Twisting through the labyrinth, the sheriff led the way, down yet another staircase, and unlocked a door with an iron grating that led into a small chamber hardly large enough to hold a half dozen men pressed together. Another iron grating, no wider than a man's shoulders, lay in the floor.

This was the oubliette. In French, it meant "to forget." The chamber was shaped like a bottle, its sides smooth and impossible to climb. No food, no water was ever lowered down. Only men.

Two of the sheriff's men-at-arms heaved up the grate.

"Thou art fortunate, Robin Hood. Thou hast a chamber to thyself. At least, the last man who entered ought not to be alive. If he is, beware that he doth not gnaw thy flesh from thy bones." And, pulling Robin forward, the sheriff pushed him down the opening.

Robin fell twenty feet, landing with a squelch in the rancid filth that coated the oubliette floor, four feet thick. Whatever entered was left to rot.

Robin struggled onto his knees, his hands still bound behind him, unable to see anything except the grate being replaced over his head and then the sheriff's torch retreating. The grated door slammed and was locked. Then there was darkness, and silence, and stench.

⊕ ⊕ ⊕

At dawn the next day, Will Stutely came running into camp, where the outlaws had hardly slept, for their leader had remained missing through the night.

Anne strode forward to meet him. "What news?"

The men gathered 'round.

"Nottingham is barred," Will panted, "as though besieged. Only those with the sheriff's permission may pass in or out." He grinned. "Happily, I have a spy who is a favoured merchant."

"*Will.*"

Stutely's face tensed and he seemed to struggle within his throat. "My master is imprisoned beneath the shire hall. He was recognized in St. Mary's, by the cellarer of Rufford Abbey, and there beaten and captured. The cellarer and his novice leave Nottingham this very morning, acting as the sheriff's messengers to the king. All the town speaks of it."

Anne paled to a dead white.

Stutely's face spasmed. His eyes dropped as he remembered having to tell her, years ago, of Robin's first being outlawed.

"He wished to go alone, and I let him."

"If the sheriff expects a siege," quoth Little John, "then we shall provide it. I would rather shed every drop of my blood than have my master be hanged."

"Nay," quoth Anne. "No man here will shed his blood."

"My lady, do not doubt that we should be doughty men. As my master's right-hand man — "

"As his queen, I assure you, I hold no doubt. Yet the sheriff's men will defend their walls with every weapon at their fingertips, for they know all they have to fear from us. Robin would die before allowing one of you to breathe your last."

"We cannot remain idle, my lady, as we did when the king hunted him."

"I would not repeat those days for anything. We are not now confined to the forest. We can act. I would intercept the monk."

"An' the monk would reach the king in Derbyshire," quoth Much, "he must ride the highway that passes full near mine uncle's house. All travellers can be spied from the window of the upper room."

Anne nodded. "Thou, Little John, and Stutely will accompany me there. We must hurry so that the monk doth not slip by unseen. Will Scarlet, look well that thou keepest our trystel tree."

Scarlet assented, his face uncharacteristically hard.

Much's uncle lived in a thatch-roofed house three bays long, its timber frame clothed in a skin of lime-washed wattle and daub. Sitting upon stone foundations, its truss construction gave it its second storey, whence the outlaws could overlook the highway. The window they watched from held no glass, as only certain churches and castles could afford such a luxury. Instead, the cold morning air licked their faces, as the wooden shutters stood open to a faint breeze. Within the hour the monk came riding and with him one of the abbey's novices.

"That must be Rufford's cellarer," quoth Little John. "See his wide hood?"

Stutely nodded. "That novice is the cellarer's assistant. I met him at the Black Swan in Edwinstowe."

"Good, then thou hast reason to hail him." Anne looked to Little John. "Stay in the trees, lest thine height unsettle our travellers. We must e'en capture them."

Thus the three went down to the road, whilst Little John went down into the leaves, and the monk and his novice came almost immediately upon them.

"Hallo!" shouted Stutely. "Is this not my talkative friend from the Black Swan? Whence come ye?"

The monk looked discomfited, wishing to pass by without response, except that the three outlaws blocked the road.

The novice called back, slowing his horse to standstill. "We come from Nottingham Town."

Stutely smiled. "Tell us tidings, I you pray, of an outlaw was taken yesterday."

The monk opened his mouth to protest.

Anne, before he could, spake from beneath the hood covering her hair and much of her face. "He robbed me and my fellows of twenty marks in certain. If that outlaw be taken, for sooth we would be glad."

"So did he me," quoth the monk, his expression altering entirely, "of an hundred pound and more. I laid the first hand upon him, therefore ye may thank me."

"The sheriff ought to thank you and we shall when we may. We shall go with you, by your leave, and bring you upon your way. For Robin Hood hath many a wild fellow, I tell you in certain. If they wist ye rode this way, in faith ye should be taken yourselves."

Little John burst from the leaves. He took the monk's horse by the head. Much sprang forth. The novice's horse backed away, yet the miller's son grasped its bridle rein the next moment.

Little John clutched the monk's hood by the throat, pulling him off his horse. The monk fell, dashing his head upon the ground.

Little John drew his sword. "He is my master that thou hast brought to harm. Thou wilt never come to our king, for to tell him tales."

Anne put back her hood. "We shall read the sheriff's missive to the king now. Thou and thy novice are to remove your habits."

⊹⊹⊹

After binding the monk and his novice, Little John had conveyed them back to the outlaws' camp as prisoners, whilst the other three continued on to Castleton in Derbyshire, where King Henry was residing in his hunting lodge of Peveril Castle. The castle controlled the Forest of the Peak, whose deer had few trees to live amongst, instead ranging over craggy hills and valleys. Peveril itself clung to a high hill overlooking the town of Castleton, a sharp cliff at its back. Built in stone during the Conqueror's reign and named after the baron who did so, Peveril had passed to the crown under King Henry's grandfather, who had added the square Norman keep at the bailey's highest crest. The keep itself shone white with lime-wash, whilst the bailey was enclosed by a castellated wall-walk over seventeen feet high.

Will Stutely and Much the Miller's son shared the monk's horse.

Anne rode with them until the forest's edge, where they dismounted. "We must part here. Stutely, don the monk's robes and I shall shave thine head."

Stutely slid down, grimacing. "Why should Much not rather be tonsured?"

"Thou lookest older. He will be thy novice."

"It were better that he were the monk and ye the novice. Your woman's face makes you appear younger still. Your height would make all think you a man."

"Stutely, the king doth know my face. He hath not before seen thee, or Much." Anne drew a knife from its sheath at her waist.

The forester seemed to be writhing within his skin, as though he knew not how to move. "My lady, my tongue is awkward. Ye know well how often I say the wrong thing without meaning to."

"I shall tell thee what must be said."

Stutely shook his head. "Yet should I fail, my master's life is forfeit. When have I ever spoke fair and been considered eloquent?"

Anne stepped close to him. "Will, it must be thee. Thou didst save Robin when he first was outlawed. Thou hast kept him safe more than ten years — more than twenty years. Thou art mine oldest friend and I trust thee. Only do not talk overmuch and say what I tell thee."

Stutely locked gazes with her a moment. It did him no good, so he plopped down upon the greensward and submitted to having his crown bared.

෧෧෧

Will Stutely and Much the Miller's son had continued alone to Castleton, where they rode through the town and up the hill to Peveril's gatehouse. The rise was so steep that the path had to jag back and forth to make itself more walkable, though even with this consideration it strained the legs of all comers. No one had ever a reason so compelling that it drove them to attempt a siege of Peveril Castle.

Granted entry, Stutely and Much dismounted in the bailey, traversing its length in their coarse, white robes and black travelling cloaks, past the chapel upon the slope to their left to the new hall at the opposite, lower corner, beneath the gaze of the keep. At the new hall's far end, before an enormous fireplace set into the wall, sat King Henry at table, members of his court seated either side of him. Pointed arch windows let in sunlight through the left-hand wall, whilst servants, clerks, and petitioners milled about and spake in lowered voices. Someone asked Stutely his business.

"I . . . am the cellarer of Rufford Abbey. Sent by the Sheriff of Nottingham with news of Robin Hood." He had barely time to look about him before being ushered to the king. Next Stutely knew he had doffed his hood and was down upon his knee saying, "God you save, my liege lord. Jesus save you!" The back of his neck burned. "God you save, my liege king!" He arose, giving the sheriff's letters into the king's own hand.

The king, his second eyelid drooping like the first, unfolded the missive to read. "So might I thrive. There was never yeoman in merry England I longed so sore to see." He smiled broadly. "Truly this is Nottingham's seal and, is it really true? Robin Hood is to be hanged?"

"At your pleasure, my liege lord." Stutely did not dare to meet the king's joyful gaze.

"Then let it be so! Take mine order, with my seal back to Nottingham immediately. This fellow be so slippery, the business is best done soon, e'en though I may not bring my court to see it. Take also twenty pounds in certain, as reward for thy services."

"Is not the reward for Robin Hood one thousand pounds, my liege?" Stutely's teeth clamped down, grazing the tip of his tongue, but the words had already escaped.

The king smiled. "It is, monk. Better for thy vows of poverty that the sum be delivered to thine abbey, rather than to thyself."

Stutely bowed, rejoining Much at the foot of the hall. They collected the king's sealed order and returned to Sherwood Forest.

⟡⟡⟡

They met Anne along the road to Nottingham, telling her all that had happened as they travelled. She assumed the novice's robes from Much, who rode to send Will Scarlet to meet them farther upon the road. If they would free Robin from prison with only a small party, then Will was most skilled at breaking locks. Stutely gave the monk's robes to him.

When Anne and Will Scarlet came to Nottingham, all the gates still stood barred.

Will called up to the porter in a voice both soft and clear, "What be the cause, that thou dost bar the gates so fast?"

"Because of Robin Hood," the porter called back, "cast deep in the shire hall's oubliette. His men, for sooth as I you say, will come to slay our men upon our walls."

"Thou needest not fear two monks, my friend. See here, we bear the king's seal. He doth address the Sheriff of Nottingham and we must deliver this missive into thy master's hands."

The porter, upon the wall, squinted down before replying. "Where is the monk that bore the sheriff's letter to the king?"

"The king felt so fond of his good news that he hath made him lord Abbot of Westminster. We hail from Roche Abbey." Scarlet lifted the seal that the porter might better see it.

In they went at the gate, wending through the roads until reaching High Pavement, where stood St. Mary's and the shire hall. They reached the latter as night was falling, the king's seal granting them entry. Within moments, the sheriff came down to read their missive. Anne bowed her head to hide her face in her hood, and Will kept up his to conceal that he had no tonsure.

The sheriff released a long, shallow lungful. "I am commanded to hang Robin Hood in the morning." He drew a small breath that escaped the next moment. "Praise God, I have waited long for this day. Friend monks, ye must stay the night here and join me in wine of the best. Come morning, ye can bear witness for the king how well I carry out his order."

"'Twould be our pleasure indeed, sir sheriff." Will's lips curled.

Before the night grew old, the sheriff slept heavily with wine, and all had gone to bed in anticipation of the early work they would have to perform.

The sheriff had given Anne and Will a room and a bed to share. Anne paced whilst Will lay down upon the bed and closed his eyes to rest them.

"How thou canst sleep now baffles me."

"My good lady aunt," Scarlet replied without raising his eyelids, "I am conserving my strength, and listening for silence. We ought not to go down to the gaol until we have heard no footfalls in a long while."

Anne ceased to pace, bracing her back against a stone wall. "He is in this very building, Will, yet he knows not that we are coming — and he is in the oubliette."

"By morning he will not be."

Anne crouched to the floor, still pressing her back hard upon the stone. "He has not eaten in two days."

"Mine uncle fasts often."

"He is in the oubliette, Will."

"It matters not; no one has nor will forget Robin Hood."

When all lay silent and had for some time, Anne caught up a candle and they took the way unto the gaol.

"Gaoler," Scarlet called through the oaken door, "rise anon, for Robin Hood hath broken prison, and out of here is gone."

The gaoler, who had been sleeping, sprang from his thin mattress and unbarred the door, fear clouding his mind with visions of the sheriff's wrath.

The instant the door peeped open, Scarlet dashed through it, his sword ready, pinning the gaoler to the wall. All his muscles taut, Will's voice remained soft. "Now shall I be porter, and take the keys in hand. Lead the way, man. We seek Robin Hood."

Anne used the candle to light a torch she took from the wall. She looked about, finding a coil of rope.

The gaoler swallowed. "That is to be Robin Hood's noose."

Anne's face blackened. "Then thou shouldst bear it to him."

Barring the door behind them, they followed the gaoler down into the sandstone caves.

Voices swayed out from the darkness as they passed, to step ever deeper into the earth. The weight of it all, pressing down above them, made it seem impossible that there could be anything but rock above their heads.

At last they reached the grated door leading to the oubliette chamber. Scarlet unlocked it. Inside they found the grate in the floor, with just enough space to stand 'round it. The stench swelled up through the bars.

Anne's throat swelled with unshed tears.

Scarlet called, "Uncle?"

No answer came.

Anne went to her knees, shouting down through the grate. "Robin!"

"Anne?"

She rolled her eyes up to Scarlet. "Get this off of him."

Will sheathed his sword, buffeting the gaoler so the man fell senseless to the floor. Will bent, lifting off the grate. "We've brought a rope, Uncle."

"I cannot grasp it. Mine hands are bound."

Anne set aside the torch and candle. "Lower me." She tied a loop in one end of the rope, to use as a stirrup. Sitting upon the oubliette's edge, she took up the candle again.

Will took up the rope's slack, bracing his feet either side of the opening.

Anne let herself slip down. Scarlet eased her slowly into the pit. She felt herself choked by its narrow neck, then swallowed up as it widened, smooth and arched, with nothing to grasp or lay foot to.

Robin stood shin-deep in the swampy refuse clogging the oubliette, his arms twisted behind him, squinting even in the faint candlelight. "Will — stop."

Anne stepped out of the stirrup, sinking alongside Robin. "I do not mind." She pulled her feet up, slogging behind him and setting down the candle to cut the ropes with her knife.

Robin flinched as he eased his arms back to their accustomed posture. "I do not dream, then, an' I can feel such a pain and thou dost not vanish."

"My love." Anne pressed his face in both her hands and kissed him.

"I am sorry, my fair one. I feared so much that our last words would be spoke in anger."

"Surely thou dost know that wherever thou goest I follow."

"Aye. As I hold thine heart in my breast."

"And I hold thine in mine." She offered him the stirrup.

Robin hesitated. "I would have thee ascend first, my love."

"Thou art injured, and I would see that thou dost not fall. Worry not; I follow."

Robin kissed Anne's forehead longingly, and took the rope. "Will! Take him up gently."

Both Robin and Anne were pulled from the oubliette, and the unconscious gaoler bound with the would-be noose. Scarlet replaced the grate and locked the door behind them. Though Robin's arms and body ached, his legs could carry him well, racing faster and faster as he sensed they neared the surface, where was the air, the sky, and the freedom of the greenwood.

Anne dowsed the torch as they locked the gaol behind them, and blew out the candle as they left the shire hall, Will locking that as well. The stars were enough to see by, especially for Robin's eyes, so long in pitch blackness. They raced without sound through the empty streets, to where the wall stood lowest, and from there they leapt down and fled Nottingham. By the time they reached the trees, the sun had begun to lighten the sky, and they found their way easily enough.

When the cock crowed and the day began to spring, the sheriff awoke, groggy but eager. He was dressed with great care for his shining moment, and then proceeded down to the gaol. When the gaoler did not answer his hails, he grew nervous and had the door broken in. He raced down to the oubliette as quickly as he might without slipping upon the slick stone. There he found the gaoler bound with the noose, and the oubliette empty.

The sheriff wasted no time, but rang the common bell. He made a cry throughout all the town to any, whether he be yeoman or knave, that could bring him Robin Hood, bountiful reward he should have. His men searched every street and alley. They found no sign.

When the king heard what had happened, how Robin Hood had gone missing, along with the two monks that had borne his seal, he made an oath that he would hang the Sheriff of Nottingham, had not the outlaws deceived him as well. As it was, the sheriff was content not to show his face but let the king hear of the escape from others, fearing that he still might be hanged if the king clapped eyes upon him.

Robin returned to camp, content to bathe, jest with Will Stutely about the latter's tonsure, and spend his days with Anne, as he allowed his wounds to heal.

Chapter Nineteen
Hazel

THAT SUMMER, WHEN THE LEAVES sprang, and blossoms upon every bough, the birds sang in the merry woods. Robin set off with a large number of his yeomen to discover some new quest. They set themselves upon a lesser known path to Nottingham and waited to see who might come.

Passing through to Nottingham's market came a potter, towing a wagon piled with pans and pots of tin and clay, some bent, some broke. There were pale red and green and blue, brown, yellow and white. There were tall thin ones, short stout ones, the like people drank from, others that resembled kettles. Whatever they were, they rattled as the potter bumped along the road.

"I bethink me," quoth Robin, "that yon potter hath never once paid us toll in the three years and more he hath journeyed through the forest. I shall have a bout with him, to erase the debt."

"Nay, good master," returned Little John. "For thine own sake do not. Yon potter is the terror of Nottingham Town; be thou warned by me."

"This faint, little man?" Robin smiled. "Doth even my right-hand man fear him?"

"Jest not, master, for thou knowest my skill at the quarterstaff, and yet once I came together with this man at Wentbridge, and he gave me a beating such as I shall not soon forget. He carries no mercy in him and did not fight clean. Moreover, whilst I am seven feet and more, thou art no taller than him, I wot, so no advantage there. In sooth, I doubt a man amongst us could win over him, yet I would give forty shillings to see one try."[4]

"There done!" quoth Robin, throwing down his purse. "I shall face this man and, attend my words, John, *he* will be the one to give over."

Robin strode out from the brush where his men hid, them lamenting not having stayed him, and Little John cursing himself for daring his master to this confrontation.

"Hold, friend potter," called the outlaw, "I would have words with thee."

The potter stopped, looking none too pleased, and one could tell he debated using his staff to sweep this fellow from his path, as he would sweep a fly from a table.

"Be at ease, friend," quoth Robin, drawing his sword. "I but wish a bout with thee, for I have heard of thy prowess and would fain match it with mine own."

The potter scoffed. His limbs seemed thick as tree trunks, his face scattered with a half-grown beard. "What manner of rogue art thou, jumping from bushes to challenge honest men?"

---

4   This is a fifth of Little John's wages for the year.

"Art thou a man, truly? For it soundeth as if thou wouldst not accept."

"I accept and whole-heartedly. Come, fellow, if thou wantest thine hide basted, I might as well do it as some vagabond."

Not giving Robin a chance to respond, the potter fell to with great might, nearly tipping the outlaw, for he had not expected the potter to attack without warning, though Little John had said the man did not fight honestly.

The band watched, concealed, whilst the men in the road went to with the strength of two winds, each trying to force the other back as he had come. This was nigh the fiercest opponent Robin Hood had faced in combat, and the band marvelled to see him so skilfully hold his own.

Scarcely could the outlaw try a tap at the potter, for so furious and fast came the other's blows.

Robin once managed to graze the potter, yet not as forcefully as he would have liked. The blade only scraped the man's side and did not cause him to fight less wildly.

The potter landed several buffets, hitting Robin twice in the ribs, once cuffing his ear, many a time striking at his elbows or striving for his knees so the outlaw's joints would give out. Some praised this practice as strategic, despite its circumvention of matching skill against skill in a pure competition.

At last Robin landed such a blow with the flat of his blade that rang in the potter's ears. As the man recovered, Robin waited, his sword tip hovering just above the soil.

Of a sudden, the potter spun 'round, catching Robin in the neck before the outlaw could block, sending him to the ground. As the potter raised his staff for the final blow, full four-score stout yeomen pounced upon him. They took his staff and bound his hands fast behind him with a bowstring.

Little John helped up Robin, saying, "Mine heart regrets this full sore, good master. I should never have let thee fight this man. Prytell, what shall we do that he might learn fair play?"

The merry men gazed menacingly at the potter and he returned their glares.

Robin thought, then a sly look passed o'er his face. He approached the potter, saying, "Now, fellow, thou art no fair fighter, as honest men are like to be. Yet thou didst call thyself one. Here, then, is a test for thine honesty: I shall take thy clothes and cart, and venture to Nottingham Town. Meanwhile, we shall tie thee to a tree. An' thou wilt await my return, thou wilt have paid thy punishment and be pardoned. If thou art gone, we shall know thee as a coward and braggart for shunning thy debt to us, and we shall keep thy wares and the profits therefrom. Is this fair to thy minds, my merry men all?"

Grunts and chuckles came from the band, making the potter wonder if they would carry out this threat or simply cut his throat.

Later that day, a potter entered the city gates pulling a wagon; meanwhile, another man awaited his return in the greenwood, his outer clothes missing, his arms lashed 'round a tree trunk and antlers fixed to his head.

The market heaved in its fullness. Robin began calling his wares and sold them for so little that a crowd of wives and widows surrounded him. He gave five pots for the price of three. He gave four cracked pans for a farthing. All came away satisfied, and many proclaimed they had never met a more charming potter.

Even the sheriff's servants were taken in. When Robin learned who these were, he hit upon a plan to show their master that the effect of his capture of Robin Hood had proved as fleeting as the captivity itself.

He told these servants he should like to give the rest of his wares to their mistress as a gift of good will. They thought the craftsman exceedingly chivalrous for purposing such a deed.

With Robin pulling his cart in their midst, the sheriff's servants led him through the castle gates and into the kitchen.

One servant fled to fetch the mistress, whilst the others bid the outlaw rest. When Lady Nottingham appeared in the doorway, the outlaw arose and bowed before her.

"Greetings, sir potter," quoth she. "'Tis not every day one greets such a generous visitor as thyself."

"Many thanks, milady," quoth Robin, kissing the hand she offered. "It is not every day one has the pleasure of pleasing a beautiful woman, let alone one as yourself."

The potter appeared so polite and complimentary, Lady Nottingham invited him to dinner, mostly for the pleasure of seeing her husband's expression. He abhorred the poor and their manners, yet this craftsman treated her as if she were a queen.

Candles lit the hall, where the men dining sat upon benches behind long tables. Robin kept his hood close over his face, and in the dimming light his features were indiscernible. He sat near the sheriff, yet not near enough to be recognized.

As the meal progressed, Robin feigned drunkenness, and began to tell of having stumbled upon a camp in the woodlands where the foresters roasted the king's deer, rather than guarding them.

The sheriff harkened. "Potter, how did these foresters look?"

"There were one, sir, tall as a tree — great 'ulkin' lad, 'e was. Seven feet, maybe more. A minstrel, too. Fairest voice I ever 'eard, and with 'im a lady. But, sheriff sir, the lead one I wouldn't wish as enemy 'pon any man. 'E split one o' 'is own arrows at three 'undred paces."

Lifting his head, the sheriff inquired, "Hath this man yellow hair and beard?"

"Yes, sir. An' I remember me right, blue eyes. Is it so?"

"Tell me," the sheriff leaned across the man seated next to him, "couldst thou find this camp again if so inclined?"

Lady Nottingham arose, disgusted that the man who had been so courtly before could be no more than a drunkard and one her husband found amusing.

The potter considered. "'Twere dark, sir, but well do I ken the woods, and there be no doubt in me mind but I can."

"Wouldst thou take me there, I wonder?"

"Sir, ye 'ave shown me such kindness I would in a trice, yet why wish it?"

"Because," quoth the sheriff, "though for years I have sought, never have I found this camp before today. Gilbert! show our guest his room. Rest well, man; we depart early."

By dawn, a potter rode out with the sheriff and three of his guard. Meanwhile, after an exceedingly uncomfortable night tied to a tree, another man called for and was freed by some foresters, never to see his wagon again.

෧෧෧

Noontide found the sheriff's nerves grated thin, for his guide seemed not to know front from back, let alone north from south. Nottingham's protector wished to be in his stronghold, enjoying wine and beef and sweet music — not hungered and fatigued amongst leaves that slapped the back of his neck and trickled dew down his collar. He forgot himself, snapping, "The devil take thee, show me the camp this instant!"

"As ye wish, my liege," replied the potter, pulling a horn out from his clothes and blowing three blasts.

The sheriff's eyes flew wide, for he recognized the sound. He jerked the bridle to turn his horse's head. Too slowly, for Robin laid hold of the rein as the sheriff's men fled back to town, thinking him behind them.

"Had I wist at Nottingham who thou wert, thou shouldst not have entered the forest in a thousand years," quoth the sheriff, the sound of four hundred feet echoing nearer.

"That wot I well," Robin said. "And I thank God that ye be here."

"Why do this to me, Robin of the Hood?"

"Ye did so first, sir sheriff."

"Why not let me in peace? What wantest thou from me?"

Robin's eyes cut the sheriff's breast. Blood shone in them. His voice dipped almost to a growl. Only for an instant. "I would have back the last ten years of my wife's and my men's lives."

Men in Lincoln green came from what seemed the very trunks of the trees.

Little John stepped forward. "Master, what is this that thou bringest the High Sheriff of Nottingham?"

"He felt keen to come, and we have had no guests for so long I dared not refuse him. Busk ye, men; we must ready a feast! Sheriff, here is your blindfold and fear not — loyal Stutely will lead your horse."

The sheriff gave Robin such a look that, had it a dram more intensity, the outlaw would have died where he sat.

Some men hurried ahead, whilst others escorted the sheriff by such long and rambling paths that Nottingham's protector thought he would end in Cathay. The smell of roasting flesh told him what his eyes could not: that he had indeed found his enemies' camp.

The sheriff was yanked from his mount and plopped upon his feet. When the blindfold was removed, he saw Little John had brought him down. Feeling quarrelsome, the sheriff spat, "Reynold Greenleaf, thou art coward and traitor."

Little John laughingly replied, "Friend sheriff, I was traitor long before entering thine household."

Nottingham's protector was then enticed to sit upon the greensward and watch as Little John and David of Doncaster battled with quarterstaffs. Soon he was cheering so loudly for David that he forgot his anger and present danger.

At last Little John, who had consented to go easy upon him, thumped David's ribs as the meal was being set upon the table, causing the youth to fall and agree that the giant had won.

Robin bid the sheriff sit at his right hand. The latter seemed like to refuse, yet four hundred eyes made his nerve drop, recalling the quarterstaffs' blows and how fast they fell.

These simple woodsmen made fair company. In sooth, had they not the forest to protect them, many would not have survived so long. Here was meat and drink for all, with virtually no cause for disease. None entering this wooded haven could resist its charm, nor the charm of those living there. So with the sheriff. He ate and drank aplenty when he had resolved to fast.

Quoth Robin, "I am glad to see you enjoy your fare, sir sheriff. Upon the last occasion but one when ye gave me hospitality, ye did neglect to give me any food at all. Having decided to offer you the chance to make up this fault, I found upon my visit last night much better courtesy."

The sheriff set down the bread he had been about to eat. "Thou canst not reproach me for having done my duty."

"Can I not, when ye did promise seven years ago to no longer hunt us?"

"How could I continue to keep such a promise, when thou didst make an enemy last year of the Bishop of Hereford, and then of the king? I would lose mine office. It is not merely my livelihood, but my fulfillment. Thou must expect me to take any threat toward it to heart."

"As when ye did hire me to hang Will Stutely, my boyhood friend, or when ye would have hanged steadfast Little John?"

The sheriff gestured to Anne, who sat upon his right. "Perhaps as when thou didst tempt away thy mentor and my friend Baron Fitzwalter's dearest daughter."

Robin smiled at her. "Ye know not my wife, sheriff, an' ye do not think her able to choose her own path through life."

"I welcomed thee into mine home, as he did." The sheriff glanced down the length of the table at the scores of outlaws staring at him or whispering to one another. "What wilt thou do to me now I am here, having set aside mine old promise? Hang me or slit my throat?"

"Why pain God by putting such a sin upon my soul?"

"Thou couldst be rid of a great enemy."

"'Twould make no difference. Another would take your place as easily."

"Yet to have thy revenge . . . "

"There lies a difference between anger and malice," quoth Robin, "yet there lies no difference between you and myself."

"Upon the contrary, there are a great many."

"Perhaps a few, for I was outlawed and excommunicated when I broke the forest law, poaching one of the king's deer, and slaying one of his foresters. Ye were neither when ye broke the forest law, paying foresters by Rufford Abbey for the destruction of the vert and denying me sanctuary in order to see me hanged."

"Thou hast said thyself that thou art an outlaw and excommunicated."

"Yet ye do not treat all outlaws so, for ye would have let the murderous Guy of Guisbourne go free, and rewarded him with silver, to boot."

The sheriff's voice lowered. "That was the Bishop of Hereford's bargain."

"I have long thought, sir sheriff, that there is hardly an honest way to become an outlaw, yet one must strive to be honest e'en after the deed is done. We are the same, for we are both corrupt. Ye exploit the law for your gain when ye should uphold it. I uphold the law when I should break it, for it no longer binds me. Ye are no better a sheriff than I am an outlaw."

"Thou dost demand far greater sums from those thou dost fine than do I."

"Ye see, sir sheriff, I cannot even corrupt mine office so well as ye do yours."

Nottingham's protector paused to seethe whilst the outlaws laughed. "When thou wert a boy at Baron Fitzwalter's, and I would dine or see thee training, I ever knew thou wert too cocky to become a great knight. Little did I know then that thou wouldst fail to become a knight at all."

"Sir sheriff," quoth Robin, "ye must know how to pull a bowstring and swing a sword. Why not take a weapon yourself? Such sport is rare in our humble greenwood."

Nottingham's protector turned whiter than a daisy, for he thought then they meant to kill him under this pretence of fair play.

"Fetch the sheriff a bow and shaft."

Before he could refuse, the weapons were handed him and a wand set at one hundred fifty paces.

"Come, lording, let us stand and strive to split the wand."

The sheriff did as commanded. He had not loosed a shaft in many years, having had his position since young manhood, with plenty of archers in his personal guard. Awkwardly did he draw the string, his grip upon the bow infirm.

All kept silent that he might concentrate, and so, breathing a prayer, the sheriff loosed his arrow.

'Twas not an altogether bad shot, though it failed to cleave the wand. The distance being none too great, he thought himself disgraced. Yet the band shouted, "Fairly shot, lording."

When offered a second chance he refused, so Robin Hood laid his own shaft to his bow and, aiming it in the most thoughtless manner, splintered the wand.

"Long indeed have I wished to shoot with you. Come, lads, show the sheriff how ye wield your swords."

Up jumped two-score men to arrange a tournament. The sheriff kept a stony face, but felt impressed and, though he would never admit so to any man living, he wondered little that he had not hanged these outlaws, for his own men were not so skilled. The band battled with swords and bucklers until one lad remained.

Again they feasted, and again the merry men earned their name. Venison pasty and poached eggs from fowls the band kept, fat capon and meat pies, leeks and onions, boiled greens and carrots, even mushrooms attended the meal. Wine and nut-brown ale were on hand, and the sheriff set upon these heartily.

Laughter roared amongst the trees as if a lion pride lived in Sherwood. At last the light dimmed so the sheriff insisted that he must take his leave.

His horse was brought with the one Robin had ridden. Before the sheriff mounted, the outlaw handed him a little, gold ring. "I bid you give this to your wife, sir, for I fear much that I offended her kind invitation last evening with my coarse behaviour."

The sheriff stared at the ring a moment, then looked his enemy full in the face. "Robin," said he solemnly, "I have no money with me to pay for thy feast nor entertainment. I beg thee let me in peace, for I would truly pay had I the means at hand."

"Fear not, lording," quoth Robin. "I believe ye tell true. Your fare, sir sheriff, is free."

Nottingham's protector mounted his horse, again donning the blindfold. Whilst being led back to the highway he thought upon what the outlaw had said. Never before had Robin Hood let go a rich man without fee, and never before had he spoke so viciously as when he had revealed himself. The sheriff thought upon all this as he wondered what he ought to do.

The outlaws of Sherwood and Barnesdale dwelt in peace four years, occasionally receiving a visitor to pay their livings. Many feasts were held and the days filled with sport. The outlaws made nary a sound when Allan a Dale touched his lute, telling his own ballads and others'. Storytelling was common, and the best tales came from Anne, who told of Robin's childhood.

Today's tale was an old one, in sooth, the oldest. It was the story of how Robin and Anne had first met. Every man came to listen and, once all was quiet, she began.

"Draw near and listen yeomen all that be of freeborn blood, for I shall tell you of a good archer, his name is Robin Hood. Robin will be a proud outlaw as long as he walks the ground; such a courteous outlaw as he is shall never since be found.

"Robert draws near the age of seven and must away to train for knighthood. He will reside at Baron Fitzwalter's castle and learn a page's duties. His parents accompany him to the household he will join.

"Baron Fitzwalter greets them warmly. 'Well met, sir earl, and sincerest wishes to you, milady. Be this Robert? Greetings, lad, and welcome. Are ye excited to begin your knightly training?'

"'Yes sir, very eager,' replies the boy, bowing. Even this fine etiquette cannot contain his bold spirit.

"'Follow me, then,' chuckles the baron. 'We shall survey your accommodations.'

"With glowing eyes the lad follows, excited to explore his new home.

"The ladies-in-waiting call him a sweet darling, the servants a stout little lad. The last met are the baron's family. At this time there are but three daughters.

"Entering the great hall, Robert beholds a woman and a pair of young girls. The woman is Lady Fitzwalter, tall and stern-faced. The elder lass is Mirabelle, and the younger Sophia, but two years old.

"'Where is Marian?' asks the baron.

"'She practises archery,' Lady Fitzwalter replies with distaste.

"'We must discuss arrangements,' says the earl. 'Robert, find the maid Marian and see if thou mayest help her shoot.'

"With direction from Lady Fitzwalter, Robert finds the missing daughter. The lass pulling back bowstring stands no taller than he. She hath long, brown hair, and a dress of light blue. The target stands twenty yards distant. Her arrow lands two fingers' breadth from the clout's centre.

"'Thou shootest exceeding well, milady.'

"Marian spins 'round, surprised. 'Who art thou, boy?'

"Robert comes closer and dips. 'Forgive me. I am Robert of Huntington. Baron Fitzwalter hath graciously accepted me as page. Thou art Maid Marian?'

"'Canst thou use a bow?'

"'As well as thee. My father taught me. He is a wondrous archer and knows tricks.'

"'Canst thou perform any?'

"'Not well,' the lad admits.

"'Nock an arrow and we shall see.' Handing him the bow, Marian steps back.

"Robert takes careful aim. The shaft flies to the target's centre. 'Wouldst thou care to learn that?'

"'If thou canst teach it.'

"The pair spend nigh two hours talking and laughing. They are the best of friends from the start.

"Days later Robert comes to stay, his eyes red. He is split from his family and will see them none too often. This new world daunts him, the excitement of knighthood looming only in the distant future.

"Whilst Marian aids Robert in arranging his quarters, they speak of many things. One is the local boys Marian ranges with.

"'Hast thou met William Stutely?' she inquires.

"'Aye, the yeoman's son,' Robert replies absently.

"'I call him "Struts." He would go 'round as if lord of the manor. It used to be "Strutely," but "Struts" is more glib to say. The next day thou hast free, mayhap the three of us could explore the country.'

"The next day is spent introducing duties and learning the schedule of training. Thus Robert of Huntington enters service as a page. Mornings bring his lessons in swordplay and other knightly weapons, whilst afternoons bear duties for the ladies of the household. If he finishes these quickly enough, he seeks his mates.

"Upon Sunday, after hearing mass, Robert is given the afternoon. Marian collects Stutely and they set out to see what might be seen, to find what might be found. Over fields to the west they go, to a castle nearby. A boy outside is waving a wooden sword and prancing. Seeing them approach, the lad stops, standing to stare.

"'Harold, come! We show Robert the countryside. He is my father's new page.'

"'I know a mud wallow from the rain yesterday,' Harold says. 'Truly, 'tis the largest ever seen. I wot we could haul water from the stream to make it good as any pond.'

"The children think this a novel idea, mud being of endless fascination to them and grief to their parents.

"For an hour and more they haul water. Resting afterward, they sing ballads to which they know but half the lines, and so they laughingly shout out senseless new ones. This puts them in a silly mood, and before long they are wading through the mud. It sucks at their feet and, being up to their knees, threatens at times to consume them.

"Robert stares at the brown water sloshing his legs. Sparks fly through his mind. Grinning thoughtfully, he collects a handful of mud, lobbing it at Stutely's shoulder. Gobs of mud are soon sailing, splashing trees, bushes, and children.

"As it doth grow late, the small ones think it best to be off. Whilst Stutely takes a more discreet entrance, Robert escorts Marian through the main door, both covered top to toe in mud.

"That evening both children are scrubbed 'til their skins glisten red. Though thoroughly reprimanded, they continue adventuring together.

"Robert always remains devoted to his mother and admiring of his father, minding his first archery lessons at the age of four. Although all but raised upon the yeoman's standards in the baron's household, Robert hath never forgotten the chivalric lessons of his knightly training. The lad's father passes into heaven, with Robert a mere seventeen years old. For his mother's sake, he aways to Huntington to govern for his absent brother. Again misfortune befalls Robert when, six months later, he is outlawed, yet even this black cat landeth upon feet all four. For though Robert has not become what he thought to be, he is better than a knight — he is a king."

CHAPTER TWENTY
Yew

IN THE YEAR OF OUR Lord 1272, England's gracious sovereign of fifty-six years, Henry III, passed away. His son, Edward I, greatest of the medieval warrior kings, returned to England two years later, having been upon crusade, and travelled through his kingdom for local lords to pledge him their loyalty.

The streets stood full crowded when the king and his wife, escorted by five-score stout fellows, rode into Nottingham. Edward's hair was turning from fair to dark. He had handsome features, though his left eyelid drooped like his father's. It has been said that no man ever possessed such strength for wielding a sword, and that his long legs saved him from falling when his horse galloped or leapt.

The sheriff rode to greet the king upon a black horse with elegant scarlet trappings. "My king." The sheriff bowed without dismounting, for his clothes were fine and new, and he cared not to dirty them. "Your accommodations await. Never hath our city been so graced as today." He bowed again.

When the king remained silent, the sheriff continued, "Rest assured my loyalty is yours."

Quoth Edward of England, "Thou hast a high horse, sir sheriff. Canst thou not dismount, even for thy king?"

Discomfort passed over the sheriff's face. He turned his mount's head to lead the king to Nottingham Castle.

The crowd's cheerings were horrendous yet, coming to one spot in the crowd, a particularly loud shout of, "God save you, brave king!" rose to Edward's ears, turning his head.

He spotted a patch of green amidst the jumbled colours: two hundred twenty men, and with them a stout friar, to whom the voice belonged.

"Safe journey, my king!"

The men with the friar appeared foresters: a dainty fellow, a giant, and a young lad with a fair lass upon his arm. One man, but a hair shorter than the king, circled his arm around a lady of nigh identical height. His stature set him apart. The others kept an unspoke respect for him.

"Who is that man?" Edward asked the sheriff.

"A forester, most likely," Nottingham's protector stuttered.

"He doth seem to command extraordinary loyalty from those near him," quoth the king. "And somehow he doth look familiar; methinks I have seen him before. Bring him to me."

"But — my king, he will not come." The sheriff turned purple, fearing he might be relieved of his position.

"Sir sheriff," spake the king evenly, "if thou dost disobey mine orders but one time more, thine head shall be sent to France, whilst thy body remains in England. Fetch me that man!"

"Guard," the sheriff called, then whispered to his man, "tell Robin Hood the king wisheth his company."

The procession halted.

Robin came before the king, behind him a dozen stout yeomen. Each one knelt.

"What be thy name, fellow?" asked the king.

"My king, if it please you, my name is Robin Hood."

The crowd hushed.

"Hast thou no sense in thine head, man?" quoth the king. "What dost thou do in Nottingham? Here ride thy two great enemies — the sheriff and myself — with twelve hundred pounds upon thine head."

"Ye are my king," the outlaw replied, still kneeling. "I would not be loyal had I shunned this day."

The king considered, and a plan formed in his mind. Long had tales of Robin Hood been told him, e'en by his own parents. "Go in peace, sir outlaw," quoth he, "and mind thyself."

Rising to his feet, Robin bent in another bow and left for Sherwood, followed by all his yeomanry.

Before the sheriff recovered himself, a near deafening cheer arose from the crowd, not unlike those heard when a Roman emperor showed mercy to a favoured gladiator.

Even once the castle gates were closed, and the sheriff and the king stood in the keep, the shouts remained.

"Sire, why did ye let him go? Full thirteen *years* — and something more — these northern parts he hath vexed sore. Ye did have him before you — ye could have beheaded him with your sword — he was so *near!*"

"Silence thyself!" roared the king, in a voice to awaken fear beneath the sheriff's breast. "Art thou such a fool to think I,

King of all England, would let this upstart slip my grasp? He is clever, I know full well, else he would not still live. Didst thou hear how the people cheered? Had I struck him down, dost thou imagine they would be still rejoicing?"

A servant entered with goblets and drink.

"Pour the wine, my lad," quoth the king. "We must toast this: the end of outlawry in Sherwood Forest."

The servant poured with trembling hands. He admired the outlaws and gave them word if he could of any danger from the sheriff.

That night this same servant, upon the sheriff's black horse, set out for the castle of Sir Richard at the Lea.

⊕·⊕·⊕

Early next morn six friars, their hoods shadowing their faces, travelled through Sherwood's shades. Noontide saw the men worn and impatient.

The head friar cried, "Is there no place to eat in this accursed wood?"

In answer, a man, who acted the imp yet stood much too tall, appeared from the leaves. He pushed back his hood and bowed, then replaced it and spake thusly: "Greetings, friar. Mayhap I can help thee. My brothers and I run an inn, yet we have not hosted a visitor in over a fortnight."

"How if we should refuse, peasant? What wouldst thy brothers do?"

"Why," replied the outlaw, "without paying guests, we should be forced to poach of the king's deer."

"If thou wert caught, hanged wouldst thou be." Anger curdled in the friar's voice.

"I think it not so, for our gracious king hath many fine animals, and little would he lose to share his good fortune with the hungry of his land."

"Dost thou condemn our king, vagabond?"

"Only God hath that right, sir friar. Doth our Lord not say, 'He who condemneth will himself be condemned?' Nay, I speak not against our king. I hear he is an honest and honourable man; I hold him in respect." Laying hold of the friar's bridle rein, the outlaw put a silver horn to his lips, blowing three loud blasts.

The friars looked about them. The air began to quake. Then rustling leaves could be heard. The ground quivered so the horses shifted their feet.

Nine-score great fellows burst onto the path.

"Oh who are these," quoth the head friar, "come so quickly at thy call?"

"These are my yeomen, the stoutest outlaws England hath ever seen."

"Thou braggest. These men are not as good as the king's."

Robin smiled. "All men are made alike in God's image, sir friar. Yet, according to the law of this great land, outlaws are not men but ravenous wolves to be butchered. Therefore, I may lawfully prate as much as I wish."

With heads bowed the six friars were led into the heart of the greenwood. Around them, the forest pulsed like a sea, yet lay still.

↭↭↭

The camp buzzed, readying a feast: some setting the cloth, others roasting deer upon spits, and more rolling casks of fine ale, flattening the grass.

"Hilloa, brethren! and my wholehearted welcome. A wondrous day to breathe, is it not? My name be Friar Tuck. It hath been long since mine eyes beheld other churchmen." His cheeks grew rosy at walking whilst he roared.

"I would not think a churchman should associate with thieves, brother," answered the head friar, now his party had been unhorsed.

Tuck laughed. "Did not our Lord come to the tax collectors and prostitutes? Was His ministry not for the sinful — for us all? My sermons do more good here than when I was a hermit at Fountain Dale. And here I need not pay for my meat and drink."

The friar chortled. "Truly, thou art right to stay if table scraps are what thou wantest."

"Table scraps!" rumbled Tuck. "Taste what we of Sherwood call a meal and thou wilt freely pay our fee, for the fare is better than what good King Edward eateth at Nottingham!" Having spoke his piece, Tuck watched the scattering outlaws about their duties.

David of Doncaster fetched them for the feast. He had grown much since joining the band. A foot at least. He was now the tallest member, beside Little John. His shoulders had also broadened, making him the best wrestler amongst the band.

The head friar was seated upon Robin's right hand. After Friar Tuck had said grace, everyone set to.

"Be of good cheer, sir friar," quoth Robin, setting a chunk of gooey venison before him. "Eat thy fill, for we have much."

"Is it not treason to eat of the king's deer?" quoth the friar, though in sooth this pasty looked the most appetizing dish ever set before him.

Robin replied, "Thou art a right loyal man to our king, especially for a clergyman, and I tell thee plainly I like thy company. Now I shall share two points of interest with thee. The first being that if the king is fool enough to abuse his power, starving peasants for meddling in his entertainment, he be not fit to wear the crown. The second being that though dead men cannot commit treason, they grow hungry enough."

"Thou dost hate the king for carrying out his justice." He reached for the venison.

"Not so, dear friar," quoth Robin, returning his attention to eating. "I like our king much and bear no ill will for myself — right justly was I outlawed — yet there is more than one man whose only crime was hunger."

"Indeed," quoth another friar, overhearing, "if hunger is a crime, no wonder thy men are outlaws."

The company laughed, for they all loved a good venison pasty.

Throughout the meal laughter never ceased. The head friar found it hard not to be merry himself, though Robin Hood's words troubled him. He had believed these men ordinary outlaws, yet now saw they were still loyal, obeying the laws, save those against poaching for food, and thieving for drink. Even when persecuted, they had neither turned against women, nor poor.

"Now, good friars, ye will see what we do for sport." Robin grinned.

The band clamoured to retrieve their bows and arrow bags.

The friars thought they would be shot. Instead, a rose garland, not more than three hand's breadths wide, was set at three hundred yards.

"Come, my merry men all," quoth Robin, "every man must shoot three shafts through yon garland, causing not a single flower to fall, else he receive a buffet from our good Will Scarlet."

"Is that wise?" interrupted the head friar, so only Robin might hear. "Is he not the outlaw who killed a man with a buffet to the head?"

Laughing, Robin replied, "'Twill encourage the men to try their best, will it not?"

The first three yeomen did well, yet when Henry o' Lincoln Town came up he could not steady his hands for the shot. His arrow rawly missed the edge of the garland, yet went through. Upon his second shot, he became overconfident, and his arrow skimmed the flowers upon the outside, causing petals to fall.

Those assembled hooted, and Henry looked pitifully at Will Scarlet, his eyes begging mercy. Feet dragging beneath him, he approached Will with as much reluctance as King John had surely felt when he approached to sign the Magna Carta. Henry trembled, bracing his feet, knowing full well this could be the last breath he drew.

Will was casually rolling up his sleeve, as if about to weed his garden, though like as not he had never touched soil in all his life.

Now both seemed ready, Henry signalling by shutting his eyes.

Will drew back his elbow and his enormous muscles, such as one would wonder to find upon so dainty a fledgling, rippled to his skin's surface. Lumbering forward with the might of a bear, he swung, and poor Henry thudded onto his back.

When he did not stir, some yeomen wondered if he were dead. Presently, Henry's eyes twitched, then his arms. He sat up dizzily, half expecting to be dead, yet seeming to be not.

The men shouted laughter as they beheld his face.

"Well done, Henry," quoth Robin, Will lowering his brawny arm as assistance. "I doubt not thou wilt have the arrows cleanly through the next time."

The friars watched as outlaw after outlaw came to the mark. The wreath was a hard thing to hit through, yet even those who missed never did so by more than a finger's breadth.

After all had gone (except for Will Scarlet and Anne o' th' Woods, for Will had his own work, and Anne refused to play at games thought up "by the brawn and not the brain of a man"), a shout arose from the men for their master to try his hand.

Winking to the head friar, Robin Hood obliged. He made short work of the three shots, pulling the string and letting it twang without any seeming note of care or aim. The first shot went through; the second followed. Yet the third arrow had an ill feather and veered left, missing the garland entirely.

At first there was silence, then low repining, and then Will Scarlet spake in his soft, melodic voice. "Come hither, Uncle. It seemeth I have a fee to pay thee and shall take pleasure in doing so."

There seemed nothing for it but to endure his lumps, yet Robin had no desire to feel Will's clout again in his lifetime.

"Nay," quoth he. "It was not a fair contest. A feather was bent askew. I felt it as it left my fingers. Give me a clean shaft, and I shall cleave the wand that doth hold the garland."

"The challenge was for three arrows, dear Uncle, not four."

Robin found no sympathetic faces, and resigned himself to receiving a blow, yet even in this he stayed stubborn. "Thou wilt not have the pleasure, Will, for I am king here, and no one may strike his king. These friars are not of our forest world. I surrender myself to their leader, for e'en a king is subject to God's justice. Wouldst thou be so kind, sir?"

The lead friar chuckled. "With all mine heart, good outlaw." He stepped up and Robin did not flinch, fearing no knock a churchman could give.

"'Twould be wise," quoth the friar, "if thou wouldst place thy feet farther apart, else thou mightest be felled."

"Truly, good friar," returned Robin, "if thou canst fell me, free will your fare and entertainment be."

With no other words, the friar drew back his fist, hurling it forward with all speed.

Robin stood prepared for nothing of the kind, and flopped to the greensward. He sat up to the most ecstatic laughter Sherwood Forest had ever heard. Even the friars took part.

There came a thundering and a trampling of underbrush. Weapons drawn, the outlaws steeled themselves for an ambush.

Half a score of mounted men-at-arms crashed into camp. Whilst the others reined in their beasts, the leader leapt from his horse, striding up to Robin Hood.

Robin rose to his feet, ears ringing. "Greetings, Sir Richard," quoth he. "Tell us your news, for 'tis plainly urgent."

"Indeed." The knight spake so he barely saved himself tripping over the words. "Robin, thou art in cold danger. I received word the king *himself* cometh this day to purge Sherwood of outlawry. Quickly — we must away! Thou and thy men may stay with me. Even should bold Edward come to my door, I shall not let them take thee; this is my promise."

Nodding and turning to his men, Robin spake. "Time doth stand against us. Take only what ye can carry and keep your feet fleet. We have a full day's journey ahead."

"Do not trouble yourselves," quoth the head friar. "There be no cause to fear our king."

"Not for thee, mayhap, but we are the king's sworn enemies, and must flee to keep our lives. Thou hast earned passage through the greenwood. We can escort ye from the forest, yet I fear our ways may soon part."

"Yet I say our paths are the same." The friar thrust back his hood.

Sir Richard filled with fear, dropping to his knees.

When the outlaws recognized King Edward, they knelt one and all, removing their hoods and bowing their heads.

The other friars revealed themselves as the king's most loyal knights.

Sir Richard saw them and cried out. "My son! Thou who wert outlawed — can this be thee?"

"It is, Father," the youngest knight replied. Strong sun had turned his face darker than his fair hair. "I joined the king upon crusade to the Holy Land." He turned to Edward. "Pray, sir, what fate lieth before my father?"

Quoth Edward grimly, "By law he should be hanged, for he willed treason and hath admitted as much. Canst thou defend thyself, Sir Richard?"

Sir Richard nodded, though near trembling. His own words calmed him. "My king, when my son was outlawed I sold everything to save him. Had not Robin Hood and his men given me the money to repay my debts, mine house and lands would have been lost and my family forced into beggary. I owe all I have to these outlaws, and to keep mine honour I must be willing to sacrifice all to repay them."

Far more still than any statue stood King Edward as he contemplated the fate of Sir Richard at the Lea. "Very well, sir knight," quoth he at last, "thy pardon is granted, for thine intentions were noble. Yet know this: If ever I hear again a treasonous word rear from betwixt thy lips, be sure that thy tongue shall soon be shorn."

Humbly, for he knew he had escaped death by a narrow pass, the knight replied, "I thank you from my very depths, gracious king. Ye can be sure I shall be the most loyal of your subjects henceforth. I pledge all I have and more to you, ever hoping our gracious king will find favour in my deeds."

Edward nodded and turned his attention toward Robin Hood. "Sir outlaw, thou hast said this day what thou thinkest of England and myself. Thou hast the interests of the people near thine heart, and that is indeed valuable. I ventured here to be satisfied, and well have I been rewarded. Wilt thou join me at court, Robin?"

"I would, my lord," replied the outlaw, raising his head to look the king in the eye, "yet cannot show my face outside this forest for fear of being hanged."

"Bear in mind I hold the power to pardon thee. However, before I do," quoth the king artfully, "I would have thee pledge loyalty to me, for thou art as powerful as the barons and officials of this land, and dost carry the hope and faith of the people."

Placing his hand over his heart, Robin Hood spake with neither pause nor reservation. "My king, here before my men and before God Himself, I give you mine undying word that my loyalty will be to you. I shall perform your will, whatever it be, for the good of England's people."

Drawing his sword, Edward placed the flat of it upon Robin's right shoulder, arching it above the outlaw's head to the left, and back again. King Edward spake: "By the power given me from God as King of England, I dub thee Sir Robin of the Hood, henceforth to join my court. Now, sir knight, thou hast thy pardon. Come, tell me, what else can I grant thee? Lands, perhaps — or a castle?"

"Truly, my king," quoth Robin, tangled in surprise, "already ye have proved your generosity, and I thank you devotedly. I cannot expect more. Yet if ye are willing, I ask one thing further."

"Prytell, what may it be?" the king returned, straightening to his lofty height.

"Please, my king, could ye grant pardon to these people?" Robin motioned to his band. "They are all honest, and most outlawed by circumstance. I ask that they be relieved of worrying for their lives at every shift of the wind."

Edward bore a hard look upon his face. "It is done, then."

The air hung still. None knew what to think, for nothing seemed real. Anne and Stutely exchanged looks. Little John glanced toward Will Scarlet who, for once, appeared flustered.

"Arise, all, for there is much planning and celebration ahead!"

The outlaws sprang to their feet with shouts of "Long live King Edward," and "Praise our fair king." The cloth was again set with all gathered 'round: Robin Hood and his band, Sir Richard and his men, King Edward and his knights.

After the feast, each stayed by the cloth to laze about in their new safety. It was then Edward began to discuss their futures.

"Robin," quoth he, "thou wilt come to court, where I might keep watch over thee, yet if thy men remain here I have no guarantee that they will take honest work. Therefore, I shall give to any who favour it the position of king's forester."

"Our king is more than generous," Robin returned. "We owe you our very lives, and still ye give more."

"Be ready tomorrow," replied the king, as if he had not heard. "We leave for Nottingham at first light."

⟡⟡⟡

Next morn, the greenwood wished master and mistress farewell. The band came up each in turn, a melancholy curl to their mouths.

Friar Tuck conducted a short service, and Robin and Anne exchanged special goodbyes with Will Stutely, their comrade from childhood; Will Scarlet, their cousin; and last of all Little John, who bid his farewell shedding some tears at being parted from his master and friend of thirteen years. Allan and Edith a Dale were bound for London as well, chosen by the king as attendants to Robin and Anne.

At last, the four mounted and were off. They travelled through the morning, reaching Nottingham by noon. Much did the townspeople stare upon seeing Robin Hood ride by, and with the King of England, no less.

At the gatehouse of Nottingham Castle stood the sheriff, ready with a score of men to escort Robin Hood to the gaol below. "Gramercy, oh king," his eyes shone upon Robin with a mad glint of elation. "Deliver this outlaw into mine hands, and I pledge my word he shall be hanged before the day doth flee."

"Not so, sir sheriff," returned the king, "for this man is bound with me for London."

"But, my king," the sheriff panted, his beard greying in the sunlight, "long have I chased this vile outlaw. Would ye have me not see justice upon his head? Please, sire — *reconsider*."

Edward motioned to a group of stableboys, who leapt forward to fetch the mounts. Edward, also, leapt from his horse and started for the castle.

"Ready two rooms for thy guests, sir sheriff. I wot it hath been long since thou hast hosted a knight of such standing."

"My king?"

Edward turned upon his heel, having endured enough of Nottingham's protector and his incompetence. "Question mine orders but once more, and I shall strike thee down. Ready a room for Sir Robin of the Hood and for his attendants."

Dazed, the sheriff called a servant and commanded what the king had said. The greatest outlaw England ever knew was now a knight of the court, when he should be dangling from a noose. Many times had the sheriff imagined this execution, how he would make it a grand ceremony, how he would be revered; it had become his obsession.

Now he underwent the torture of playing host for this man he considered his mortal enemy. An outlaw dwelt under his roof, feasting at his table, sleeping in his bed — an outlaw who had outwitted him time and another. This maddened the sheriff, a galling insult to his authority. Robin Hood had murdered and stolen, yet he, the High Sheriff of Nottingham — who had loyally preserved the king's honour — was looked upon as the criminal. Had the sheriff ceased to hunt the outlaws, he would not now look a fool. Yet, had he ceased, he would have been evicted from his office or, worse yet, called traitor. There was no justice for Nottingham. Worst was the king's favour toward the enemy, and the knowledge that, if he showed anything short of courtesy, his office would be wrenched away.

Nottingham's protector vowed that, when the opportunity presented, he would finally slay Robin Hood.

Part Five

CHAPTER TWENTY-ONE
Cornel

T HE NEXT FOUR YEARS BROUGHT much. Baron Fitzwalter died. His estate was divided into four lots, one for each daughter, aside from Anne, who had been disinherited when she came to live in the forest.

Will Scarlet returned home to find his father passed away and his mother soon to follow. The only one left him was Meg. They had been young sweethearts, speaking of marriage a time or two, and Will expected to find her wed years ago. Days after his mother's death, a caller came to pay respects. It was Meg. After a year-long engagement they married, and lived happily at Gamewell.

Little John shepherded near the woodland shades. Though not used to a quiet life, it was simple, which suited him. The rich grasses by Sherwood caused John's sheep to grow stout and woolly. In quiet moments, he relived the days spent with Robin Hood's merry band, smiling as he watched the sun cross the sky.

Some of the band returned to their old professions, or became yeomen farmers. Others, like Will Stutely, became foresters, and still others, like David of Doncaster, travelled town to town, showing their skill and spreading tales of Sherwood.

As for Robin Hood, he had gone to court with King Edward. The journey to London was a cheerful one, with the outlaws spinning tales of their adventures, and the knights telling of their battles in the Holy Land. London appeared before them in a mist, the old city wet with night's dew. Through the streets to the Tower they rode and, though it was early, people swarmed, cheering the safe return of their king. After two days' rest from their journey, Robin was given a night for vigil and a grand knighting before Queen Eleanor and her daughter-in-law.

Robin and Anne had two children. The first was Michael in 1275, named for the archangel and looking exactly as his father. The next year brought Mary, named for the Virgin and having the same shade hair as her mother. Allan and Edith a Dale also were blessed with children, and the two families lived happily at court.

This could be our story's end. However, there is one tale further, though I hate to tell it, of how this great legend met his end.

Llywelyn ap Gruffydd, Prince of Wales, had realized Henry III as his lord, but refused Edward. The year 1277 saw knights and soldiers sent west. Finding the Welsh preferred guerrilla attacks, the English army circled the coast, leaving strongholds in their wake, at last killing Llywelyn. After seven years Wales was finally conquered.

After the first year of fighting and killing, Robin returned to England, having seen too much bloodshed. Amongst other battles, he had helped to capture Anglesey. Edward agreed Robin's promise of faithful service had been valiantly kept. Thus did Sir Robin of Sherwood leave court life.

With his wife, children, and the Dales, Robin returned to Nottinghamshire, where the king had granted him an estate. All wanted to see the old camp and home of nearly fourteen years, which they would pass upon their way. Robin needed no persuasion, for he carried a great longing to be an outlaw again, if only for a moment. The Tower in London had not the bright sun nor the birds' song. All was grey and smelled of soot. Just to see the camp before continuing on would assure them they had indeed come home.

Letting the carts go on ahead, and ducking through the trees, the party was at last forced to dismount, for the forest fronds had grown denser in their absence.

Michael asked in a wide-eyed whisper, "Are there wild beasts?"

"Not here." Robin smiled. "Listen and thou wilt find it so."

As they neared the clearing, the horses bowed their heads to enter. Sunlight lay ahead, and the underbrush gave way to slender grass.

The party emerged from the trees onto the greensward.

The old greenwood tree looked stiffer, reflecting the age of its friends. Its branches still reached, as if trying to grasp what stretched just beyond its fingertips.

One wrinkled branch lay upon the ground, seemingly frozen whilst writhing in pain at its separation. A glimmer could be seen beneath its greying leaves. Robin crouched, to find the golden arrow won at Nottingham Fair, when he had seen Anne again after months apart.

To the left rested the path to the smaller clearing, where Robin had spent his first night as an outlaw and where they had planned to rescue Edith a Dale. At the back of the clearing, peeking from the tree line, stood the battered ruins of the huts used during rainy nights, such as the one of Will Stutely's capture. Beside were the fire pits and a few rusted spits. The table showed eerily bare — of food, of platters, of cloths. Beyond the brambles hid the treasury. Here waited the wealth of monks, bishops, and noblemen, the Sheriff of Nottingham, the Bishop of Hereford, and the brothers of Fountains Abbey, though King Edward had won back his own coins.

Robin stood, tears itching his eyes. He placed his silver horn (which he still carried) to his lips, longing to hear the notes echo from tree to tree, as if the forest were haunted with the ghosts of men dead under the law. Three blasts he sounded, as in the days of old.

And as the notes wound through Sherwood, the forest moved.

Everyone looked to the trees, forgetting they had been pardoned and need no longer fear.

Foresters broke through the leaves, several bands. The man that led them was of average height and muscle. Scruffy blonde hair peered at angles from under his cap. The face looked aged, yet familiar as always. Beholding Robin, he wasted never a moment, but knelt, crying, "Master! Robin Hood come home!" The others followed his example. These were the former outlaws of Sherwood, now foresters captained by Will Stutely.

This loyalty pricked Robin's heart. Tears rimmed his eyes, and he bade them all rise. He meant to say that he bid them God's blessings in their new lives.

Robin thought how merry their adventures had been, and how he had longed to live free during all his time at court. Thus, what came was quite different from what he willed his lips to say.

"My men, let what ill-fortune tore us apart never do so again! Let us live in the greenwood the rest of our days, and we shall die free men. Once more shall we eat and drink as we please, once more protect those seeking help and defy those who would plunder the poor. What say ye, my merry men all?"

In voices choked like their master's, they cheered. A cheer for a king returned.

⊕⊕⊕

News of Robin Hood returning to the greenwood and taking up his old name travelled throughout the countryside. Fresh to the sheriff's mind came every humiliation Robin Hood had caused him: enraging King Henry, forming the largest gang in England, evading traps, thwarting hangings, robbing those the sheriff protected, robbing the sheriff himself and, finally, invading Nottingham Castle as a guest and not a prisoner. The sheriff's revenge had been to tour England, stopping at or sending letters to each monastery, beseeching the destruction of all documents mentioning Robin Hood or his band. The monks agreed, for the church's overly rich had always been the Hood's victims. Thus, the great outlaw king was stricken from history.

Unsatisfied, the sheriff had bided his time. Now an opportunity sat before him. He cared not for the fifteen hundred pound reward but, whilst nearly all the outlaws returned to greenwood life, gathered an army. He would march upon the camp with one standing order: Robin Hood was to be captured alive, for the sheriff himself to slaughter.

Word of this spread, as word does, piercing Sherwood's deep walls.

"Master," quoth Little John, as they stood alone by the stream, "let us away to Barnesdale, as in days of old, for we cannot stand against the sheriff's force without bloodshed."

Robin turned this in his mind. It seemed he would agree, and meant to, yet if they ran the sheriff's army would follow, and they would be forever running, outlaws or no. Until each hung dead in the trees around Nottingham.

His men had spent their youth upon adventures; now was the time for rest. The sheriff would pursue until his own death, and by then Robin's children might be grown. Half his men dead, never knowing safety. Robin felt tired of the fight. He wanted to give his wife the time he had never been able to. He wanted to visit his brother, whom he had not seen since childhood. He wanted to know peace for the first time in his adult years.

Robin cleared his head so only logic remained: the only way to stop the sheriff endangering his family and his band was to kill. The sacrifice could be worth it. It certainly seemed the easier route.

Therefore quoth he, "Nay, Little John, that we shall not do. I say the sheriff doth not rule this land — it is ours! The sheriff doth not protect this land — that do we. We shall settle this matter, and the sheriff hath chosen the day."

"But master," said Little John, "'twould mean battle. Our men would be killed."

"Can they not shoot? We shall establish an ambush."

"Men would still die."

Robin smiled sadly. "'Tis the only way change can be wrought sometimes."

Thus with retribution, leaving larger gashes until life is wasted.

Not a month before, Robin had stood proud with that great warrior King Edward, knowing his children had whatever they desired. The king would not twice grant a pardon. Robin had trapped his family and friends a second time, letting them flock to him in death. They looked to him for guidance, never acknowledging him a murderer, a thief.

All he could think of at times was his daughter, Mary, huddled and cold all through winter in a Barnesdale cave, and this alone scared him so he dared not flee. He could not raise his children into fear. His men might begin doubting his word if he recanted.

Then morality would slip into his head and tell him he should run.

Many times Little John drew aside his master, urging flight, and Anne twice as many times again, yet Robin would only reply, "I hate it much as thou dost, yet 'tis the only way that I can see. These men deserve to live out their days in happiness. They will have only one further day's fight to attain this, for I cannot ask more. My children will not spend their lives in hiding for a mistake I made eighteen years ago."

The outlaws readied themselves for battle.

Upon the seventh day of the week, two hours after sunrise, a pair of spies sprinted into camp. All looked to Robin, face hard, though his eyes swam with sadness.

"Come, my men — let us drive out the villainous Sheriff of Nottingham. We fight for the freedom of all under his power who have had their own voices stripped from them. Away and await my signal!"

Two hundred men disappeared in the instant, as if mist. Only the children and women remained.

Meanwhile, the sheriff's army marched through the trees, knowing only the camp's direction. The sheriff rode in their midst, where he could best be guarded. Much of this army hailed from Nottingham's men-at-arms, yet there also marched foresters and less than a score of villagers, now considered traitors by their neighbours. The villagers crept, shoulders tense, clutching staffs or axes. The men-at-arms rode with contempt, the grips of their sheathed blades next to their palms. The foresters advanced with stealth, their darting eyes combing the brush, though most often the movement seen was only a change in sunlight.

Entering a long, narrow clearing, the foresters moved more cautiously, and the men-at-arms lost cockiness. These trees seemed to take breath, denying them air.

A horn blasted the silence. The sky loosed clouds of arrows. They blew down like wind.

Foresters and villagers fell to the ground, and even the sheriff's men-at-arms, for in the hands of an English archer the longbow could strike with the force to cleave armour and still pin a man to his horse.

At nightfall the band returned to camp. The battle had ended hours before, yet they had remained to dig a mass grave for the dead. The outlaws had survived without injury, yet were no longer merry, for each had killed; all of the sheriff's men lay dead.

⊸⊷⊸

Word of the massacre in the greenwood, and of the sheriff's death, tore through the country. Three hundred seven men had died; Robin Hood had turned bloodthirsty.

Solemn after the battle, the band had somewhat recovered their spirits by the tenth day. Robin had not.

Men had been killed without mercy — men who could not defend themselves. Hundreds of souls had vanished from the earth, their blood poured into his hands, and he could not hope to hold it. Robin refused food, sleeping only when exhausted, and even then his guilt marauded in ghoulish nightmares.

"My lady Anne?" Will Stutely approached the stream behind the outlaws' camp.

She sat beside it, not as though she had intended to, but as though she had crumpled.

"My lady?"

"He cannot shake the sickness. The weight of his guilt hath turned him weak."

Stutely came forward, dropping beside her upon the stream bank, feeling the wet grass slither beneath his palms. "'Twas war."

"'Twas war — in Wales. Here, it was murder. It was always murder. He knew it."

Stutely snorted; it sounded like a growl.

"He did his pretending before, thou dost thine now. God shall forgive thee, Will."

Stutely snorted again, rubbing his hands upon the grass 'til it wore away. "My master is strong. He will recover."

"He believes every one of their deaths his fault. As if he had shot each in turn. Life cannot be simple, when such pride lives in the same body with such morality."

"Where are your children? They would put him in better spirits."

"With Edith a Dale. They should not see their father this way. 'Tis not him."

"Not since the day we were pardoned."

"Though it is more him than in a great while. He is gentle again."

The dirt grated Stutely's skin; it was the only way he could feel it. "Thou shouldst not cry."

Blues had washed into the lines of Anne's neck, the sockets of her eyes, making them appear hollow. "Dost thou remember when King Henry hunted him? Thou didst come to me here, and I told thee, Will, that I could have no life without him. I feel myself dying."

Stutely drove his fingers into the dirt, digging a glob and hurling it in the stream. "God save — be quiet!"

"Robin doth believe he deserves to die, yet he clings to life for our sakes, as he loves us and would not have us suffer. Yet his conscience — "

"I won't listen." Will stood, slapping the earth from his hands. "All in the forest know my master lies ill. I shall away to the Blue Boar and find a healer. They will have flocked there, wanting to aid. Weep alone, if ye must."

"God will forgive thee the bloodshed, if thou dost ask it." Anne seemed to be speaking to another through him.

Stutely found two more outlaws who could not sit still, and they went.

The Blue Boar sat nearly as quiet as the camp. Though full, few spake, and those only murmured. The smell of the place — bread and ale — seemed to have gone stale and sour.

Stutely strode up to the keeper. "Be there healers here? Robin Hood bears need for one." He felt himself tugged from behind.

A chin etched with wrinkles was all one could see of the woman's face. She hunched, her tattered garments richly stained. "Lead me to your camp, good sirs, for I know an ancient remedy that may bring your master peace."

"Yes — yes." Will shook the place with the loudness of his voice though, in sooth, he spake no louder than usual. "Thank you, good woman. Follow us straight away." He could not help but think this a good omen, to meet a second time in Sherwood with a woman healer. Finding Aveline had allowed him to slay the killer wolf, as well as to help his master end the crimes of Rufford Abbey's monks. Surely, this woman would allow him to do something even greater and save the best man he had ever known.

They led the old woman in leaps and bounds, and she kept pace. The hems of her hooded mantle frayed, as if an animal had clawed them, and for all her shoon helped her she might have gone barefoot. Yet her appearance did not weigh upon her mind as she tramped the dark forest paths.

When they reached the camp, the old woman did not seem tired, as though she often walked briskly through the woods. A few of the band looked up as this party passed them by toward the small clearing adjacent the camp.

Little John stood with an arm around Anne, tears trickling silently down their faces. Upon the greensward, surrounded by furs, lay Robin Hood, shivering and sweating the same moment. His open eyes did not seem to acknowledge he was ill, only that men were dead and he stood at fault.

The woman took in this scene. "Leave all, and worry not; I shall take care of this man." The leaves quivered at her voice.

With lingering looks they trudged from the clearing, the boughs surrounding it having grown withered and black.

From beneath her mantle, the woman produced a skin pouch. She removed its knotted leather tie and a rancid odour crept into the air. Tilting Robin's head, she poured the liquid down his throat. At last he noticed her.

"Dost thou know me, outlaw?" she asked. "Nay, how couldst thou? Yet thou didst meet mine husband once: a forester, Roger of Doncaster. Thou didst shoot him dead. Nigh one-score years have I been biding time. I have raised my children alone. Thy widow will find herself in the like position. I know thou dost love her." Rage accumulated in the woman's voice. "The way she looks at thee I can see thou hast loved her. I loved Roger, and I pity thy children, as I did mine. I had six. Didst thou know two marched with the sheriff? Many times I have renewed my vow to spill thy blood in thine own realm. Thou shalt suffer in death, as I have suffered in life. Ten minutes before the poison takes thee, and let it be known that he whom no man could touch, a woman has finally snared."

She grasped the outlaw's wrist, slashing deep with a dagger she had concealed.

Robin's eyes jolted wide and he cried out. Though he had been dealt many blows, none stung with the venom this carried. Its pain revived him.

The woman was gone into the woods, thence never to be seen, having fulfilled her purpose.

Robin lay in sweat and blood, feeling his legs grow numb, returned to the world and yet fading from it. He would never again rob a rich monk upon the highroad. He would never again feast his men, Little John at his right hand. Never would he see his children grown. And not once more would he walk with Anne in the forest shades.

The band had heard his call. Little John, Will Stutely, and Anne o' th' Woods broke into the clearing.

Seeing his bleeding wrist, Anne knelt to bind it, whilst Little John cried, "By my troth, master, that vile woman shall grieve for what she did today!"

Yet Robin spake: "Nay, John. Since when hast thou thought of harming a woman? I have caused her pain enough." He laid his hand upon his wife's, which was working to bandage the other wrist. "Leave it be, love," quoth he, "I shall die of poisoning either way. Do not worry thyself so."

"She poisoned thee?" choked Will, stuttering, "But master . . . ye cannot die."

"Aye," quoth the giant, tears welling again in his eyes. "We . . . " He stood still.

For a moment all was quiet. Robin called to mind all he had planned to say during his days lying in and out of delirium, reciting what he could remember. "Tell the men to live always by the code of the yeoman, and obey God's commands. John, tell them how grateful I am for all they have done.

"When I am gone, return to your lives — Sherwood has seen outlaws enough — and empty our treasury to those who have need of it." There was more, yet his thoughts slipped away like a stream. "Bury me under the greenwood tree, and let my grave be not disturbed. Keep safe the shades of the greenwood, and remember the days we had. Thou hast been a true friend, Little John. Return to thy sheep. Find a wife with rosy cheeks to fuss over thee. Stutely, do not waste thy loyalty upon one unworthy of it. Thou hast never failed me, not even today."

Stutely looked ready to protest. A rockslide seemed to seal his throat. His voice paralyzed, he could hardly feel himself breathe.

"Thou couldst not have been more true to me wert thou mine own brother of blood and flesh." Robin's eyes came to meet Anne's, reading everything, as he always could. He tried to squeeze her hand — yearning for warmth — yet could not be sure his fingers moved. "I repent for the pain caused thee, dearest. Never let Mary sacrifice what thou didst. Be sure she weds an honest man. I know thou wilt teach Michael the rules of chivalry and the use of arms. Raise him to be honourable; do not allow him down the path I have chosen. Have a care also for thyself, love. Go to Gamewell — Will shall look after you three." Talking so much set him panting. "I love thee as I could no other."

"Thou *art* honourable, Robin. More than any man living."

He read her eyes, and she meant it. She had argued him nearly hoarse before the ambush. Yet knowing all he had done and thought, she meant it, this most stubbornly moral of women. She who had known he would die.

Robin, too, knew he would soon depart, for his arms were stone, and he could no longer feel his wife's hand in his. "Dearest, be in no hurry to see me again. I do not die; thou art half my soul, Ivy."

At the pet name he had never spoke before anyone but her, Anne kissed Robin's lips. "I love thee. Robert."

His eyes jolted wider, though no others could see what they saw. Robin gasped, "Jesu cometh . . . "

His chest ceased to rise and fall. His gentle heart ceased to beat.

Stutely pointed to the gash in Robin's arm. "Look." The blood had ceased to flow.

A cry pierced the greenwood. Men heard it in every clearing, upon every path. They heard it echo through the Blue Boar.

The king had died.

Upon that day, the forest grew dark. Leaves shrivelled and were wind-whipped from the trees. Branches sagged under invisible weights. Trunks toppled, to rot back into the earth.

Afterward, there were no more outlaws in Sherwood Forest. All the band had gone, and no other wolf's-head dared tread the paths, where Robin Hood is king.

⚬⚬⚬

The forest has changed since that time, with aged trees felled to make space for farms and cities. Yet there is one clearing, grown quite small, which no human foot has entered since the reign of Edward I.

At the head of this clearing stands a stout greenwood tree, over one thousand years old. Beneath it rests a stone, free in the sweet air, etched with the language of high medieval England. These words it bares:

Robert, born at Huntington,
Lies under this little stone.
No archer was as he so good;
His wildness named him Robin Hood.
Full thirteen years, and something more,
These northern parts he vexed full sore.
Such outlaws as he and his men
Shall England never know again.

Historical Note

The scarlet forest, clothed in blood and gold,
As aged as time yet never aging.
Rich men line the leaves with gold;
Outlaws bathe the sward in blood.

WHO WAS ROBIN HOOD? No one knows. The outlaw who could not be captured is still on the loose. Robin may be a real man whose exploits were exaggerated. He may be a compilation of numerous medieval outlaws. He may never have existed outside of a storyteller's imagination. His legend has survived through the medieval period, the Reformation and Civil Wars, the Industrial Revolution, and two world wars, over eight tumultuous centuries. As his story is retold, it is changed to suit a new audience. Robin's tales have been embellished and disoriented through time. As always, he is a master of disguise.

This novel has tried to blend true history with many of the legend's popular historical inaccuracies (as well as some of my own). What follows is a brief overview of what can be said about the original figure of Robin Hood, who was the subject of my graduate dissertation at the University of Nottingham.

Dozens, if not hundreds, of different stories about Robin Hood were told during the Middle Ages, but we have copies of only five: *A Gest of Robyn Hode*, *Robin Hood and the Monk*, *Robin Hood and the Potter*, *Robin Hood and Guy of Gisborne*, and version A of *Robin Hoode his Death*. It is difficult to say when these stories were written down and even more difficult to say when they were first composed, since each was likely circulating generations before being put on the page. During this time these accounts were changing; *Robin Hood and the Potter* and the later *Robin Hood and the Butcher* probably started as the same story. Our versions of the five medieval ballads likely date from the 1400s, while Robin Hood, if he was real, almost certainly operated as an outlaw between 1200 and 1262 or, if he wasn't real, almost certainly was invented during this interval. That is about two hundred years for the "game of telephone" to distort, replace, invent, or discard. The year 1200 is a good starting date, as deeply entrenched elements in the medieval ballads (how sheriffs operated, for example) are specific to the thirteenth century. The year 1262 is when thief William, son of Robert le Fevere, was renamed William Robehod in a legal record, indicating that the legend had become relatively well-known by then. Any Robin Hoods after 1262 (those having adopted the name due to the legend, as well as those not) may have had their exploits confused with and put into the legend. A real Robin Hood or a character named Robin Hood, if either existed, would have had to exist before this year.

Although two centuries too new, the five medieval ballads all agree that while outlawed Robin lived in Barnsdale, Yorkshire. The minute local details included would have been, and for centuries were, unknown to outsiders, so that we can be heavily confident of the legend being formed in what is now West Yorkshire. Robin Hood and his men only visited Nottingham and Sherwood Forest, which were approximately fifty and forty miles away respectively (this distance often being traversed in unnaturally record time). A forest in medieval England did not necessarily mean woods, but an area under forest law, which could include fields and villages as well as trees. Barnsdale was not a forest. It is difficult to say whether it had many trees. Barnsdale was so small (only about five square miles) that, wooded or not, Robin's men were not really hiding. What made Barnsdale such an advantageous place for outlaws was instead its location. Travellers journeying the popular north-south road would have to pass right by Robin Hood's stronghold, which meant plenty of opportunities for theft. We know that people in the 1300s feared being robbed when passing through Barnsdale. Whether this was due to real danger or due to stories, true or not, of Robin Hood, we cannot be sure.

The way Robin stole from his victims, the way his men hunted, and his expertise with the bow all point to Robin having been not a noble (the Earl of Huntington identity was added in the 1500s), but a forester. Most likely, Robin was a walking forester, meaning he patrolled his section of forest on foot everyday, often exploiting fines and poaching. Many alien elements were added to the legend in the 1500s, including Robin being from Locksley, an association with King Richard I, and robbing the rich to feed the poor. Not every addition came from the 1500s, of course. The ideas of Robin supporting oppressed villeins or Saxons against lords or Normans are very modern ones. Additionally, it was a falsified family tree from the 1700s that gave Robin the surname Fitzooth. Part of why he is so difficult to track down is that Robin and Hood were common names. We find them over and over in medieval records, but there is no solid evidence of anyone being the real Robin Hood. The name is almost certainly an alias, anyway. Where taxation is a major issue in later retellings, the medieval ballads only once mention it: Robin says he will impose a tax on the potter for travelling through the band's territory. The potter is also the only medieval character to fight with a quarterstaff. As a yeoman, it was below Robin's dignity to use such a weapon. In the ballads, Robin refers to himself as a yeoman (a social position sort of approaching a middle class) many times, and Little John calls him a yeoman of the forest, a term meaning "forester." A real Robin Hood could possibly have started out as a forester in Sherwood, been outlawed for taking advantage of his position, and retreated north to Barnsdale, nearer his family connections, where he continued to behave as an overzealous forester, this time with no forest law to support or hamper him.

Foresters, especially those from Nottinghamshire, were known in the Middle Ages for their skill at archery. They had to be able to aid the king when he came to hunt, and to defend themselves from poachers. A myth was started in the 1800s that the longbow came to England from Wales, and at sometime during the 1200s, possibly after the legend's genesis. While the medieval ballads never use the word longbow — this term was not used until the very end of the period, long after the ballads' origin — Robin's archery feats could only have been performed with what we now call a longbow. Such bows were certainly present in England throughout the 1200s, and all of the ballads' archery feats are entirely possible with this weapon. (Splitting an arrow end to end was added many centuries later.) Robin's signature trick in the ballads was splitting the approximately one inch in diameter wand that supported a garland target: the most difficult shot in archery. In the five medieval ballads we have, usually only a handful of Robin's companions are given names: Little John, Will Scarlok, and Much the Miller's son. Gilbert with the White Hand and Reynold are each mentioned once, but Reynold Greenleaf is also the alias Little John uses to trick the sheriff, so this becomes ambiguous. The band's names unanimously appear to be aliases. Scarlok means lock breaker or picker, and millers were widely thought to cheat and steal from their customers. Little John's nickname likely would have been acquired before adulthood, there being no indication in the medieval ballads that he was either short or a giant, and so susceptible to such an epithet.

Characters like Maid Marian, Friar Tuck, and Allin a Dale were later additions. Maid Marian comes from French literature, her lover a different Robin. Her character and Robin Hood's were brought together in the May Games around the year 1500. It is also possible that their association came about due to Marian's link with a friar character. Stories about Robin Hood and a friar were probably circulating during the Middle Ages. From at least 1417 to 1429 a highwayman named Robert Stafford operated in southern England under the alias Friar Tuck; this is likely where Robin's friar comes from and how they became linked.

The only king named in the medieval ballads is Edward, in all probability Edward II (r. 1307–1327). If Robin Hood was real, he would actually have lived during the reign of John (1199–1216), formerly Prince John, or Henry III (1216–1272, nine years old when he became king), or both. This helps to illustrate that even the medieval ballads, by *far* our best source for Robin Hood's legend, being written down at least two centuries after the fact, still cannot be relied upon too heavily. However, since they were written at least two centuries after the fact, they cannot be relied upon too heavily.

It can sometimes prove frustrating, searching for elements that are genuine. At Blidworth's St. Mary of the Purification (part of the Mansfield Deanery rumoured to be connected with Will Scarlet), there is an unusually shaped stone alleged to mark his grave. This connection with St. Mary could have been inspired by the church's 1608 monument to a Sherwood Forest ranger, featuring his hunting paraphernalia. Meanwhile, Little John has three supposed graves. The Hathersage one, excavated in 1784, allegedly held a thigh bone belonging to a man over seven feet tall. This bone was subsequently stolen off a windowsill by a baronet, so there is no remaining physical proof of the grave belonging to a giant, though the medieval Little John is never said to be a giant anyway.

Gest and *Death* contain versions of Robin going to be bled (a common medical treatment) by the Prioress of Kirklees. She plots against Robin with her lover, Roger. *Death* says that Robin is buried nearby, probably along a road called Nun Bank Lane, and there is a grave there, but no bones. The tombstone is modern and, when excavated, the earth beneath it was found never to have been disturbed. It is possible that a real Robin Hood could be buried somewhere along Nun Bank Lane — just not where his tombstone stands. He could actually be buried anywhere, or nowhere.

Perhaps the most frustrating thing — and the thing that keeps drawing us back — is that no one can prove whether or not Robin Hood existed. There remain compelling arguments in favour and equally compelling arguments against. At present, we cannot know who he was, how many he was, or even if he was. When looking at the evidence, it is by all means *possible* that Robin Hood was real. The closest thing we have, however, is a fictional Robin created many generations after the fact.

I hope this book has brought you to acquire Robin Hood as a hero. He has been one of my heroes since I was four years old. In spite of others' expectations, he lives by his principles: courtesy, honesty, generosity, and devotion. In defiance of becoming a criminal, he becomes an ideal. And though Robin Hood the man may be dead, his legend shall never be slain.

SELECT BIBLIOGRAPHY
FOR HISTORICAL NOTE

Almond, Richard, and A. J. Pollard. "The Yeomanry of Robin Hood and Social Terminology in Fifteenth-Century England." *Past and Present*. February 2001: 52–77.

Bradbury, Jim. *The Medieval Archer*. Woodbridge: The Boydell Press, 1985.

Chandler, Amy Elizabeth. "Discovering Robin Hood." Diss. University of Nottingham, 2012.

Crook, David. "Notes and Documents: Some Further Evidence Concerning the Dating of the Origins of the Legend of Robin Hood." *The English Historical Review* 99 (1984): 530–534.

Dobson, R. B., and J. Taylor. *Rymes of Robyn Hood: An Introduction to the English Outlaw*. 3rd ed. Stroud: Sutton, 1997.

Holt, J. C. *Robin Hood*. 2nd ed. London: Thames and Hudson Ltd., 1989.

Holt, J. C. "The Origins and Audience of the Ballads of Robin Hood." *Past and Present*. November 1960: 89–110.

Knight, Stephen, and Thomas H. Ohlgren, eds. *Robin Hood and Other Outlaw Tales*. Kalamazoo: Medieval Institute Publications, 1997.

Pollard, A. J. *Imagining Robin Hood*. Abingdon: Routledge, 2004.

Glossary

alaunt: large hunting dog

buckler: small, round shield

cellarer: minds a convent's cellars and stores

distrain: to seize goods in order to enforce a court appearance

engrosser: buys large amounts to increase the price of something

fermisoun season: the season for hunting hinds, lasting from the close of the season for harts until Lent

fewterer: man in charge of holding and releasing greyhounds during a hunt

fortnight: two weeks

gaol: jail

good den: a greeting

hart: six-year-old male red deer

hind: female red deer three years or older

hogshead: liquid measurement, varying between thirty and sixty-three gallons

malmsey: a sweet wine

murrain: disease affecting deer and cattle

palmer: pilgrim

score: twenty (for example, ten-score is two hundred)

sennight: one week

stag: five-year-old male red deer

trysting or trystel tree: a tree one goes to, derived from a hunting term

waster: wooden practice sword

wight: powerful

wolf's-head: outlaw

wot: know